Bridg
Gulf

Malcolm Hollingdrake

One Man's Fight for Justice

Also by

Malcolm Hollingdrake

Shadows from the Past
Short Stories for Short Journeys

For my wife Debbie.
For your love, help and support.
x

Prologue

1998

His mind was blank, he was without clear thought and had been for longer than he would have wished. It was as though his thought processes had been paralysed. At first, they had joked about the periods of blackness, his 'dark side', as they had referred to it. It had steadily grown until the light and the dark merged and they laughed little at that stage: Concern and fear had forced themselves inevitably into their lives bringing with them uncertainty; as the creeping inability grew, their laughter faded.

It had been worse for their son who had never really understood his father's moods, the complete swings from happiness to anger. They were too hidden and he was too young, but swings they definitely were, swings that brought anger, violence, frustration and pity within one short moment of life. The family was crumbling before their eyes and there was nothing to be done. How quickly the avenues of hope dried up and the tears grew.

Vicky had threatened to leave twice but failed to act; her love for this man was stronger than she had imagined. They had so much to live for, their son and the baby she carried.

***

The wind tugged gently at his clothes and he was impervious to the drizzle. He was alone, wrapped in an anger and blackness that had enveloped his being. He knew not from where he had come from. He scrambled onto the parapet of the bridge looking down into the void and the green, dark waters of the ship canal that glittered like a snail's track along a wet stone. His eyes followed its length. In the distance, amongst twinkling lights was his house; it was no longer his home.

The dawn was on the horizon and the sky hung heavily. Behind him his car's hazard lights flashed their warning but the passing motorists failed to notice the sad, lonely figure of humanity high up on the bridge, their myopic vision concentrating on the strip of tarmac ahead through the spray.

The low aircraft, strobes flashing brightly against the low cloud, flew above clawing its way to land. It would be the last thing on which he focused. To him it was an aggressor, here to inflict pain, bring death. For seconds he was back in the Gulf War, the rain, the cold, the noise flooded his confusion; he was terrified and alone. He tried to keep the moving lights in view as his stomach-wrenching fall began. No scream came to his lips as he plummeted through the darkness. He remembered nothing after hitting the water. At last he had found peace.

***

The body was found much later in the day and only then did the true horror of the incident come to light. The police had received no response from the house of the deceased and only after questioning neighbours and hearing their concerns did they break through the back door. It did not matter how long you had served in the force you never got used to the uglier side of policing, and the sight that greeted the officers was neither pretty nor understandable.

Even though there were no external marks of violence to the body, the child was dead, alone on the bed surrounded by his toys, his wide, unblinking eyes staring through the polythene bag at the swinging mobile. In the next room lay his mother, she had suffered a terrible beating; she would neither walk nor see again. It would have been far kinder for her life to have been taken that night, with her children and her husband.

***

The press coverage of the tragedy was graphic with varying degrees of sensitivity. The television news also gained its pound of flesh as it ran and re-ran pictures of the house and the motorway bridge. It was the name that struck Roy Hanna first and made him stop and think. He had known this man well in the past. They had fought together and they had sought help for their symptoms after the fighting had ceased. He knew what he had faced. His battle was over but Roy's was only just beginning.

Malcolm Hollingdrake

Chapter One

1999

The bridge spanned not only the Douglas Valley with its meagre river, trickling brown through the lush reeds that tried to choke it, but the canal and railway as well. Above him streamed the constant flow of traffic heading north and south, pounding the bridge relentlessly day and night, three hundred and sixty-five days a year. Even as dusk approached it was clear that night came early to the valley and with it a reduction in man-made sounds.

The canal towpath, always a popular recreational highway, gave easy pedestrian access to the bridge. Over the years, many foolhardy youths had challenged themselves to the task of balancing along the beams that traversed the pillars, to emblazon the bridge's flanks with aerosol initials. It was clear too that one slip, one startled pigeon, could cause a loss of balance and a predictable conclusion after falling twenty-two metres.

The bridge's span was approximately two hundred metres supported by sixteen concrete cylindrical legs. Strong. By contrast, the Semtex B was like a ball of grey plasticine: no smell, no weight and at this stage without menace. Within the bag were ten pieces of identical size and weight, a small palmtop computer and a set of night glasses, as well as detonators, pliers, tape, grease, a strong tube of construction grip adhesive and wire. Roy Hanna followed the canal towpath whistling quietly to himself, to focus the mind. His suit had been left in the car and he wore lightweight canvas climbing boots, jeans and a thin, breathable jacket. On his head was a peaked baseball cap.

The light from the lock-keeper's cottage was the only visible electric light under the bridge. It stood next to the locks as if turning its back on its reason for life. The main windows looked over the woods, river and the motorway bridge. Its occupants were going to have a grandstand seat! Once over the locks, a narrow path led through a pasture towards the railway line that ran down the valley. Crossing, Roy stopped to watch the silhouetted flight of a heron returning to its nesting site. The great, majestic bird flew gracefully above him, its legs thrusting rearward in an attempt to streamline its form. Roy continued following the path leading up the banking and onto the underside beams of the bridge. The beams ran onto the large, concrete lintel, semi submerged into the banking, making it ridiculously easy to climb along them. Three metres high and finished at their base like an inverted "T", the beams gave ample foot space and the enclosed back not only afforded security but obscurity. About two metres above the outside girder ran steel drainage pipes, perfectly positioned for handholds; the task was now so easy. He soon followed the path of the graffiti artists, walking on the girders, right gloved hand sliding along the pipe above, his whistling echoing alongside the sharp, metallic rattle of vehicles. He always worked alone, always had. It felt better that way.

His eyes soon settled to the dark and he could see before him his pathway along the girder. Spaced every three metres was a cross piece securing ten parallel beams, every alternate one was cross braced. Roy rested at these. Securing his bag to his chest, he began to move, cautiously at first until he felt a rhythm develop. The evening breeze was stronger here and the need for caution stopped the whistling.

Once above the second row of supporting columns he rested, feeling a sense of security brought about by the proximity of the surrounding cold steel and the wide concrete lintel just below. The rattle of cars gave him company as he reached right-handed into the bag.

Six months earlier, two hundred miles away the same hand and the same bag had been in a similar position; the same care and eye for detail had the mark of a craftsman, a man who took pride in the job, a man who now looked only forward to forget the past.

Beneath the span the light had almost disappeared and even though Roy's eyes were accustomed to the gloom, he found it difficult to continue. He began whistling again, lightly, as from the side pocket of his bag he brought out the night glasses. With care he removed his cap and placed the glasses over his eyes. Immediately the underside of the bridge took on a green, ethereal charm. Corners previously obscured from sight became clear. The graffiti artists certainly had wit but not an anatomical eye! Looking down into the valley below brought surprises. A couple leaned on the concrete support in an embrace, hands eagerly searching within clothing. Roy watched; feeling voyeuristic brought a smile to his face and a stiffness between his legs. The couple moved to the bank and it was clear there was going to be only one ending as they locked together. Roy watched and waited. Passion was soon spent, their faint giggling meeting his ears. They moved away slowly across the railway to the locks before walking wrapped in each other's arms, unaware their passion had been witnessed.

Roy went back to work. The Semtex was carefully laid, concealed in grease that was liberally smeared on the supporting bearing, as he had been taught, to cause the maximum disruption to the structural integrity of the bridge. Securing his grip he moved again, further out over the void, carefully placing feet and hands until he reached the centre span. At this point Roy was twenty-two metres above the ground: river to his left, canal to his right. He placed the Semtex as before with care, the thin black wire being tucked into the joints and greased as he moved along the lintel. The detonators were placed, waiting. The height and the breeze, firmer at this point as it channelled under the bridge, gave him a strange feeling in his groin that warned of danger. He secured his last Semtex, the delay connectors placed to give sequential blasting of twenty-five milliseconds; this would enhance the shatter force. In thirty minutes he would be back on the towpath heading home. Once all the wires were in place the palmtop, scrubbed of serial numbers and marks, was glued in position. The alarm had been set in keeping with the plan. Carefully the wire to the explosives was connected to the computer, the TPU, the timer and power unit. It could not now be removed. Roy glanced round making a final check before returning.

***

The bed was warm and snug, occupied by a solitary female, tucked up with a whisper snore. The red glow from the bedside clock seemed to fill the room. Roy had said he would be late; the meeting in Liverpool would go on until all the details had been ironed out.

Joan had known Roy for a year now and it was their mutual love of the outdoors that had brought them together; it would be three months before they shared his bed. Initially she would leave at 2am to return home, the smell of him still in her hair; her parents still expected her home. Their concern for her was stronger now than at any other time. They wanted her to succeed within her profession and failed to understand her. They both believed that she was staying out far too late when she had to rise at seven to prepare for her day in the classroom. Now, thankfully that was behind her. She still felt, however, that she knew too little about him but she loved him and time would release all the information she needed.

The clock showed 11pm, the vertical blinds blew gently in the breeze ringing occasionally on the Venetian glass bowl on the window ledge. She moved in her sleep uneasily.

***

The car, a grey Subaru Impreza Turbo was left in the car park of the canal side pub accompanied by many others. Last orders was a term only loosely applied here, many cars would remain until quite late. As Roy approached the road which was

8

carried over the canal by a small humpbacked bridge, he was startled by a runner who darted from beneath it.

"Evening," spluttered the small, sweating middle-aged man as he skirted Roy.

"Evening," replied Roy as he stood watching the figure pounding along the towpath in the direction of the motorway lights. "Bloody crackers!"

The car locks sprang open with the depression of the remote. He opened the boot, removed his bag from his shoulder placing it carefully to the side before covering it with his jacket. He took a small stainless steel Thermos and poured a steaming coffee before settling into the driver's seat. The digital clock on the dashboard showed 11.30. He removed his soft climbing boots and slipped his feet into his shoes.

The engine fired and the grey Subaru moved towards the road. A right turn took him away from the nearer motorway junction but by habit and a sense of keeping the faith he wanted to drive over his latest bridge; the knowledge that beneath him was enough explosive to destroy the bridge and those on it, made him grin. The road from the canal twisted and built up but the houses soon thinned. As his foot responded to the conditions, the car began to move quickly. His preparation was good. His foot lifted from the throttle before the school sign and moments later the Gatso speed camera slept on. A left turn swiftly brought the M6 into view, the line of white centre lights running north/south signalled its fast approach.

Once on the slip road the four-wheel drive reached 70mph effortlessly and soon a chuckle came as the valley passed below. Within twenty-minutes he would leave the M6 for the M62, one of the fiercest roads he had known in the wintertime but this summer night it was but a friend and three of its bridges were his. He cruised at 90mph cresting the Pennine moors at just past midnight, their darkness rich velvet. Soon to his left would be Halifax glittering below in the valley and he was almost there.

West Street was home, a row of terraced houses like many others in Bradford; true, honest stone houses that would stand for another hundred years. The house was past its best but as he said, "Home was home".

The car alarm armed itself as Roy moved to the house. He opened the door with difficulty and went in, his arms full of suit, bag and boots. The hallway led to the stairs. Two doors were to his left, the first to the lounge, the second to the dining room and kitchen. He took the second. He hung up the jacket and bag after removing the night sights; they were locked in the cellar. He rinsed out the flask before retracing his steps and moved swiftly upstairs. The bedroom door was ajar and he heard the ring of the blind on the bowl. He showered before sliding into bed.

The quilt was kicked to one side exposing Joan's breasts and flat stomach. His mind drifted to the couple under the bridge and their frantic coupling. His penis again began to react in concert with his hand that moved up Joan's belly to the firm breast. He took the nipple between finger and thumb and squeezed and rolled. It responded and Joan turned inwards towards him.

***

From the radio, 'The Prayer for the Day', broke the silence of the morning. Both stirred but it was Roy who moved first. "Thought you were asleep when I got in!"

"Seduced whilst sleeping. You men are despicable," she murmured sleepily with a broad grin. "How about doing it again in slow motion?"

She kicked off the quilt and spread her legs invitingly.

"You've a class to teach ... and me, I've one hundred and one things to sort out from yesterday's meeting."

"Did everything go well?" enquired Joan as she curled under the quilt.

"We're getting there. There's another meeting planned for Thursday just to nail everything down. I'm in the office today".

The conversation was broken by the sound of the shower and Roy's infuriating whistle.

Slipping on her dressing gown she went downstairs and filled the kettle. The sun seldom hit the back garden but it still looked colourful with its hanging baskets and pots. Before her arrival it had been a desolate yard, colourless as a winter sky.

Roy moved behind her wrapping his arms around her waist. "Nearly as pretty as you". He kissed the nape of her neck. "Kettle on?"

Joan moved from his grasp and took the full kettle she was still holding and plugged it in, touching her forelock obediently. Their eyes smiled.

"What time were you in?"

"Not too late. The motorway was a piece of cake, a pleasure really. Sorry if I disturbed you." His grin said it all. "You get sorted, toast will be ready in ten". She went to shower.

Joan had packed her school bag the previous night and Roy carried it to the small Vauxhall Corsa parked on the street. She opened the boot and he placed it with care.

"Home usual time?" asked Roy as he opened the driver's door with his right hand, his left, unnaturally stiff, touched his forelock as she had done earlier. She took his hand and kissed its cold surface before reaching on her toes to kiss his lips.

"Hope so. Shall we eat out?"

"I'll be home for six, we'll decide then."

Roy closed the door. The car started and moved away, pausing at the street entrance before disappearing from view. Roy stayed motionless for a moment before returning to the house.

The house had belonged to his parents and on their untimely death he had been sole beneficiary. Little had changed for he saw no need to alter anything, after all home was home. He went into the kitchen and loaded the breakfast things into the dishwasher, one of Joan's contributions to the home. The sight of his jacket brought the previous night to mind and a smile to his mouth. Just three more and he would be in business.

Chapter Two

In 1986, Roy had enjoyed his final twelve months at school but he needed a break away from the claustrophobic atmosphere. His parents, both in their mid-forties, were desperate that he realise his true potential and go to university, after all he had the necessary qualifications. His peers were eager to experience the freedom education on this level could bring. They talked ceaselessly if not optimistically about parties, the sex, the laughs that would follow as if by right. Roy found the talk puerile and he felt decidedly uneasy; these were his troubled days.

It was a colourful advert in a magazine that first attracted his imagination to his future path, a future that could have been no further from his mind. The advertisement was a catalyst, it did something to him, it captured his imagination and set the ball rolling with its promise of adventure. The library was to continue the momentum when "Who Dares Wins" by Tony Geraghty became his reading. He remembered the Iranian Embassy siege in the May of 1980 and the elusive men dressed in black, who had within eleven minutes prevented the deaths of the innocent by bringing death to the 'guilty', with what we were led to believe was perfect precision. Although he had no yearning for the SAS he could see that a short career in the forces might be the elixir he needed to expand his mind and take him away from his home.

Roy had never travelled abroad with his parents but had been to Germany with his school when he was sixteen. They had travelled by coach and he remembered the nausea. The culture, the architecture, the history fascinated him. He knew Bradford a small part of a large world and he yearned to see as much as he could. On his return his enthusiasm was to be lost on his parents and he felt sad for them.

***

Roy locked the front door of the house and pressed the remote on the key ring. The central locking responded and within minutes he was heading towards work. An unfeeling thumb pressed the cassette into the machine and music filled the car. His musical taste was varied but Blues was a regular companion. It normally took fifteen minutes door to door and today was no exception.

Drew was already there ... Drew was always there. The company, D.M. Business Machines had been started by Drew McKenna, an amicable Scot, on his return from America. Originally gestating in a corner shop in West Street before making the grade, it had then relocated to purpose-built premises in one of the many industrial sites around the city's ring road. The trade was now more computers than general office equipment and the competition was fierce. Drew had been looking for a book-keeper in those early days and Roy's mother had fit the bill. It was this connection that had enabled the maimed Roy to re-establish himself into society, giving him the will to carry on and, as it turned out, the finances to even the score.

The business had certainly rewarded Drew with a home in Harrogate and a horse; his build was evidence of his early aspirations to be a jockey. It had under Drew's reign grown into a successful, respectable business. However, it had taken its toll. Mrs McKenna was no longer at home. An expensive divorce had nearly put paid to the company and Drew on more than one occasion. He was small but was made of strong stuff. Times were now good.

"Morning Roy, be with ya in a jiff. Everything go well in Liverpool?"

"Fine, the one computer is now three and they also need a copier, some faxes and some furniture. Didn't need to discount too much either. The Director says he remembers you as a salesman in Phoenix in about 1961."

"Good man, he can remember me from wherever he likes providing he places orders like that. Your mail's on your desk. Be in later."

Roy, taking the hint, moved through to the office that was his; the desk with leather chair, copier, filing cabinet, settee and a window which looked out onto another identical building. To the left, however, was a view of the motorway and a bridge that spanned the narrow valley linking with the M62. This bridge would never be his; too close to home.

There was a brief knock and Emma, the secretary, appeared. "Coffee, Roy?"

"Morning. Love one."

She smiled and closed the door. Within minutes she had returned to place the fresh coffee, black and steaming on his desk. "POETS day thank goodness," she smiled again and left.

Roy read the mail, filed what was necessary and checked his messages. On his desk was his palmtop and under 'Agenda' he brought up the week's diary. He had grown to like this little electronic wizard, so much so he had discovered its full ability with the help of the technicians with whom he worked. It was this machine and its diary that would make all the difference to the planning that he had embarked on all that time ago and that was so close to fruition. Three more bridges would bring the number to fifty-seven.

The palmtops had been easily purchased as part of his job was selling them, but the explosives had been difficult, certainly the most risky and definitely the most expensive. Yet his travelling and his involvement with the import of business machines, linked with the connections made during his time in the forces, alongside endless patience and thought made anything possible.

The coffee was good and soon all was in order. He rang a couple of customers to make appointments before leaving. He straightened a photograph on the wall to the left of his desk of himself in a different life, a life that had been cut short. The uniform made him look older than his years. He was proud and having the time of his life. He rubbed his left hand. It was cold and motionless. Sometimes he would wear a glove but now he felt people had to live with it just as he did, but it made him angry, bloody angry. He glanced back at the photograph and then at his hand.

He rang home leaving a message for Joan. "Appointments in Leeds and Wakefield. Call me on the mobile should you need me. I'll be home by 5."

The motorway was busier than usual, Fridays did affect the traffic making it unpredictable and as Emma had so succinctly pointed out, it was POETS day. The Subaru gurgled its way through the traffic. The only giveaway to its 208 BHP was the radiator scoop on the bonnet. The car itself was simple, almost family saloon in its configuration, certainly not the usual rep machinery.

During the afternoon Roy had covered seventy-two miles, had been interrupted four times by phone but most importantly he had chuckled three times: he had driven over three of his bridges. He arrived home slightly later than anticipated and Joan was in the garden to the back of the house. He watched her briefly from the dining room. She moved slowly, carefully deadheading her baskets. He tapped on the window; it made her jump. She smiled and came in.

"You're earlier than I thought, made me jump!"

They chatted briefly before Roy went into the cellar to prepare. Joan returned to the garden. The cellar was, for want of a better title, Roy's workroom. He had always used it from being a child and the walls still reflected the different phases of childhood. His father had converted the waste space for him. Once it had been the store for food and coal but now with its insulation and heating it made an ideal workspace, secret by being subterranean. There was a workbench and tool racks, cupboards and a timber store. Suspended from the low ceiling the plastic model aircraft he had made, each collecting dust that covered the various colour schemes so painstakingly applied. It was in this room that Roy not only designed his bombs but also stored the necessary equipment, and it was here that he was going to prepare the last three. Each device had been carefully thought out, not one was identical other than the TPU. He had taken into consideration the site, the type of bridge, its construction and design and the location. Some devices had intricate anti-handling features and he was pleased with his originality.

The thrill of construction was immense but no match for the excitement level he reached in placing the bombs. The hours of planning and preparation were drawing to a close and the testing time would start. He only hoped he would be able to keep control of the situation and see the plan through to fruition. Only time would tell. He had these to plant and then the clock would start. The following week he would plant all three. He could hardly wait. He was like a child on Christmas Eve. His excitement bubbled.

***

The following Thursday was damp and overcast and the journey to Preston was without incident. Business over, Roy took the A59 out of town stopping in a lay-by close to a hotel and restaurant that overlooked the River Ribble. It was 10pm. The new bridges over the river had been completed months earlier to take the ever-increasing demands of traffic. They towered over the old stone bridge, lights aglow. Roy knew this was to be the last, his fifty-seventh. They were all similar: all large spans, all heavy traffic carriers, all key sites, all vital to the movement around the country and all expensive to replace. They were all his or they would be. Now he could, should he wish to do so, turn back, cease this game of death but it excited him more than anything he had done before. In twenty-one-days it would start and nobody but he would be able to stop it. The bridges would certainly all collapse unless they agreed to meet his demands.

He checked across at the hotel which seemed busy. A man stood by the front revolving doors with a cigarette. He looked like a waiter. Roy moved to the rear of the car and removed his bag. His night shift had started.

Chapter Three

Famagusta, known to the Turkish inhabitants as Gazimagusa, is still one of the most unspoiled ports in the Mediterranean, one of the old Cyprus ports with its heavy fortification and cathedral. It now languishes within the Turkish side of the island after the invasion of 1974. Ancient and mystical, Christian and Muslim mingle together. Scars of the war are still visible but tourism is beginning to discover its unspoiled charms. It was here Roy relaxed. This was his home, where he felt at ease. He liked the Turkish Cypriots, their way of life.

He had managed to buy a small flat in a suburb, facing fields with an unrestricted view of the mountains in the far distance. He had liked the peace of this side of the island, a seclusion he had found when friends from his regiment were discovering the sins of Ayia Napa. Roy had been captivated by this town since being based in Dhekelia, a large army garrison on the Greek side of Cyprus. He had explored its streets, its port and enjoyed the relaxed freedom it offered. It suited his intellect.

The posting to Cyprus in 1988 had been an inspiring part of his career in the army. Much of his basic training had been carried out in England and Germany with one tour in Northern Ireland. Cyprus was where he really wanted to be. The garrison spread for many acres and resembled Britain apart from the days of constant blue sky. There was everything that Britain had to offer from its best to its worst. There was order from its pavemented roads to the rows of red bricked houses, each with its own garden, front and rear, play areas and schools that resembled any garrison in any country. The N.A.A.F.I epitomised its quintessential Englishness and its bars.

To the young squaddy, however, the bars in Ayia Napa drew like magnets; drink was cheap and the female English holidaymakers easy, with the added advantage they would be gone in a fortnight. To Roy that held no attraction but the Turkish side drew him with a fascination he could not understand. The United Nations, whose peacekeeping role kept the Greeks and Turks from killing each other, patrolled the "Green line", the buffer zone separating the hostile sides. They also sent out vehicles to parts of Turkish Cyprus that were still occupied by the Greeks, these enclaves nestling on what was foreign soil. Roy was always eager to fill any empty seat on these patrols. The UN also knew what was good for them too, they would use Salamis, an area of coast unspoiled by development but wrapped in the ruins of the island's Roman past and pine forests. Here they relaxed, learned to sail and swim.

The ancient city of Salamis was once large and prosperous, founded in 1184BC after the Trojan Wars and it remained the principle city until the Romans transferred the island's capital to Paphos, an area Roy knew. It was the earthquakes that had seen an end to the once fine town and harbour, and the ruins had remained hidden by sand dunes until excavation. Roy often swam and snorkelled above the stones of the old harbour, the marble white in the clear water, collecting fragments of tile and pots, running them through his fingers like a blind man trying to make contact with the distant past. The water was warm and blue and he was in heaven.

Set back a few metres from the sea was the excavated ruin of the Roman theatre; its staged seating rising twenty metres to give the several thousand spectators a clear view of the stage. It was here, as evening approached, that Roy let his mind drift, a solitary figure surrounded by stone. Thoughts of his parents at home in their Bradford terrace, rain inevitably falling. They had believed their life was good. If only he could bring them here, transport them in an instant so they could watch the sky change as dusk approached, walk along the water's edge, feel the warmth of the sea on their hands, smell the heat and the heady aroma of pine, maybe then they would understand his deep desires to leave the industrial north, its shiny wet streets and its inhibitions. He would often whistle, the sound filling the silence, a habit he was to develop.

***

It was in the autumn of '88 that Roy was called to see his CO.

"Sit down. I'm sorry Roy but your parents have been involved in a road accident. The details are sketchy but as far as I'm aware they are both alive but in a critical condition. I've arranged a flight for you leaving Akrotiri tonight. Your parents are in Leeds Infirmary and that's all I know at present. We're all so sorry, Roy. If there's anything we can do let us know. All the travel information is here." He handed Roy an envelope containing details of his compassionate leave, timetables and tickets.

Roy learned forward, numb at what he had heard. The words seemed to tumble round his head in a disjointed way and for a moment he could not speak only look at the brown envelope in his hands. The CO moved from behind his desk and rested a hand on the young man's shoulders, aware of the turmoil with which he was trying to get to grips.

"Come on. We have to look on the positive side of this, remember we're here if we can do anything to help, you mustn't hesitate."

Roy cleared his throat, "Thank you, sir". He rose before standing to attention, saluted and left the room.

***

The TriStar flight was uneventful, landing at Brize Norton where a car was waiting to take him to Leeds. The time difference was in his favour.

Both parents were much worse than he had imagined. He found himself waiting in a small room. The hospital was quiet. "Mr Hanna?" a young nurse queried. "Your parents are

21

responding to treatment; they are stable but critical. There is little you can do here. Go home and rest, we'll call if there's any change".

"I'll wait."

His reply was curt and he knew it; a short smile conveyed an apology. "I'll wait through there if that's okay?"

Even at this traumatic time he did not fail to notice the nurse's ankles as she walked away, a bit of light relief in what was to be a gloomy twenty-four hours.

***

The intensive care unit was bright with light, monitors repeatedly sounding that life was still there. The steady metronome of life support was the soporific Roy needed. The nurse with the attractive ankles covered him with a red blanket and let him sleep.

"Mr Hanna, Mr Hanna!"

Roy jumped to attention; thoughts of his father rushed immediately to mind hearing the title.

"Mr Hanna, this is Doctor Elliot."

Doctor Elliot shook Roy's hand firmly. "Mr Hanna please sit down. I'm very sorry, but your mother passed away minutes ago, there was really nothing further we could do. Your father remains stable. Would you like to see your mother?"

Roy stared blankly, still feeling he was asleep. It was only the firm hand on his shoulder and the concerned stare of the doctor that brought him to his senses. "Yes, yes. Thank you doctor." He rubbed his eyes and smoothed his hair instinctively as he did before seeing her. She would always comment on his appearance.

His mother now looked so frail but somehow more human as the pipes and tubes had been removed. The bruising and cuts to her face did not distract him. He bent over and kissed her. "Why?" he muttered to himself.

"Is there anyone you would like me to call?" the nurse asked gently, laying her hand in condolence on his shoulder, sensitive to her intrusion.

"No, no, thank you. But could you get me some coffee please? Black."

Roy held his mother's small hand in his before stroking her forehead with his left hand. He began to weep. There was so much he needed to say, so much, but now that was impossible. The nurse entered with some coffee.

"I'm outside should you need me, take all the time you need, Mr Hanna."

His short smile and wet eyes said it all.

When he eventually left the room, he had said all he had needed to say when she was alive. The nurse was busy working with other patients. He was now immune to the sounds. A policeman was sitting alone by the door, coffee in hand and looking at his feet. He turned to look at Roy.

"Mr Hanna. PC Clark, sir. Is it convenient to talk? I'm sorry to hear your mother has passed away."

"About the accident?"

"Sir, I wonder if you might be able to help."

Chapter Four

The Cyprus morning had a beauty all of its own, kept at bay by the shuttered windows. It never ceased to amaze Joan just how dark and cool they made the room. She knew Roy was up and about but carried on drifting in and out of sleep.

Roy always liked to rise early when in Cyprus. He would dress in shorts, vest and Reeboks before descending the marble steps to the garden gate. He always turned left taking the road to the end. The corner house was home to a large dog that always greeted Roy with snarls and barks as it tried to slip the leash. A pomegranate tree grew at the corner and he enjoyed looking at the remnants of last year's crop that had the appearance of fossilised fruit. The road led through buildings that housed light industry flanking the Dhekelia Road, a way Roy had travelled down as a young squaddy and that had altered less than he. He turned right, breathing well and increasing his stride as the gradient increased. The road led to the border, the Green Line, No Man's Land. The view of the plain began to fill his peripheral vision, broad and vast, spreading to the mountains to the north.

The gradient increased and soon the masts of the British army base climbed vertically, pointers to the bastion that nestled over the hill some four miles ahead. The road levelled and within minutes the barrier signalling the end of the road came into view. Half a mile further on he waved at the relaxed Turkish police and soldiers. They recognised him and called out in Turkish. He smiled and headed home feeling better for the exercise, the air and the chance to think.

Breathing heavily, he momentarily stood at the gate. A car passed, horn sounding a morning greeting and a friendly arm waved. He lifted the key from under the mat and walked slowly up the stairs to the flat. He showered, the cold water refreshed him and he prepared breakfast.

The bedroom was suddenly filled with light as Roy pushed open the shutters allowing the slight breath of breeze to stir the stagnant air. Joan buried her face into the pillow.

"Shit!"

"Whatever happened to good morning?"

She lifted her head off the pillow to see the man in her life totally naked holding a tray on which was balanced a glass of freshly squeezed orange juice, toast and coffee.

"Madam has a choice today. She may have what is proffered on the tray or ..."

He pushed her back onto the bed his good hand slipping between her legs. The Cyprus morning was beautiful but it could always be enhanced.

"This toast is cold!" Joan chuckled.

"Never bloody satisfied some guests. Please put your complaint in writing to the management."

They smiled and held each other.

***

The road out of Famagusta was the main Nicosia road that ran past the airport. New housing had been constructed nearby behind eucalyptus trees that offered shelter from the summer sun's intensity. The way ran almost straight before bending, passing factory buildings and then the farmland of the Mesarya Plain.

The plain was hot and the road shimmered. The car was slow in comparison to the Subaru but it did its job. It had been hired for their stay from Tongus, a local garage owner Roy had known for years. They often met in London when Tongus visited his many relatives who now resided in England. The Suzuki jeep had certainly seen better times but it was reliable and was a convertible. The road was straight and the convenience of travelling on the left as in England caused no confusion, but hazards there were; grazing sheep, stopping buses and the many Turkish wagons with steering wheels on the 'wrong' side would often dice with the lives of others as they struggled to overtake. Roy on more than one occasion had to pull off the road.

The air was warm in Joan's hair as she sat, feet on the dashboard, the open-topped jeep allowing the breeze to penetrate the openings of her clothing. As they approached Nicosia they headed towards the mountains, Buffavento and Girne, one of the most spectacular bays you could ever wish to see. The road saddled the mountains at their lowest points but even so the climbs were twisting and breath-taking.

Roy had visited the area many times in 1988. Later, he had often brought his parents there and they had talked of retiring to a small house in the mountains, maybe Karmi, a village that nestled to the west of Girne. Just below the castle was their ideal and if they had relocated, they would have been alive today. The thoughts of his parents strolling around Girne in the hot summer sun upset him. He directed his thoughts to his fifty-seven bridges in England each secretly carrying Semtex and each having its own alarm, set like sleepers in Arthurian legend waiting for the right month, right day, right hour, minute and second; ticking like the life support machine that signalled life from death before the destined time when they would rise and bring destruction, turning the key to unlock his dreams.

The heavy air horn of the approaching wagon shook him bringing all his attention to the present. He steered the jeep straight with his right hand.

"Okay Roy?"

"Mm, just thinking about your early breakfast," he lied.

She placed her hand on his bare knee and squeezed it. "Where's this surprise?"

"Soon, soon."

***

The policeman walked Roy away from the noise of the intensive care suite.

"I'm sorry to hear the news of your mother, sir. A tragedy."

Roy could only nod. "Where was the accident?"

"I don't know if you're aware but there is a great number of road works on the M1 near Doncaster and traffic reduced to single lanes, something to do with strengthening all the bridges to meet a new EEC weight ruling. A right bloody mess if you ask me."

Roy's look said enough.

"Sorry, sir. Out of order. It appears that a maintenance vehicle rolled into the lane hitting your parents' car. There was no driver or workmen near the vehicle. We believe youths may have let the brake free. It's a tragedy, sir."

"What time was this?"

"We believe the accident occurred at about 4am on the sixteenth. At that time there was very little traffic but one other witness believes he saw youths in the area. The emergency services reached them as soon as possible. When it's convenient we would like to talk to your ..."

The conversation was interrupted by the nurse. "Mr Hanna your father is failing, please come."

Roy turned and followed the nurse but he was already too late, the silence from the life support said it all.

"God no!"

***

The forested mountains of Cyprus have a fragrance of their own; pine and thyme mix to form a heady concoction that fills the nostrils and warms the heart. Roy swung the jeep left following the signs. The blue sea below looked inviting and cold.

"If you're a good girl I might let you swim this afternoon."

"I've no costume young sir."

27

"Then swimming is definitely the order of the day!"

Soon the trees obscured the sea as they climbed higher. Before them in the distance they could see the castle perched on the pinnacle of rock where it had towered for over 900 years, a bastion in troubled times, and Roy's bastion, his haven. Although in this ruined, skeletal form the fortress was still awe-inspiring.

The thin black line of tarmac ran between the brown clay that rose sharply on either side of the vehicle, cutting out the sun and generating an unnatural cold even though the sky above was blue and clear. The road swept round bends and curves until again the castle faced them. To the left was a flat piece of land that was obviously levelled by man. Roy swung the jeep over, its wheels kicking up brown dust. He stood up holding the windscreen and then helped Joan. She stood on the seat. Roy inhaled deeply and the cool mountain air crashed into his lungs almost making him cough. He removed his Ray Ban sunglasses.

"Before you ask it's not a football pitch," he said squeezing Joan round the waist. "It's the original tilting ground from the time when knights were bold and ladies were for the taking."

"It's really beautiful Roy." Her face was masked by a deep admiration for the scale of it all.

"On the right is a small tower. It's now part of the Turkish Army base and they use the tilting ground as their gunnery range. You can make out the butts at the far end. The soldiers are probably watching you right now," he said in a mock Russian accent.

She laughed and kissed him gently. "Then we'd better give them something to report!"

"Wicked woman!" He kissed her.

Roy pulled her back into the seat, started the engine and selected first gear without breaking off the kiss. The jeep began to move slowly and she grabbed the dashboard. He laughed and accelerated onto the road towards the castle.

As the jeep pulled into the parking area beside a red Seat, the temperature was noticeably colder than on the plain. He jumped out, walked around the back of the Suzuki and held out his hand. "This way madam for the guided tour. The castle built by the Byzantines was named after a hermit named Hilarion. It was also surrendered to the English Crusading army under Richard the Lionheart in about 1191. It was later strengthened under the Lusignans and, believe it or not, became a summer palace. Cool yes?"

"You really surprise me. Where do you get all this bullshit, don't tell me you read it up?"

As they stood at the side of the road, their backs to the castle and looking over the twisting track that had led past the tilting ground, Roy briefly mentioned his time in the forces. His enthusiasm was clear. "Head's just full of nonsense," he announced almost apologetically. His mind was focused on his bridges, waiting. They passed through the vaulted passageway in the gatehouse before climbing the steep path. The temperature even at two thousand feet brought sweat to them both and the conversation ceased. Roy whistled gently as if concentrating his mind on the footpath. He paused a moment to allow them both to rest.

He had noticed a difference in his general health from the time he had returned from the Gulf; it was an indescribable lethargy, originally only momentary but these episodes escalated and there were some days that seemed to be cast in inertia. It was only in the last sixteen months that the true reality of the situation had brought fear and a deep resentment.

"Are you all right, Sir Galahad?"

"Yes, just had my breath taken away by the view; I never tire of it."

They carried on until they perched on the highest part. The breeze blew their hair, feeling chill against their damp, sweaty bodies.

Girne spread below them like white china on green baize, its castle and its harbour, its sports stadium and hotels. The coast, deckle-edged blue, ran as far as the eye could see.

"Roy, this is the most beautiful place I've ever seen." Joan leaned her head on his shoulder. Her outstretched hand pointed to a smattering of white houses that appeared like torn paper.

"Karmi," Roy answered without hearing the question.

To the east the mountain range ran away into the blue haze, broken periodically by shadows. Roy's thoughts ran wild. The injustice of it all, the thought of his parents, the war, the bridges ... the bridges. The knowledge of it all was as safe as the castle on which they sat, trapped in the memory of his palmtop; waiting like they had made him wait, as they carried on doing, but not for much longer. He was now in control.

The journey down was a delight and six or seven kilometres brought warmth and the comfort of people. Roy parked the jeep near the service station. A brief walk through the narrow streets brought them to the relatively quiet harbour. They stopped at one of the small cafes and ordered beers. At a pinch they could still see the mountain on which the castle sat but the ruins blended with the rock. Roy smiled. "To my castle, my love and the future." He lifted his glass and drank thirstily. The horseshoe shaped harbour was surrounded by traditional, four storey buildings that were originally built as warehouses. Now they were becoming homes, hotels and bars. In the harbour waters lay a variety of vessels, from brightly painted fishing boats to millionaires' yachts but there was still an air of space, as if this part of the Mediterranean was now forgotten.

"Your castle was a lovely surprise, Roy, and my day has been perfect, thank you."

He smiled, paid the bill and walked with her around the harbour wall. Water as clear as ice licked one side of the wall in a frenzy, its waves breaking, foaming white whilst the water in the harbour remained still and calm. Roy was the same, on the one hand he was serene and relaxed, enjoying his holiday whilst inside he was constantly mulling over the plan, sweeping every avenue ensuring nothing was left to chance. He had but this one opportunity, and it had to be right.

The journey back, including their picnic stop, was as perfect as the day itself. They stopped to buy groceries before heading home. Near the Government buildings and the Post Office was a small rusting train, wheel high in long grass, a remnant of the railway that once ran here. "Made in Leeds," announced Roy. "Makes me feel at home."

"Sad man," Joan nodded her head and tutted.

Roy parked the jeep in the shade of a palm tree that grew yards from the flat. A lizard scurried in the grass disturbing leaves, causing him to look down; you always seemed to hear them but never saw them, their camouflage was just perfect.

***

The airport at Ercan was fairly quiet as they prepared for their return journey. The calm was about to end for Roy, if only Joan knew that the storm was just around the corner. The 737 to Istanbul arrived on time and soon they would be home. Thoughts of the holiday were tossed in his mind as the aircraft shuddered gently in the turbulent air. He squeezed Joan's hand.

The change of plane was uneventful, a transfer he had made many times before. Strange how he could never pass through this airport without thinking of 'Midnight Express'! The flight over Europe was relaxing, a fitting end to the holiday. He had again seen Joan in a different light, he had grown contented in her company.

The pilot announced that the weather in Manchester was wet. It always is, thought Joan, as she raised her eyebrows. They fastened their seat belts in readiness for landing. Grey clouds swirled menacingly outside the aircraft window and the plane shuddered as it descended into the grey stratus. The noise in the cabin increased as the plane touched down. Joan gripped Roy hard, instinctively.

Once through customs they made their way to the car park. The Subaru was there, dusty but with all its glass in the right place and not in pieces around it.

"Glad to be on our way home?" quizzed Roy.

Joan said little as she stared at the wet motorway interrupted by sweeping windscreen wipers and rain. "I could live there, Roy. I could leave all this tomorrow." She began to cry.

"Find some music, please," he requested, in the hope of easing away the post-holiday depression. "One day we'll do just that and maybe sooner than you think."

The last word was drowned out by music from the stereo.

Chapter Five

Drew was in the office earlier than usual and Roy's early start was noted. They talked briefly about the holiday before Drew brought Roy up to date with the happenings in the business machine industry. Roy was pleased to hear some cold calls had been rewarded with firm orders. Emma brought in coffee and asked about Cyprus. Roy retrieved from his bag what was obviously a bottle.

"A little thank you. Hope you enjoy it. The best from Turkish Cyprus."

Emma blushed at the unexpected gift, she thanked Roy and grinned before leaving the room.

"I'm going to be busy today Drew so I'll be in the office all day. Lunch later?"

"Sounds good. Glad you're back."

Roy went into his office placing his case on the floor near the desk before returning to retrieve his coffee. He sat behind his desk swivelling the leather chair until he was facing the wall on which hung a picture of himself as a younger man. He was sitting against the side of a Warrior armoured vehicle dressed in desert pattern army fatigues. The strange mottled light caused by the scrim net; the camouflaged netting that festooned the vehicle created an unreal image; a tranquil, ethereal marking on everything beneath. His face was smiling and confident, a face that had yet to experience death, mutilation and the evil of which man was so easily capable.

Roy remembered receiving news of his call to the Gulf, it had excited him more than he expected. He had been preparing for this, it was his job. Some soldiers never have the opportunity to fight in a real war situation. All too often they had a 'hands tied' role as peacekeepers and this was frustrating, one-sided and bloody dangerous. His first tour of

Ireland brought these facts home to him as clearly as a slap in the face.

From before the outset of Operation Desert Storm on 17th January 1991 Roy had been with his fusiliers in the Gulf. He had arrived from Hanover one of fifteen thousand troops making up the second wave, others had been there longer and the air force was well and truly established. Originally flying into Dhahran in Saudi Arabia, their primary role at that time was one of protecting Saudi from the possible attack from Iraq. He had spent twenty-four hours at the Black Adder lines, the receiving point for British troops, named after the comedy programme, before moving into the desert and front line positions for training. It soon became clear to all that Saddam had no intention of leaving his new found territory of Kuwait without some kind of push and now the number of troops and weapons amassing at the borders would certainly give him the Father of all Battles.

Once in position the troops cleaned weapons and practised to be totally prepared for what was to come. However, none would be prepared for the awesome speed that the push would take, the confusion, the atrocious weather, the anxiety over gas attack and amidst all this the very real possibility of fratricide. Troops had been allocated NBC suits and body armour and all vehicles, including Roy's, were decorated with an inverted 'V' using fluorescent and reflective tape, a universal sign of friendly force to the hundreds of aircraft and other heavy ground machines that trundled, eager for action, through the desert. By February 23rd Roy's Warrior, fully equipped, was within the leading attack group. They were ready and the following day with pennants and flags flying from the rats' tail aerials, they were moving over the desert, red identification tail lights ablaze; they were hunting. The radio inside the Warrior hummed with the constant noise of war as orders and information passed backwards and forwards. The groups often dealt with Iraqis, who more often than not surrendered quickly after heavy guns attacked their positions.

The Iraqi troops, often ill, poorly dressed and badly fed would prove no match.

Roy's Warrior, Delta Six, and its partner, Echo Eight, were instructed to deal with an Iraqi Chemical stockpile and even though Roy, as leading commander of the two vehicles, protested that this was not really his job, he, with his explosives' knowledge, found little difficulty in seeing the job through. It seemed strange to him afterwards that he entered the area totally unprepared for any effects of the sinister stockpile of lethal weapons or the effects of the aftermath. The job had to be done swiftly and as efficiently as possible. The removal and burial of the drums was easily achieved. The area was marked on the charts and the co-ordinates taken from the Global Positioning equipment in the Warrior were relayed to HQ.

The two Warriors had been separated from the group for twenty-four hours and rested. The weather was showing signs of improvement, the clouds were lifting and light was beginning to break into the sky, blue was visible. It was then it happened. They had feared this from the outset but there was nothing they could do. Two American A10 tank buster aircraft had dropped from the gloom, decided the Warriors were enemy and lined up for the kill. The Maverick missiles launched and accurately found the cold targets. Roy's Warrior was hit first. The explosion was immense. Roy standing in the turret was blown clear of the main body of the vehicle but the men inside were less fortunate, all died instantly. The second missile was less forgiving; it completely destroyed machine and men. Of fourteen, Roy was the only survivor. However, he was injured. His left hand had been crushed.

The two aircraft had disappeared into the cloud before they had seen the hits but they soon returned to view their kills. Roy in pain cursed their inability to see their Arabic 8, their reverse 'V', before the pain of his injured hand caused him to pass out.

***

The shrill ringing of the phone brought Roy back to his senses. It was Joan. "Missing you. Seems strange not having you near after two weeks together."

"Thought you were teaching."

"Some non-contact, wanted to let you know how much I love you."

"I love you too. Strange to be back. Just can't seem to get motivated, I feel so bloody low ... post-holiday blues I guess."

"Must go, Roy. Will you be home early?"

"The sooner the better today. See you tonight,"

The morning passed with most of the work only being completed with great determination and grit, he was having a bad day and it was out of his control, they were definitely worse now than before. He'd had all the tests, corresponded with others from the Gulf who had similar symptoms but it seemed that there was little tolerance or understanding for the syndrome. He was, he felt, lucky. Some peoples' lives had been totally devastated by what they believed were the side effects of injected substances each and every serving soldier had endured in order to remain safe from Saddam's noxious gasses that could bring death, horrible death, in seconds. The daily NAPS, washed down with tea three times a day were also untested other than in the Gulf. By March 1991 it was rumoured that troops had been exposed to mustard gas and Sarin, fallout from damaged storage dumps; all denied emphatically.

It had become clear to Roy that his condition was neither hereditary nor something contracted recently, but that had its incubation in the desert at the hands of his own government, the same government who now refused to accept any responsibility for turning men into the sick and dying. Even their offspring were, if not born with serious defects, showing early signs of genetic disorders. It was even rumoured that thousands of health records, along with Roy's, showed glaring irregularities and had been accidentally wiped from the MOD computer before any investigation could take place. He had known three fusiliers who had died since their return; they too had suffered similar symptoms. One had grown so depressed he had taken his own life after murdering his wife and child. These were a few of the many. There was something wrong, something needed investigating.

It was this frustration, this battling with the subterfuge of immorality that welded with the need for his personal battle, a battle that if successful might pave the way for a realistic settlement for those he knew. He was going out but he was going to go out fighting, in the only way he knew. To hit where there would be pain, pain like they had never felt before. They would not be in a position to ignore, pass the buck, they would be totally exposed. Even if demands were secret, the public would bring pressure to bear. Their fear and confusion would force an outcome, an outcome that would be swift and just. This was his only chance to bridge the gap in his life and its uncertain future that had been created, in his opinion, by the Gulf War.

The telephone again broke his train of thought. It angered him. It clearly sounded in his voice. "Yes?"

"You all right, Roy?" questioned Drew, obviously taken aback by the forthright reception.

"Shit, sorry. Not feeling too bright. How about an earlier lunch than planned, I need to talk to you."

"Thought you'd locked yourself away, it's 12.30 now."

Roy grabbed his jacket from the chair and crossed the room glancing back at the photograph.

"Jesus, why me!" He flung the door open to meet Drew who was just leaving his office. Their eyes met and Drew realised Roy was worse than he had thought, it was more than just a bad day. He too had noticed that the man was changing.

Drew's early recollections of Roy were as a schoolboy, when he had first moved into the premises in West Street. He had memories of telling off the youth for playing football and loitering in the doorway on wet nights; in those impoverished days the flat above the shop was Drew's home, a far cry from today. He had been kept informed of the young man's progress when Mrs Hanna worked for him. The initial disappointment she showed in his career choice soon grew into pride. On her desk was a photograph of a handsome soldier, her son. There had been concerns too during his time in Belfast and Operation Desert Storm. Drew felt he knew Roy but he also was aware of a metamorphosis. He had seen changes, not purely the physical but the psychological. He had never quizzed him about the Gulf conflict, he had only been his support.

"We'll take my car as you need a drink. I'll run you home afterwards. The car's safe enough here."

Roy smiled, a smile of genuine gratitude. He lifted his hand and touched Drew's shoulder. "I owe you."

"Go to the car and I'll be with you in a tick."

Roy left the reception area. Drew made it clear to Emma that Roy would be out for the rest of the day. "Don't call me unless it's urgent. See the lads in the warehouse or put it off until I get back. I'll bring you back some prawn crackers." He winked and left. Roy was already in the car.

The journey seemed long, neither spoke. Instead of the usual pub Drew pulled into the car park of an upmarket Chinese restaurant. "Have you eaten here before?"

"Yes, must be two years ago. Special birthday treat for ... Christ can't even remember her name."

"There's been so many? You are having a bad day."

The restaurant was quiet, as Drew had hoped. It was obvious that he was a regular by the greeting he received. They were soon shown to a table pointed out by Drew during the handshake and welcome. A pint of lager and a Perrier arrived soon after they were seated.

"How hungry do you feel?" challenged Drew as he passed the menu. "The duck's bloody good."

"Cheers. Thanks for the time." Roy drank deeply before placing the frosted glass in front of him. He ran his finger round the cold rim. "Do you know, Drew, the depressions are coming thick and fast. The doctor says there's nothing wrong, I'm in fine form apart from the obvious." Roy lifted his left hand. "Do you believe there's something in this Gulf War Syndrome?"

"Well apart from the Government denying any knowledge of the problem, it seems to me, if you want the opinion of a salesman, that someone is sitting on fucking info that's explosive. There's so much being covered up that if it blows, litigation is going to fall on the heads of the powers that be like confetti at a spring bride's wedding. There's absolutely no chance of the truth coming to the surface. The files will no doubt be lost, people will deny any knowledge of error, mistake, malpractice or incompetence. In fact, the only way, in my opinion, that the truth will ever come out is if America spills the beans. What are your real beliefs and fears, Roy?"

During the course of the meal, Roy spelled it out clearly as he saw the situation. He tried to give a clear, honest picture of what troops on the ground faced during their time in the war. The seemingly endless injections, the removal and destruction of arms dumps; huge arsenals stockpiled with God only knew what! The destruction of identified chemical weapon factories and the fumes from burning oil wells that turned day into night, Kuwait into Golgotha. Roy had clearly made an impact. Drew had barely touched his meal.

"Is the food not good today, Mr McKenna?" enquired the waiter, genuinely concerned that his guests were insulted by the food.

"Er ... no, no sorry. The food was delicious. It was my appetite that was at fault. I've never had a bad meal here yet and you haven't let us down today. Thank you." The waiter's interruption had broken the spell and brought them back from 1991, away from the cold wet desert. "I never realised it was like that, even though I watched the reports on television and read the coverage in the press. I just never thought about the sinister implications. Can I help in any way?"

"You're helping just by being here. There'll come a time in the not too distant future when I may feel like this every day, feel as though I can't get out of bed, can't work. Some days I feel so desperately tired I haven't the energy to wash and shave. You really just can't imagine the feeling, the frustration and the humiliation. I'm still a young man for fuck's sake!"

Roy's eyes filled, more in frustration than hurt or self-pity. He couldn't remember a time he had felt such anguish, such a feeling of impotence.

Drew felt for the young man, a sympathy that was real and deep. He truly had no idea of the depths of Roy's inner confusion but sitting opposite as tears filled his friend's eyes he saw it, only faintly at first but it was there, he saw it grow and swell within the tears that hung in each eye: a resentment so deep it caused him to sit back. His expression brought uncertainty and he could clearly see a stranger opposite, a stranger who was capable of unthinkable deeds.

"I'm sorry, Drew. You really don't need to hear all this. I'm sorry. I think you might need to start thinking about finding someone to replace me. Sooner rather than later I'll be no good to myself let alone you. I'll be knackered, not worth a toss. Maybe I was the unlucky one from the Warrior." His anger was palpable.

"You'll be there, you'll be there my friend. Another beer?" Drew immediately realised Roy had hardly touched the one he had. "Come on, I'll take you home. You certainly need some rest."

The journey was again a silent, thoughtful passage but both men were aware of the need for silence; it marked a respect. The car swung to the kerb outside the terraced house.

"Thanks, Drew. Coffee?"

"No thanks. You get yourself a brandy and get some rest. I'll give Joan a ring tonight. Keep your chin up mate."

Roy smiled, closed the door and stood back. Drew waved and pulled away.

Chapter Six

Once inside the house, Roy moved upstairs. He closed the bedroom curtains and lay on the bed and wept, wept like he'd never wept before. He was a well of frustration oozing out of control. No matter to whom he turned there was a sympathetic ear, a pat on the back but nothing concrete, no decision or admission. He could see that he would become a statistic of Government manipulation. His anger welled up, drowning the frustration and he moved to the other bedroom, his study. There on the desk next to a piece of the Warrior that had been destroyed so long ago in the desert was his palmtop computer, identical in every way to the ones he'd used to power and time the explosives on all fifty-seven bridges; expensive, accurate and very, very reliable.

He sat and looked briefly out of the window before lifting the lid, almost like opening an oyster shell, to reveal the keypad and screen. He pressed the 'on' command and a request for the password appeared on screen. He typed in 'Arthur' and immediately the agenda file appeared. Using the menu he typed in the word 'Bridge' and the date came up on screen. 'Gathurst, M6. Sept 7th 17:59 hours'. He had chosen the time to cause limited personal injury, the warning should ensure that, but maximum disruption and inconvenience; the M6 at this time was chaotic and with north and south lanes closed it would become a policeman's worst nightmare! The leniency was only temporary.

If the Government failed to follow his instructions then the warning times would grow dangerously short and lives would certainly be at risk. He hoped that they would meet all his demands without a single life being lost but he was prepared to risk all: he was prepared to see all fifty-seven bridges destroyed, and people with them, if that was what it would take.

He checked his watch, 4th September. Just three days. He had planned to send a warning for the first three bridges using the code word, 'Gulf'. He hoped that it might throw them off track for a short time, possibly consider fundamentalists until they received forensic evidence. If he were to be really lucky this charade might continue beyond the first tranche.

The coded message would be sent to the Automobile Association using their vehicle breakdown free phone number. If they failed to pass the message on, believing it to be the work of a crank, then someone would be aware of the error and the police would eventually be involved, but he was sure in these times that procedures would be in place to deal with this type of call. He also believed that the calls were recorded or a number stored. He had chosen the call box with care, away from prying eyes. He had checked the boxes thoroughly whilst planning the bridges. There was obviously an element of risk with this as it had never ceased to amaze him what a small world it was and that one could bump into acquaintances at the most inopportune times, but hopefully not in the country well away from home. It was a calculated risk he feared but one he was equally prepared to accept.

Roy heard the key in the lock and Joan entered and began to climb the stairs. She would not be expecting him home with the car not being parked in the street. He called her name but she was still shaken.

"What are you doing home? I didn't see the car."

"Had an absolutely shit morning and Drew took me for lunch. Good pair of ears has Drew and I kind of moaned on. He was terrific Joan."

"How are you feeling now? Can I get you anything?"

"A kiss would be a tonic."

Joan moved towards him and kissed him lovingly, breaking away to whisper, "I love you," before resuming.

"I had a rest this afternoon so right now I'm not feeling too bad. Probably an early night will do me good."

"Thought you were ill," she goaded mischievously.

"Sorry, not tonight my flower," sighed Roy with a true sense of loss. "I could make you a coffee though, fancy?"

"Lovely, I'm going to take a shower and I'll be down in a few minutes."

Roy pressed the off key and closed the list on the palmtop before turning along the landing. Joan came out of the bedroom naked. She was fit and trim. She had been a member of a local gym for years and the hard work and dedication was reflected in an athletic figure. Her breasts were small and firm and her stomach flat. They kissed but Roy, against his manly instincts, pulled himself away. He moved downstairs and into the kitchen.

As the coffee was poured Joan came into the kitchen wearing her robe.

"Smells good."

They chatted about their work before settling on the sofa. For the first time in the day he felt in control.

***

Drew phoned at 8am the next day. Roy answered. "Listen, I don't expect you to be in the office today but I do expect you to see a friend of mine. His name is Bill O'Brien, he's a psychiatrist. I've known him a long time, in fact without him whilst I was going through my divorce, I think I might have topped myself. If you can ring him on this number and sort out an appointment; he's expecting you to call but would appreciate it before 9.30 this morning. I'm sending your car round with one of the warehouse lads under threat of death that he does no more than 30mph. I'll talk with you later." He hung up before Roy could protest or be abusive.

Roy knew his friend was acting in his best interest but still felt there was nothing to be gained. He gave it half an hour and then rang the number.

Bill O'Brien was driving into work when his mobile rang. "O'Brien," was always his curt answer.

"Hello, my name's Roy Hanna, Drew McKenna suggested I should ring you this morning."

"Hello, yes good to hear you've taken his advice. He's very concerned by the threat of losing his best man. Do you feel you can meet me today? I can make two o'clock or if that doesn't suit maybe tomorrow."

"Two o'clock is fine. Where can we meet?"

Bill gave the address of his clinic over the phone, wished him goodbye and hung up.

The meeting was more fruitful than Roy had hoped yet he was disappointed as they relaxed on two soft easy chairs.

"No couch?" posed Roy to ease his nerves.

"There is if you would prefer but I'm sure you are more comfortable here."

It was obvious that Bill was not only up to date with the psychological symptoms of those who had fought in the war but also he was involved in the latest diagnoses from his colleagues in the States. It was apparent that there was a clear acknowledgement of the problem and that this acceptance was half way to solving it. Bill had requested information from the Internet with some success. However, a colleague with whom he'd worked was practising in a hospital in Florida and was involved in the counselling of a number of critical Gulf War troops.

The discussion lasted just over the hour and although relaxed was certainly intense. Roy found himself telling his life story to a complete stranger. It was, however, good to talk. It seemed to release a pressure that grew and grew with the anxieties of everyday life until it was all-consuming, until his head seemed full of clashing thoughts, ideas that not only conflicted but grew almost tumour-like, eating away any positive ideals that might have been there. It was in this mental cauldron of contempt that the maelstrom of his plans was conceived and strangely, no matter how deeply Bill would delve, these would remain hidden. These secrets were Roy's only lifeline of hope and he was going to cling on to them no matter how cotton thin they were.

They agreed to meet again in a week using the same venue. They shook hands and Roy left. Passing through reception he smiled at the young secretary. She returned his smile out of politeness. "See you again we hope."

On leaving the clinic he walked along the street that was now busy. There was a florist's shop on the corner with the most beautiful arrangements of cut flowers. He stopped to look. He chose twenty large yellow carnations for Joan, a sort of good-girl present for putting up with him. They would certainly make her day.

Roy quickly found the car and put the flowers in the boot. He dialled work.

"D.M. Business Machines, Emma speaking how may I help you?" How that now standard answer grated on his nerves. He must speak to Drew and work out a more original greeting.

"Emma it's Roy. Is Drew free, please?"

"Sorry to hear you were under the weather. You need another holiday." She giggled at her own joke. "The wine was lovely, thank you. I'll just try him for you." The earpiece filled with the sound of Jerusalem as if played on a Jew's harp. "He's on the other line but he says he'll call you back shortly. Are you on your mobile?"

"Yes. Thanks Emma. See you later this week."

He started the car and drove carefully towards the pay booth. As he handed his ticket over the phone rang. He paid before answering.

"Roy, Drew. How did it go?"

"Quite some man your Dr O'Brien." He was interrupted by the sound of a horn. The driver behind in the queue grew anxious that Roy was taking too long at the pay booth. "Shit!" He selected first gear and waved an apology to the guy behind. Pulling into the traffic he continued his conversation. "He certainly is aware. We seemed to get on well and he now has some background to the situation so who knows, he may turn out to be the tonic I need."

"Let's hope so, my friend, let's hope so. I've cancelled any meetings you had arranged until Friday to give you some breathing space but only return when you feel up to the job."

"I'll ring you at home tonight. Drew, thanks, I really appreciate your concern and support."

Roy was soon out of the worst traffic. The weather was fine. Two more days, just two. He felt the tension in the pit of his stomach rise. Thursday would be the day.

Joan was delighted with the flowers and everything stopped until they were arranged and placed on the table.

"They're lovely Roy. You shouldn't have but I'm glad you did. She kissed him. Fancy a shower?" she quizzed hoping to draw him out.

"Love one."

The cool water flowed through their hair as they kissed. She soaped his body into a lather and then he hers. She raised a leg placing it being his back and they made love.

Chapter Seven

The next two days moved slowly. Even though Roy went into work, he could not believe how the clock seemed to stand still. It reminded him of when he was a child waiting for Christmas or a birthday. His nights were on the whole uninterrupted. He slept well.

On the morning of the 7th, he was pleased to see the sunshine. Radio Four filled the room. Joan stirred and he kissed her. "You shower first and I'll sort out breakfast."

He was keen to start, to get over the initial explosion. Once the ball was rolling he would, he thought, feel better, more in control knowing that his device had worked. The strange thing about a bomb was that there was no guarantee.

He moved to the study and checked the details on his palmtop once more. There it was in green and black timed for 17.59. Could he remain normal, if ever he had been normal since the Gulf or at all for that matter? Could he mask his anxiety or was there a touch of excitement eager to erupt?

He went downstairs and turned on the radio. No real news but how quickly that was going to change. Tomorrow morning would certainly be different and that would be all his doing. He, Roy Hanna, invalid, Gulf War veteran ignored by many, particularly the government, would begin to bring pressure to bear. Tomorrow's news would be his.

***

Those days in February 1991 had been just the same; it was in the desert that he had felt these bursts of emotion, watching fellow soldiers writing home, maybe for the last time. It amazed him the thoughts that were juggled in the mind at moments like these. All personal photographs that might compromise the captured soldier were stored and left behind, only the mental images of girlfriends and wives floated in a mind that dimmed and blurred the edges of familiar faces. Fear, passion and anticipation had the power to do this. The night in the desert separated from the main group, the cold, the comradeship, the fear; the moment standing in the turret knowing that split second that something was wrong, the tingling in the body that overpowered movement, speech, and thought raced back into Roy's mind. He was sweating as he flipped closed the palmtop with the same ease the missiles had closed the chapter on fourteen young lives. He stared at the black cased computer as if it were his own coffin. He would see it through today. He placed it on the table and moved downstairs.

***

The Subaru pulled up some way from the telephone box Roy had earmarked. It was situated in a quiet, isolated spot away from heavy traffic both pedestrian and vehicular. He sat quietly in the car for a while checking the area to ensure his first impressions of the site were accurate. His heart was beating and he felt as though its thumping filled the car. "This is it," he said to himself and broke into a whistle that naturally concealed his apprehension. He jumped out and again checked the free phone number of the breakdown service before strolling to the red telephone box. He went through his speech carefully in his head before picking up the receiver in his gloved hand and dialling, placing the suffix 141 to prevent the call from being automatically traced. The call was answered immediately by a request for a membership number.

"Please listen, this is very important as your ability to relay this message could save lives. Bomb, Gathurst Bridge on M6. Timed to blow 17.59 today. Give them this code. GULF. If they think it's a hoax tell them to wait until they hear the bang!" It was now out of his hands. They had fifty-seven minutes to react.

Sarah had worked as a telephonist with the breakdown service for just short of twelve months. Her training had been good; an extensive part of her risk assessment management had covered this very problem. At the time, like most, she thought it would never happen to her but today it had, today she had felt a chill run down her spine as this man, possibly a terrorist had spoken to her. Her action had, after, the initial shock, been one driven by instinct. She knew the message was recording as he spoke and she looked for the details of the call area and if possible, the call box. The system for locating a call to a specific box was not as yet complete but there was hope. No, the actual box was not noted but the dialling code area was shown. Her mouth was dry and sweat beaded her forehead. She called the supervisor. Her mind raced.

"I've just taken a bomb threat, I'm sorry but he didn't give me any time he just spoke without gaps. There remain only fifty-seven minutes."

The supervisor immediately called the police using 999 and played the threat to them, in turn they recorded the message. It took eleven minutes from the call being received to the motorway warning signals beginning to slow the traffic, issuing speed limits to traffic approaching the bridge in both directions. Police vehicles too were moving into position.

Peter Jones had been sitting in his police Range Rover on a slip road off the motorway completing paperwork, he was due off shift within the hour. The traffic had been increasing and it astonished him how foolish drivers could be. He had his own equation: the greater the traffic, the more hazardous the conditions the faster the traffic. It also never ceased to amaze him the effect the distinctive livery of his vehicle had on the drivers' brakes, there was a distinct slowing when they noticed it waiting! He had seen it all. Large drops of rain mixed with the remnants of squashed flies on the windscreen when the call came through. "Shit, that's all I need! Lights, siren, action!" he shouted out loud as he selected both and swung the Range Rover onto the hard shoulder.

As if by magic the traffic to his right slowed more in keeping with the electronic speed restriction signals. He moved into the inside lane and then the middle slowing the traffic in all lanes down to 30mph. The Pied Piper had nothing on this. It was obvious from the change of traffic flow southbound that the same was happening further north on the opposite carriageway. Another Range Rover, all lights aglow, streamed down the hard shoulder and took up station to his left. Peter moved further to the outside lane. The line of traffic behind was going to leave the motorway at the next junction whether they liked it or not. "What a fucking time to explode a bomb, if there is a bomb," he thought to himself. He had one eye on the mirror. Up ahead was junction 26. They would hold the three lanes of snarling vehicles and then lead them away down the slip road whilst other police vehicles blocked the motorway. The speed was reduced to a walking pace and then a to a standstill. Both police vehicles held station. The passenger in the second vehicle climbed out and moved to the rear of the Range Rover. Peter took out a pile of cones and ran ahead placing them across the three lanes at an angle to lead the cars and wagons off. He then pointed to the cars in the inside lane to move toward the slip road. They obeyed his instruction. The rain continued to fall.

It was obvious to Peter that the operation for the southbound track had been successful as no vehicles passed on the other side. It was going to be a long night. Another Range Rover travelled quickly up the opposite, now empty carriageway and dropped off three policemen, more reinforcements to help deal with the traffic as it snarled to a standstill at the bottom of the slip road. Soon it would be moving, if only very slowly.

The bomb squad had been called immediately and were to be helicoptered in, landing on the empty carriageway ahead of the traffic. Further men and equipment would travel in Transac Bomb disposal vehicles up the now empty southbound carriageway. It would be impossible to move north now any other way. Each vehicle would carry all the necessary equipment to deal with any threat. If this were a hoax it would just cause a delay to traffic for a couple of hours; if it were for real, God only knew what the outcome would be.

The Aerospatiale AS 355F Twin Squirrel touched down bringing spray up from the road surface. Its blades cut the air noisily sending out turbulence that rocked the very close central reservation lighting standards. Two men, dressed in waterproof high visibility police clothing climbed out. Peter's Range Rover was requested to move close. Some equipment was lifted from the helicopter and carried to the waiting vehicle. The helicopter lifted off. The men climbed into the Rover. They quickly introduced themselves.

The helicopter travelled north, gaining height. Wispy grey cloud hung like tentacles.

"He's going to check for any strange packages in deserted vehicles that might be on the bridge." The officer was linked with his own communicator and headset.

"Paul, there's nothing visible here. Going around one more time. Be back on the ground in a minute."

Out of the gloom came the white Squirrel which was put down expertly on the spot. A man jumped out, waved at the pilot and the helicopter lifted off. The running man came around the Range Rover and jumped in the back.

The explosives officers knew from the coding of the threat that this was not IRA but the code GULF brought fears of fundamentalists. But why blow up a bridge in Greater Manchester? They all thought it the work of a rogue nutter who had seen too many Rambo films. The game plan was now simple. They would wait for the deadline, now only six minutes away plus thirty minutes before kitting up and going in for a look. It was clear from police reports that no vehicles were parked beneath nor were there any canal boats moored under it, so whatever the explosive device was, it had to be attached beneath the span of the bridge either to the legs or hidden within the structure.

Traffic was now tailing back ten miles in both directions. The serpent was growing at an alarming rate; not only was it extending along the motorway but the slip roads were filling up and this had a knock-on effect, it was total confusion.

The train from Wigan to Southport had left Wigan Wallgate station on time and was due to stop at Gathurst at 17.50 but was delayed due to signal problems. Although the motorway was sealed off the railway had failed to receive any information of the potential danger. The train was cleared and arrived at Gathurst station at 17.57. The old road ran parallel to the motorway but dipped into the valley, under the railway and over the canal before climbing through woodland, the same route Roy had taken on the evening he had set the explosives. This road had been closed, as had the road to the station. The few houses in the vicinity had been evacuated leaving only a patrol car by the hump-backed bridge, out of harm's way. The station was empty of passengers, the station house long since disused.

The train pulled in momentarily. Nobody left nor joined. Rain ran down the windows smearing the dirt. Patterns caused by the airflow had almost obscured the clarity of view. A push on the throttle and the diesels belched smoke as they moved the two-carriage train away slowly gaining speed. It soon crossed the country road that led to the canal. The rain was coming down harder now. The driver saw the police car, lights flashing. Blue patterns smudged against the window and illuminated his cab. He also noted the motorway bridge ahead was unusually quiet. Normally at this time it was full of traffic. "Must have been some kind of accident ... should take the train," he said to himself as he smiled. How prophetic in his innocence. The time was 17.58 and 40 seconds. This was a beautiful part of the run, the line bordered the valley side above the canal and the river and was flanked by woodland and fields.

The Senior Expo, Sam Phelps checked his watch. "If this is no hoax it's going any minu ..."

He never finished his sentence. There was a brilliant flash followed by an almighty bang as the sound waves echoed around the valley. Birds staggered into the air, flying haphazardly. Smoke and dust followed in concert; it all appeared to be happening in slow motion. The force had been huge.

"Jesus H! Is everyone intact?" Sam enquired, obviously shocked. He had truly believed this one would be a hoax. "Learned a lesson there, boy," he said to himself.

The Range Rover moved forward at the instruction of the senior officer. "Take it slowly, Peter."

Small pieces of debris hit the roof of the vehicle. There appeared to be no major damage from that distance but there surely must have been. The view of the explosion from below was quite different. The bridge itself had cracked like an egg along its expansion joints leaving gaps similar to veins in the tarmac. Some gaping holes had appeared directly above the blasts. The bridge had sunk as the bearings on which it rested had been destroyed. The crash barriers were bent and twisted and many of the drainage covers had been propelled skywards. The central reservation lights along its entire length were haphazardly set at angles like drunken men.

They called in the helicopter from its hovering position a safe distance away. It had recorded events on the video it carried. It soon landed. The Senior Expo climbed aboard and it took off quickly in case another bomb was set.

"Bloody mayhem below the bridge," said the pilot as he brought his craft sideways to give all a clear view. "I've sent for emergency support but how they'll get there ..."

Sam could not believe his eyes. The scene beneath the bridge was reminiscent of a war zone. The tranquillity had been destroyed. The lock-keeper's cottage was without roof tiles and windows, curtains flapping as if in surrender. The rain began to seep in. The underside of the bridge was blackened and pieces of steel and concrete hung, motionless. It was not these things their eyes focused on but the train that had caught the blast, it had been directly underneath. The force of the blast or some debris had jumped it off the rails. It had ploughed into one of the concrete legs as it turned over, twisting the first carriage under the second in a jack-knife motion. The driver had died as soon as his cab had hit the concrete, he did not even have time to think. The passengers were not so lucky. Death came more slowly in the tangled confusion. Although there were only twenty people, all probably on their way home, the jarring twisting metal and the ensuing fire had found each and every one. Those trapped by their arms and legs could only watch the light of the approaching flames through thickening acrid, choking fumes that tore at their throats and eyes. Those free to move but cut and bloody were soon overcome, their breathing slowing and their anguish growing. They screamed and tore at the metal until their fingers bled but slowly, they died. The pall of thick smoke rose through the bridge giving an indication to Peter and those in the Range Rover that something was wrong, terribly wrong, down below.

Sam transmitted to his team, the shock in his voice quite audible. "Major problems down below, serious damage to a train and there is an horrendous fire. I can't see there being any survivors. Did no one notify the railway of this problem? If not, someone better do it now in case there's another train on its way. What a fucking mess." Sam was more shocked than angry. "Has the backup arrived?"

"Yes, they're just arriving now."

"Kit up Paul, take Mike with you and check the bloody bridge." There was a pause but the transmit button was still down. The noise of the helicopter could still be heard "And Paul ..."

"Yes, Boss?"

"Take special care, I've got a horrible feeling about this nutter. Things aren't what they might seem."

"I'm always careful."

Two Expo Officers moved to the rear of the bomb disposal vehicles and started to prepare for their walk. Their aim was to search for any remaining devices that had been set to explode during the checking process and to take a closer look at the damage caused to the bridge. Both men were dressed in lightweight bomb disposal suits which offered protection and flexibility. The suits' helmets contained their own de-misters, essential in the wet weather and transmitters. They also had their own cooling systems which were invaluable when things grew that little too hot. Each man also carried a bag in which were a number of search mirrors. The job would be to comb all the drains and around the concealed areas on the top of the bridge. The search took more than an hour and proved that there was only the one bomb. Both men returned, pleased to be back and relieved that the bridge was clear.

The helicopter touched down. The rain had now stopped. The bomb disposal team began to clear away. Smoke continued to spiral skywards, clearly marking the burning pyre that sheltered beneath the now fragile span. The bomb had done its job.

Chapter Eight

Roy had just pulled up outside the house, his brain buzzing with anticipation. His thoughts were broken by the reality of a newsflash on the radio warning drivers that delays on the M6 were now tailing back eighteen miles and that there was serious congestion on all roads in the vicinity. He was gratified to hear that this 'problem' might last a number of days and drivers were being asked to seek an alternative route. He turned the ignition key and the engine's rumble ceased. He closed the car door and went in. Joan was sitting watching the television, a coffee in one hand. He smiled and put his jacket on a hook by the door.

"Any news?" His question was without sincerity as he was still mulling over his success and the aura he exuded sparked Joan's curiosity.

"Not really, work was as usual. Have you heard the news of the bombing?"

He tried to look surprised but replied that he had caught snippets on the radio, "Somewhere on the M6, I believe." He felt his face flush slightly and he knew that Joan had noticed. "Anyone hurt?"

"Apparently the bomb de-railed a train that was travelling under the bridge and they believe many were killed. There were no cars on the bridge as a warning had been issued. We live in a world of mad bastards. Who on earth would want to do a thing like this? What could it possibly prove and what might they gain?" She looked at Roy squarely, as she often did but on this occasion he felt uncomfortable. His eyes diverted to the television before settling back to hers when he had regained some of his composure. He was shocked. There was a genuine feeling of nausea building in his stomach, and he left and went to the bathroom. He vomited.

His appearance in the mirror was one that shocked. He suddenly looked old and his skin pale. Guilt had started to take its toll.

"Are you all right, Roy?"

He heard the sound of Joan coming up the steps and he flushed the toilet quickly and took a drink from the tap to refresh his mouth. "Yes, just a little queasy, must be something I ate at lunch."

He opened the door and smiled at her. She looked confused and concerned. She held out her hands and hugged him. "Go for a lie down. Would you like something to drink?"

"No, no I'll be fine." His mind whirled and the thoughts of the killings filled every cavity of his brain. "I'll be fine. Let's go downstairs."

He was not a murderer, he never had been. He had been taught only to kill the enemy and he found difficulty in visualising this universal pariah; all too often the propaganda posters of the World Wars came to mind and although they stirred the spirit of a nation, they only confirmed that his victory today was pyrrhic.

His night was the most disturbed he had experienced since his time in the Gulf. It was a montage of all that had been bad in his life, colourfully collated into random snippets that caused him to toss and turn, sweat and call out in his sleep. At 4am he moved from the bed and made his way to the kitchen. Light was no good to him; he needed the dark. He re-ran some of his nightmare if only to convince himself that he was a key player in this madness, it had happened to him, he too had suffered, more than he could put into words. The ignorance of the medical profession in being incapable of helping him brought a light to his process of thought; a light that would guide him, rightly or wrongly from this labyrinth. The more he juxtaposed his arguments the more brightly the light of conviction glowed until he was in the light. He returned to bed and slept.

The pictures in the morning papers failed to touch his senses. He had donned emotional armour that helped strengthen his resolve to see this through. If more deaths resulted then they were the enemy, and that was that.

***

In the days that followed he watched with growing interest the way the damage to the bridge was handled. After two days of constant repair they had succeeded in opening single lanes in either direction for cars and light goods; heavier vehicles were set the task of avoiding the area completely. The long-term prognosis was yet to be determined and he hoped that as that was reached another bridge would fall a few miles further north to add to the already confused area. He would follow the same procedure, carefully selecting the phone box. The fact that on this occasion the bomb warning was going to be a morning call meant he would need to be out bright and early himself.

He left Joan sleeping, kissed her hair before going downstairs. He did not breakfast; he was too tense. The car started with the first turn of the key. The time was 04.46. He drove out towards the motorway heading for Huddersfield. The M62 was again quiet. Pulling off he followed the brightly lit way into the centre of town before turning for Holmfirth. The road turned and snaked through housing. Some newsagents were opening. Milk floats crawled silently. Soon the trees bordered the road and Roy knew he was close. On his approach to Holmfirth he turned right. The road was steep. Soon he was nearing the top. A church nestling in trees sat on a sharp bend, a war memorial faced him. "Someone's enemy, someone's father, someone's son, someone's brother ... dead." He pulled up on the bend and looked at the white marble and black lettering. Remnants of poppy wreaths lay at its base, withering like the memories of the old. He turned right and parked the car away from the houses. He climbed out and moved to the poppy-red phone box. It was now 05.50. The sky was lightening and the clouds were a spectacular orange colour. He looked at them before taking in a lung full of the fresh morning air. He picked up the receiver and dialled the same free phone number.

Again with unwavering efficiency a friendly voice answered and Roy went through the same procedure, notifying place and time of the bomb, leaving the word GULF before hanging up. He walked back to his car. At the same time the telephonist notified his supervisor and the police were informed. They went into action with speed and precision and the traffic on the motorway was halted. The code word had brought an almost instant respect and no chances were taken. The hotel close to the bridge was also evacuated, guests hurried out, many dressed in nightclothes. The traffic moving along the A59 was also brought to a standstill. They knew that should the bomb detonate, they were in serious trouble but they were impotent, nothing could be done but wait for the deadline of 06.57. The procedure was a replica of the earlier bombing. The Expo, Sam Phelps, controlled the operation with the same degree of circumspection. The call on his mobile had woken him, he had not had time to shave just to grab his things and leave. The helicopter was waiting with two other officers. A cautious respect was being developed for the Gulf Bomber. Sam, Paul and Mike sat in the helicopter as it lifted off. No one spoke.

It never ceased to amaze Sam the number of people who would telephone the police after a major incident, claiming responsibility; some even give their names and addresses, they would even send their admission on email! The sad thing was that valuable time was consumed investigating them as one might turn out to be guilty. As the noise of the helicopter droned he was convinced in his own mind that this was not the work of one man but a group, a presumption that proved precipitate, inaccurate and one that was to cost him dearly.

The helicopter had landed away from the bridge but close enough to give them a clear view of proceedings. The morning was bright and a light mist hung over the river bringing a warmth to the scene.

"Least it's not fucking raining," chirped Mike as he jumped to the ground, arms full of equipment, his boots shining. "Not shaved chief?" He glanced at Sam and continued to unload.

As soon as the equipment was removed the helicopter left, the rotor blades biting into the peace of the morning. It hovered for a moment before flying away from the bridge to a safe height. There predator-like it hovered. Time was against them as Gulf gave little warning. Their game plan was to wait; five minutes was no time in which to ascertain the correct judgements. At the designated time the blast happened with positive effect.

The sharp anger of the initial flash seemed to make the whole bridge convulse like the spasm of a dying man, sending debris high into the air followed by a crack that echoed menacingly. Smoke, almost white, followed strangely before drifting away with the wind like a spirit.

"They've done it again. Obviously same type of device and clearly placed accurately. They're teasing us and I guess this is just the start."

As a precaution, Sam dressed in bomb suit and visor; it was heavy, weighing seventy kilograms. His first task was to check the bridge for further devices. The likelihood was that should they exist then they would be in the drains or beneath the bridge supports. The drains proved easier to check as the majority of covers had been blown away but caution had been his saviour in the past and every move was carefully planned. He approached each hole with a search mirror, its telescopic handle giving greater depth. Sam was concerned about introducing too much light into the darkness as another smaller bomb could be triggered using a light sensitive switch. The danger was always complacency, particularly when there was a lot to absorb.

The morning traffic was beginning to grow, particularly northbound. Many of the drivers, especially those in heavy goods vehicles, had spent too much time already negotiating the diversion further south and finding a total blockage again did nothing to ease the tension. Many were out of their vehicles as others patiently waited for the police to divert them away from the scene.

It was apparent that the bridge was clear. Sam now had to check below. That too was clean and to their relief the guests of the hotel were quickly ushered back inside.

Another police helicopter arrived on the scene bringing with it forensic experts, one of whom was Carl Howarth, a man in his late forties. From his inspection of fragments embedded in the concrete pillars of the Gathurst site, he had made a guess that the TPU was some kind of electronic organiser. He had also found traces of PETN, a chemical used in plastic explosives such as Semtex. He was quite clear in his mind.

Carl greeted the bomb disposal team, he knew them reasonably well, some better than others but the way things were developing they would be best of friends if the bombing rate was to continue at this pace. He shook Sam's hand firmly. "Didn't expect to see you men so soon after the last time. Seems we have a real problem on our hands, particularly if my hunch is correct and we are only dealing with the tip of the iceberg."

"Being so cheerful really keeps our chins up. Found much from the first blast?"

"TPU is in a palmtop computer lined through to Semtex is my guess. Quite straightforward stuff. Simple, and as you're experiencing, effective. He's certainly not about blowing things down, just causing enough damage to disrupt a large percentage of the traffic network in the area. His placement is accurate too. I'm amazed though that one of these devices has failed to be spotted. If he's planted a few you'd have thought some vandal scrambling under some of these bridges would have had a tug and a pull. They must be well concealed."

Sam moved with Carl Howarth towards the underside of the bridge. The main blast area was clearly visible and the damage as expected.

"Seems he's placing the charges on the bearings of the bridge and around the expansion gaps in order to cause the most damage. He also has the opportunity of concealing the stuff with grease." Sam broke off his conversation and showed where the bomb had been sited. He demonstrated that it was easily accessible and easily executed. "Clearly there's a bridge design fault but then ..." he paused as if mentally correcting his stream of thought. "Should we be making allowances for any nutter who wants to take a pot shot at his fellow men?"

Carl nodded appreciating the observation. He had experienced the aftermath of many such incidents. "There'll always be an Achilles' heel and always a Paris to exploit it. The bridges are becoming clipped birds. They're still there but fail to function. How many is he collecting?"

Their eyes met and Sam realised that he respected this man. Here was someone who saw possibly more, saw through the smoke, had empathy. Sam left him to get on with his work and walked back to his team. They were busily clearing away. The traffic was still snarled up and the day was only just beginning. For many it was miserable but for one it was a day too long and another step forward.

Chapter Nine

At the same moment in another part of the country, Roy was meeting his first appointment. He was trying to complete the agreement for a new order for a large supermarket chain. He sat with the manager negotiating the fine financial details of the deal. The new computer system was expensive and this was the culmination of long, hard tendering but it was now his order, or soon would be. They had worked together in the past and even though payment was often slow they ordered large.

The manager had been concerned about the delays to the distribution and it was conveyed to him that a further explosive device had brought chaos yet again to the M6. One of his drivers had phoned in to say he feared very long delays.

"It's all we need, Roy, more delivery delays; these bloody shysters need sitting on the bloody bomb themselves."

Roy pictured himself as a shyster and then sitting on a bomb, it was a cartoon-like image that filled his mind. He controlled the grin. "Any casualties this time?" An amazing amount of surprise in his voice.

"The driver didn't say, just that he was stationary and had been for well over an hour."

The deal was signed and Roy confirmed delivery, "Subject to bombings, of course." He realised his joke was not appreciated and left whilst ahead.

He headed back towards Bradford, his mind not fully on his driving. It would soon be time to play a key card, probably *the* key card, one that was sure to cause the greatest amount of fear as it would surely bring death. The radio was interrupted with the latest news regarding the bomb, advising drivers to stay clear of the area for the foreseeable future as both bridges had been structurally weakened. He slowed and looked in the mirror. It was working. Roy Hanna, a nobody, a

Gulf War casualty, a forgotten soldier was changing the face of today and was sure to change the face of tomorrow.

It was clear too in Whitehall. The Home Secretary wanted to see more action being taken. He needed co-operation and an involvement of the army and the police to bring a swift end to this terrorism and he wanted, nay, demanded it, sooner rather than later.

It was agreed that the armed forces and police would work closely to inspect major motorway bridges. It was becoming clearer where the devices were likely to be placed; their own experts could tell them that. The co-ordination would fall under the responsibility of the Metropolitan Police and a main operations room would be established. It was obvious to date that only the north west had suffered, but they could not at this stage make any predictions.

***

Roy enjoyed Drew's pleasure. "Well done Roy, that order is just what was needed, can't afford to lose you." He meant every word. Roy, when on form, was superb at his job but there had been changes and Drew could only watch helplessly the deterioration in his friend. However, he had noticed a more positive Roy of late. He put it down to a determination to beat it, overcome whatever it was that gnawed away inside.

Roy was pleased himself by his success. It had not been easy maintaining the concentration or motivation for sales when he was in the midst of what was to him the most important gamble of his life, but he was doing bloody well and this motivated him, fired him with a drive he had not faced since before the Gulf. It felt good, fucking good.

The next four days were a blur as he listened attentively to the news bulletins and read the papers with interest. Funeral services were being held for some of the people who had died in the blazing train, the majority had been identified from dental records. The image of a dead Iraqi soldier filled his mind's eye, famous in its gruesome detail. He had remembered clearly the photograph and it had shaken him on first seeing it. The victim was a grinning, charred Iraqi casualty killed on Multa Ridge during his attempted dash for freedom from Kuwait along with countless others. He still remembered peering from the wagon to be greeted by a corpse, its rictus smile of death grinning as if it were a last act of defiance; black teeth and hollow-eyed. He remembered he had stared at it, soaking in every detail at the time. Now he was amazed how unmoved he was at seeing the grieving relatives, even young children carrying flowers for a lost parent. The television reporting was sensitive and moving. Joan's angry responses to the images were those of a normal human being and even her anguish failed to ignite the smallest pang of doubt or guilt. He just seemed to revel silently in its blackness but his callous coldness did not go unnoticed. Joan was alive to it and it somehow disturbed her. It threw her off balance and the more it happened the more she watched. "What's going on in that head of yours, behind those icy eyes?" she asked herself more than once. She would find the heart of this man. If there was a future it was to be her goal.

"Terrible business," he heard himself say as if to destroy the embarrassing silence that was growing.

"Just to think, Roy, that could have been you or me. Those innocent people left for work that day never realising what lay in store. Some mad man blew them to pieces and for what? Some religion, some political statement or some petty grievance; remember Dunblane? It just makes me so angry." She watched his every move. *"React Roy, react. Show something!"* she shouted silently in her head. Roy moved over to her and enveloped her, squeezing her tightly.

"Let's hope they catch whoever did it soon. I worry about you when you are out and about."

She wondered; she really did. He pulled away and looked at her. He lifted her face and kissed her. He touched her face with his left hand. It was as cold as his soul. She smiled at him before moving away.

"You've been different the last few days, a new man. Whatever you are doing it's obviously having an effect."

Roy had been better in himself and she recognised that and wanted him to know. Maybe this callous streak was a way of dealing with things.

"Whatever you're doing keep doing it."

If only she knew what she was saying, thought Roy. If only she knew! He believed himself to be different, he actually felt better, it was like an emotional catharsis. "I love you, Joan," he whispered.

***

The following day was bright. The blowing blinds rang against the bowl. Roy awoke. He lay there quietly contemplating the ringing from the windowsill and soft breathing next to him.

In the Gulf they would often listen to the sound of the rain beating the Warrior with the same metronomic beat, often at night when they would be resting or sleeping under their CARM (Chemical Agent Repellent Material) which hung like half a tent from the side of the vehicle. There was never peace. Often kit had to be brought in from the rain, at night a difficult and somewhat dangerous business. Roy remembered one particular night in early February 1991 when it seemed hell had broken loose. The artillery had put up a horrendous barrage and this with the night's storm had brought what Dante imagined Hell to be to their part of the desert. Lightning, rockets and shells illuminated the night sky exploding into colours of eerie transparency, their glow showering the wet desert with the reflective heat while in reality the accompanying rain and cold wind whipped the huddled figures ferociously as they lay semi-alert beside the Warrior. It would, they hoped soon, be reveille, a time when all the team would stand to inside the vehicle for thirty minutes. It was thought that the enemy would likely strike at this time of day so all had to be ready. A klaxon sounded and the words, "Gas, Gas, Gas!" filled the air as the six sardine soldiers struggled with respirators, a routine that many could do in their sleep but it was just another false alarm. Roy knew that G day would be anytime and this filled him with a fear and an excitement that proved a stimulating cocktail. He would be in the desert eighteen more days but out of his Warriors group of six, he was to be the lucky one.

The delivery of the morning paper shook him from his reminiscing. He checked his watch, 6.30. He dressed in running gear and moved quietly downstairs, poured some fresh orange juice and retrieved the paper. The headlines were dull in comparison to recent front pages but the cartoon made him smile. Smiling in the morning. Wonderful, he thought. He drank the remaining juice and left the house.

It was 7.45 when he returned. The run had gone better than he had thought and today he felt as though he could run for ever. He showered and then woke Joan.

"You were up early, you should have woken me," her greeting seductive in its sleepiness.

He kissed her. "Breakfast won't be long, I'll run the shower for you."

"Busy day today, Roy?"

"Not too bad but I must ring Dr O'Brien, he wanted to see me this week."

Joan went to shower as Roy prepared a simple breakfast of cereal and toast. It was ready when Joan came down. They chatted about their day and Roy prepared to leave. "I may be late tonight but I'll ring you about 4.30. Will you be at home?"

"I'll be home," replied Joan.

The door closed and Joan moved to the front room window, coffee in one hand. She stood and saw Roy drive away and instinctively she waved. He was not looking and no wave was returned; she had not expected one, he would not know she was there. She watched the car leave the street and returned to the kitchen. She tried to think round the fears she had felt last night, the callous aura that she sensed was probably nothing. She knew she would have to put it into perspective. As she approached the bedroom she found herself attracted to Roy's study and instinctively she allowed herself a visit. It was organised and tidy for Roy. On the table sat his palmtop computer, it was always there. She picked it up and ran it through her fingers, her eyes unfocused. Something was not right and here, surrounded by his secret things, her female intuition was at its peak. Was there someone else?

***

When Roy had settled himself at work, he rang the psychiatrist. His secretary answered.

"Dr O'Brien is with a patient at the moment, may I take your name and number, or you can ring him between 10.30 and 10.45, he should be free then."

"Please tell him that Roy Hanna called for an appointment."

"I can make an appointment for you Mr Hanna. Have you seen the doctor previously?"

"Yes, yes but I would like to talk to Bill before making an appointment." He slipped in the doctor's Christian name to make the process slightly less formal.

"That's fine, Mr Hanna. Does the doctor have your number? Then I'll get him to ring you at his earliest convenience. Thank you for calling."

Her precision was polite and professional if somewhat cold and clinical. The return call came as a surprise at 10.15.

"Thought you'd forgotten about me," jested Bill, testing his response.

"Sorry, Bill, been hellishly busy trying to catch up on things." He lied of course.

"You sound perky. When do you wish to meet me? I'm free on Thursday later in the afternoon."

"That afternoon would suit, say 5pm?"

"Look forward to it. 5pm, my clinic? I'll see you then."

Another brisk efficient call left him holding the receiver seconds after the call was concluded. Roy was uncertain about continuing the meetings after this one, as he felt vulnerable to the inquisitive questioning; nothing could be divulged, he was too far down the road, too near his target but there was always that chance and risks were to be cut to the minimum.

That night he sat in his study after supper. Joan was marking and preparing, a side to teaching that few people outside the profession understood but one that was real and added considerably to the stress. The palmtop was open on the desk; next to it sat an electronic labelling machine. This clever little device allowed self-adhesive coloured labels to be printed. Thousands of these machines had been sold and Roy believed this was the best way to communicate his demands to the police and then the government. He pressed the 'on' button and the palmtop came to life. The agenda of his personal bombing campaign filled the small screen. He began to type the message on the labeller:

'GULF, GULF, GULF. NEXT BOMB, NO WARNING. EXPECT FIREWORKS BUT LIMITED LOSS OF LIFE FOR THE MOMENT. FULL LIST OF FUTURE DEVASTATION CAN BE HAD FOR £2,000,000. CHEAP REALLY FOR A LOST LIFE AND SO MANY TO SAVE. WILL CONTACT YOU AGAIN. IF YOU DON'T BELIEVE WHAT YOU READ, WAIT UNTIL YOU HEAR THE BANG!'

Roy could see that on Wednesday at 2am two bridges on the M25 would be blown, bringing chaos and a change from the north to the south of England. He wiped the plastic-coated label with a cloth and placed it in an envelope. This would be sent to a leading newspaper during the Tuesday night.

His agenda showed timings of the bombs and their targets written as co-ordinates. He had noted the exact position of all placements using his handheld Magellan Global Positioning System, a relatively cheap tool he had used in the Gulf. Each Warrior was equipped with one to ensure exact positioning. It also gave details of the messages to send and when to send them. Everything was in this treasure trove of information; it was the heart, the nerve centre. He switched it off and closed the lid. Considering its importance, he showed only minimal respect for its security. He knew Joan would not be able to find information within certain sections as they were protected by passwords but he was also a firm believer in fate and if the plan were to fail, then it would fail! However, he had stored all the information on a small black hard disk and that was hidden.

Chapter Ten

It was the wagon driver who had spotted it. His wagon had thrown a tyre with the customary explosion whilst cresting the hill on the motorway, a sound that filled him with despair as it would mean a late arrival home. He slowed the Volvo articulated wagon to a halt, metres before the motorway crossed a deep valley. The motorway itself was cut into a hillside and although the late afternoon was unusually warm, the wind was channelled down the grassy sides. He applied the brakes expelling a loud, sharp hiss and then banged on the steering wheel with his fists, pronouncing to the world his anger. He grabbed the phone from its cradle and hammered in the number printed on the label stuck to his windscreen for such emergencies. He had been lucky, this was only his first blowout this year. The tyre firm operated a twenty-four hour call out service and estimated they could attend in forty minutes. He gave his position and hung up. He rang the depot to explain he would be late, and then his wife. He anticipated a delay of an hour but said to expect him when she saw him. He would ring again once on the move. She had been anxious with the recent spate of bombings and he was only pleased to be able to reassure her things were fine.

He put the phone into the pocket of his fleece jacket, sidled across to the passenger seat before climbing down onto the hard shoulder. The traffic was busy. The chill made him need to urinate. Normally he would pee against the tyre of the wagon – no one would see – but for some reason, maybe the proximity of the bridge, he walked to the edge of the valley. The concrete structure slowly descended until the span grew from the grass bank. The driver walked down the incline holding the concrete wall for support until he could walk under the bridge. Even though it was out in the wilds, kids had drawn on the steel and concrete.

He unzipped his blue trousers and started to urinate initially against the wall but then he turned and began to spray down the valley like a child competing at school as to who could piss the furthest. He giggled at his own puerile behaviour but it lifted his mood. "You're bloody mad. If people could see you now!" he said out loud.

His eyes followed the span of the bridge out over the void, stopping about a third of the way along. Something was hanging loop-like between the gap of two pillars. He finished and zipped his trousers. His eyes were again drawn to the wire hanging and swaying. Had the kids who had written their names so crudely also made a swing? Surely not, this was not a playground. For one it was too far away from anywhere, and secondly the drop was too great for even the bravest. He turned and moved away and made his way back to the motorway. As he reached the barrier he noticed he was not alone. Two uniformed police officers were looking at the wagon; one was already inside the cab whilst the other stood below.

"Can I help you officer? Been for a pee."

"This your vehicle, sir?"

"Yes, as you can see had a bad blow out on the back near side. Tyre people on their way."

"The wagon seemed abandoned close to the bridge; we can't be too careful with these explosions. We'll need your documents, please."

The driver jumped into the cab next to the other officer. He reached into the compartment behind his seat producing a small case. He handed the documents to the officer.

"Please climb down and follow my colleague to the Range Rover."

He jumped down and did as he was bid, kicking the shredded tyre as he passed. Blue lights flashed brightly behind the wagon. All three climbed aboard and the documentation was cleared. Once satisfied that things were in order the officers relaxed more. The driver removed his cap.

"Listen, I don't know if it's anything," said the wagon driver, "but whilst I was having a piss, I noticed some cable or wire hanging from under the bridge, probably something and nothing but it caught my eye and who knows these days?"

The officers looked at each other, the older one of the two raised an eyebrow, "Let's take a look Tonto." He smiled at his partner and then at the wagon driver. "Can you show us please?"

All three climbed from the Range Rover and trudged past the wagon just as the tyre repair van arrived. They walked towards the van. The driver gave his instructions and the three disappeared beyond the bridge. As they edged round the concrete corner 'Tonto' slipped on the wet grass.

"Shit!"

"Piss I would have thought," jibed the other policeman. "Some detective you'd make if you can't tell the difference."

The driver laughed before apologising, although for what he was not sure.

The officer wiped himself down, now more concerned with his damp uniform than the driver's pointing finger.

"It's hanging between the second and third pillar, see it?"

"What do you think?" asked the older officer. "Forget your fuckin' pants for Christ's sake. Look!"

"I've really no idea but let's not take any chances. We'll let others make that decision." All three moved back towards the motorway, avoiding the damp patch as they went.

The tyre was off the wagon and the spare was being rolled into place.

"Shouldn't be long now!" shouted the fitter above the sound of the compressor. The police officers called in over the radio and explained the situation. The duty officer eventually connected them to bomb disposal and they described in detail what they had seen.

"Stay there, we'll enforce a speed restriction in the area and get to you as soon as possible. There's no point in closing the motorway for a child's swing," instructed Sam Phelps.

Sam had decided it was probably nothing but he could not be sure. Maybe they could catch a live one. Who knew the clues it might hold?

The car, another Range Rover, this time without the bright coloured bodywork but with blue flashing lights, ploughed its way through the traffic with siren wailing. It pulled onto the motorway and headed west. It never ceased to amaze Sam how cars spread as their drivers spotted the flashing blue lights. He often said he felt like Moses parting the Red Sea. They were soon on the spot.

The wagon had gone but the remnants of the tyre lay by the edge of the road. The position of the two vehicles certainly brought the speed of the passing traffic down. Many drivers were too busy gawping.

Sam and Mike shook hands with the officers and introduced themselves.

"Where's this mystery wire?" requested Sam in all seriousness. "Down here, mind you don't slip," said the officer smiling at his colleague. The private joke went unnoticed as the two Expos followed them. "There, can you see it?" The officer was pointing a finger out over the void.

The explosives officer followed the direction of the pointing finger and there in the dim light was the hanging wire. "Don't know, just don't know," muttered Sam, his eyes searching for a route out along the span. "Mike, we need a helmet light and a camera then we can begin." He said this in almost a whisper and the two officers were hanging on every word. They quickly hurried up the grass bank to the vehicles. He discussed the situation in more detail before moving round to the boot.

"You or me, Sam?" asked Mike.

"Sorry, my turn."

He dressed in a Bristol Armour Type Twelve search suit. This offered him the flexibility to move and climb. The helmet was fitted with intercom and lights. In a waist bag he placed a small video camera. He checked the helmet lights and then the video. "Mike, can you receive? One, two, three, four, test."

"Reading you five, Sam. Take it carefully."

Sam turned to the two officers who were standing close by. "You two need to go to the car and move clear, just in case. I'm only going for a looksee but who knows." He smiled at them both and watched them turn.

"Good luck, Sam," they both said in unison.

He left the visor of the helmet open as he moved down the banking towards the span.

"Don't slip," suggested Mike, more out of something to say rather than to be amusing.

He began to make his move along the base of the girder. The light danced on the underside of the structure as Sam's head darted from side to side, constantly scanning for clues. It was ridiculously easy to traverse the span, providing heights held no fear.

"Couldn't be easier, Mike. The girders are wide and the wind's not as strong as I'd anticipated. Not far to go." On approach Sam paused. He could see that something was not right. "I think there's something here. Can't really make it out. I'll describe as I go along. The wire is attached to what appears to be grease. The grease is smeared into the underside of the support and the support looks as though it's on a bearing. There's masses of the stuff. It seems to run along the underside towards the pillars but I can't clearly make that out."

"What's the other end of the wire in, Sam?"

"Hard to tell from this distance. I'm going onto the lintel." His fingers touched the wire. "Two core, smeared in grease running into what looks like a large blob of grease." From his bag he took the video camera and recorded the details, the bright light illuminating the nooks and crannies. "Hope it's not light sensitive." Sam put away the camera and removed a rag from the bag. The traffic noise, audible through his helmet, seemed louder or was it just the beating of his heart? He wiped some of the grease away to reveal a black, slightly corrugated case, wires leading into the back. "We've got ourselves a device here. Get the motorway closed, Mike, I'm going to check the explosives if they're there."

"Careful, careful!" Mike called base. "Able One, Able One."

"Go ahead Able One."

"Device located positive, set procedure 'Charlie' in operation immediately. Repeat, establish operation 'Charlie'. We also require back-up squad. Over."

"Roger Able One, 'Charlie' procedure. Immediate backup notified. Out."

Charlie, the code for closing and detouring motorways, had been devised after the second bombing.

Although traffic was still flowing it would not be long before an eerie silence would descend on this stretch of the motorway, and if 'Charlie' were to be effective it should alleviate some of the queuing that had been so frustratingly uncontrollable on the previous occasions.

Mike relayed that 'Charlie' was in place as Sam crested the banking, cigarette in one hand and his helmet in the other. He raised his eyebrows signifying they had found the real thing.

"I think it's Semtex B, enough too but the detector should confirm. The TPU looks like our old friend the palmtop computer but everything's just covered in bloody grease. Two core cable, strands of the stuff, is wired somehow behind. I presume the devise is glued to the bridge. Must be the GULF's. Get the detector, I'm going to confirm."

The portable detector could identify a variety of commercial and military explosives and its non-contact probe meant that if anti-handling devices were present there was little fear of triggering. The results would be instantaneous, results that would be needed when decisions were taken to defuse. Whilst Sam busied himself below, Mike watched the video on the playback.

Sam returned and confirmed his original theory.

"Coffee, Sam? There's some in the Rover."

"Good man. I would love some but must slip out of this suit."

They both strolled to the rear of the vehicle. The motorway was now still and only God knew what the traffic was like. The coffee was warming. The constantly nagging radio told its own sorry tale of the traffic congestion and confusion.

***

Roy ran his hands round Joan's waist and nibbled and kissed her neck. "How much more of that have you to do?"

She turned in her chair and smiled. "I'm through." She kissed him warmly. "It's getting no more of my attention tonight. Fancy going for a drink?"

Roy nodded his approval and they left the house hand in hand. The sky was a beautiful duck egg blue fading to almost emerald green; the sun had well set but there was an autumnal warmth. The street, full of dark areas, reminded him of his childhood, he had played in its passages and side roads, he knew them intimately. He paused and images of children playing and laughing excitedly ghosted into his memory. The screams and peals of laughter rang round his head with a strange clarity.

"Okay my man?"

The words shook him to his senses. "Fine, fine. What're you waiting for? Come on!"

Joan laughed and they moved on.

Chapter Eleven

The bomb squad took longer than expected. The traffic, even with 'Charlie' in force, was horrendous. The two vehicles, large, white vans with blue flashing lights mounted on top and the distinctive lettering, 'Bomb Disposal' marked down the flanks, arrived and pulled in behind the blue Range Rover. A twin Squirrel helicopter flew over and hovered momentarily before moving away.

Two of the people from the first vehicle Sam recognised straight away and smiled a welcome as they approached; the other was a stranger to him.

"Sam, meet Detective Superintendent Earl, Special Branch. He's co-opted to the group. Will discuss all the latest once we're sorted here." Colin Ashcroft was senior and group leader of Bomb Disposal. "What's the crack?"

"Electronic device wired to a number of explosives and reminiscent of the other GULF packages. I'm concerned by the way the TPU is attached, it doesn't allow X-ray or removal without possible triggering. We don't know if this bastard has included anti-handling devices or not, but if GULF is as warped as I think, he must have all sorts up his sleeve. Look at the video. It gives a reasonable image of the problem."

The three men huddled round the small screen. Like Sam, Colin had served his apprenticeship as an Ammunitions Technical Officer with the army before taking up the position in the police. He had risen to the rank of senior. Most ATO's moved towards the police after their army service.

"What's the chance of a controlled explosion or taking out the TPU with a laser guided shot or maybe a pigstick disrupter close to?"

"What's not clearly visible from the video is the position of the TPU to the banking, the only clear place to shoot from.

It's cleverly hidden under the girder, probably to keep it away from any nutter spending his evenings decorating the bridge with an aerosol can. I'd really like to get this one intact. I want to see what we are up against because I feel we haven't seen the end of these by any stretch of the imagination."

"So what's left?"

"Trace and cut the wires, remove the explosives and then take away the TPU." It sounded so simple the way Sam breezed through the description. "We'll have to watch for anti-handling and make sure we achieve good, clean cuts on the wire but to do that, at this stage is the best option. After all, we don't know when this little critter is due to go pop!"

At that moment, Mike, who had been listening intently, requested the task under the pretext of it being "his turn".

Sam looked at him for a while. "Okay, kit up but be careful. Full descriptions and full coverage."

Mike moved swiftly to the rear of the white Transac vehicle. He dressed in the same suit Sam had worn to afford the movement needed to traverse. He also wore a full harness round his waist, similar to those worn by climbers and the climbing rope was attached using a carabiner. This rather complicated safety feature was designed on the spot. The safety rope would run through carabiners attached to the bridge rail so that should Mike slip he would only fall a short distance, but more importantly he could launch himself away from the device at any moment should the need arise; at least that way he should be away from a direct blast. He put on the helmet, checked the lights and requested a radio check. He placed his satchel containing all the tools of his trade over his shoulder.

He gave a thumbs up sign and descended the grass banking. His security rope was attached above as another Explosives Officer kept control of the slack. He was soon out under the span, carefully balancing on the girder, the bulk of his clothing and bag making it slightly more difficult.

"Moving onto the lintel now," he said breathlessly. "Thought I was fit!" He took some wire cutters from his bag and carefully but positively cut the dangling wire, a job he had done hundreds of times in practice but one that always brought tension when done for real. Do it wrongly, cut slowly and drag the metal through the wire, or connect the two wires with careless cutting, the circuit could be joined and goodnight Vienna! It was difficult to see how many wires came from the TPU but he was sure by the damage caused by the previous explosions that there would be quite a few. Unknown to them all, the device was cleverly rigged. The cutting of the wire had started a secondary timer running. Mike had three minutes of life left. "Moving onto the TPU. Give me more slack in the rope."

"Good cut Mike."

"Scares the shit out of me for real."

"Concentrate and be careful. You're not talking to us, Mike. Keep us informed; we have to know this bastard inside out."

"The unit is attached to the bearing and sheltered, smeared with grease. I'm wiping it clean." Mike took a cloth from his bag and wiped the black box with great care, aware that a tremble switch might be concealed. "It's definitely a palmtop-come-note book style computer. Wires are running from the back and the whole shooting match is glued onto the bridge. It appears to be builders' strong adhesive. It has a lid that I'm sure would reveal a key pad but that's staying shut for the minute, maybe there's a light sensitive switch attached."

There was not and had he opened the case he would have seen the warning numbers clearly on the screen counting down!

"I'm tracing the wires visually."

"You're doing well Mike. We have a picture," reassured Sam. He was more nervous listening to the radio and would have liked to be tackling the situation below. He would have felt more in control.

"Sam, there appear to be six, each to a separate explosive. It's well executed. If I cut all of these wires successfully there's still a chance the TPU could contain a small charge. I'd like to use a controlled explosion to make sure. There's no point taking the risk at this stage. What do you want me to do?"

"Get as much visual information as you can, then do as you think best, Mike."

From his bag he removed a small charge, removed the covering to the adhesive back, stuck it to the TPU and then drew the pin. He now had less than one minute of life left as the timer counted down.

"Charge set and active. I'm just taking a last look at the computer for more clues. Make sure everyone is clear and take up any slack when I call."

It was the last message he ever sent; they were the final words he would ever speak. The clocked ticked to 00.00.

The flash was intense and the heat seared. His body was torn apart as the remnants strapped into the armoured suit and harness swung from the burning rope above the valley, a grotesque human pendulum.

The explosion shook everyone taking them by surprise; no matter how long you were in the job you still jumped when you heard the detonation. The vibration ran through their feet and instinctively everyone turned away. A buzz could be heard over the radio. It too had died.

After what seemed like minutes but in reality was seconds, Mike's remains tumbled to the valley floor as the flames burned through the taut rope. Parts of his body would be retrieved later, other parts would never be found.

"Shit! Just what are we dealing with here?"

Vestiges of the remaining day were obliterated by smoke and dust that soaked up the light like blotting paper. It was hard to tell in the remaining gloom but it appeared that the bridge suffered the same damage as the others, buckled and structurally compromised: they were losing the game.

"Get Forensics down here and get them here fucking fast! Get me a secure line through to the Chief Constable!" barked Colin. "He's not going to be too happy."

Each van carried a separate radio that allowed secure speech operation; each was fitted with digital encryption.

The paramedics waited by their Range Rovers for the call to move into the valley, an instruction that could only come once the bridge had been swept for further devices. There was no urgency to attend the smouldering, dismembered corpse below.

"Chief Constable on the line, sir," was a call from one of the Transac vehicles. Colin looked skywards for inspiration. The discussion was frosty. He was ordered to keep the press at bay and play down the situation as much as possible; public concern was rising rapidly and it had to be their priority to keep panic to a minimum.

The late news bulletin announced that a controlled explosion had been made successfully to disarm another terrorist device, there had been no casualties. Roy turned off the television. He moved to his study, opened his palmtop and scratched one item from the list in the agenda. He paused before closing it. He lay awake for some time wondering if they were searching every bridge. Surely not, but he slept uneasily. For the first time since he had started the campaign, he suffered pangs of fear and doubt.

Sam too had a restless night, a night that he knew was a gift as every other night was to be. His friend had triggered the bomb that should have been his. Maybe he would have been more careful, seen the problem that would have made the difference between living and dying. Maybe he would have made the same mistake. He would be a charred shell and Mike would be home with his family. It was not easy consoling his wife, convincing her that the cover up over her husband's murder was essential to catch the people who had widowed her. She had in her heart of hearts known that one day this call would come and she hated them all for it. Sam hated himself and the whole bloody world. The half empty brandy bottle proved it.

Chapter Twelve

The meeting was informal considering its importance, the Commissioner, Sheila Dewar, brought the meeting together. "Gentlemen, good morning. I'm sure you have all introduced yourselves but if not let me take a moment: Graham Sharp, Head of SO12, Jonathan Keen, liaising for SO13, Colin Ashcroft, Bomb Disposal, Major Perry, SATO for the military and Philip Haslem-Parr from MI5. The Home Secretary is growing increasingly concerned that we are not yet on top of this situation. The loss of the Explosives Officer yesterday only heightens the problem. I'm sure I don't have to point out that there is growing anxiety in the government and the Prime Minister faces many difficult questions, therefore they wish to see an efficient end to this matter. As most of you are fully aware, we have received another threat. Graham, will you continue, please."

"Thank you, Ma'am. We received a demand, hand delivered to a Manchester newspaper in the early hours of the morning. You all have a copy in the envelope."

Envelopes were passed round and each person eagerly opened it. They all read the single sheet and looked round the table, raised eyebrows and puzzled looks said it all.

"As you are aware, officers have been tasked to check prominent bridges throughout the country but as yet nothing has been located, the device found yesterday was spotted purely by chance. I'm sure I don't have to mention that a 'D' notice has been served on this and the press are co-operating fully. We are graced with some time on this occasion and it must count. Colin your comments, please."

"The Metropolitan Bomb Disposal Officers are working closely with our colleagues in the military and a search of all the motorway bridges on the M25 has been ordered after prioritising from the information gained so far. Should anything materialise we will operate Charlie. We must keep each other informed at all times. All information will filter through the ACPO – this, the Anti-terrorist Sub Committee will co-ordinate all GB police forces, MI5 and the military; their role will, as always, be crucial."

Graham Sharp looked at the Commissioner. "Any clues yet as to who may be behind all this?"

"We've ruled out the IRA and any Middle East faction and at present we're working on the idea we have a rogue, possibly ex-military. The GULF code is our main clue and we're searching through our records for any piece of information that may give a lead. As you are aware there are a number of ex-Gulf veterans who are allegedly suffering from symptoms that may or may not be connected with their specific duties and experiences in the Gulf and this may be the catalyst, but I assure you, gentleman, this is pure conjecture. I would hope to have more details later."

Everyone sat and played with this idea and there was a strange quiet. Jonathan Keen broke the silence. "The small sum requested also indicates a small operator, we're considering playing the game in order to save an Autumn of doubt and damage but also to catch our monkey. We'll await GULF's next communication. Providing we can ensure that by making the payment we eliminate the risk, then it may be a small price to pay but it does mean compromising our integrity as we'd be bowing to the demands of a terrorist. The Defence Select Committee will be meeting to approve this move once we receive the next communication."

It was obvious from the facial expressions of those concentrating on Jonathan Keen that they were aghast to hear that there could be payment made at this early stage. However, those who had witnessed the charred remains of one officer thought it a cheap price to pay, particularly if the reporting lid could be kept very tightly closed.

"Any more points, gentlemen?" The Commissioner made eye contact with each person around the table in turn, waited and then smiled to the general assembly. "I want a result, I want it soon and I'd prefer not to pay two million pounds to see an end to this matter. We've already made mistakes and that clearly will not do. Good afternoon."

The others rose from their seats as she left the room. They talked feverishly amongst themselves.

***

The search was methodical and three devices were located. True to form all were carefully placed and were controlled by the trademark TPU. Investigations were already in hand to check through suppliers in the sales of these computers; there might be a clue. All were disarmed using controlled charges with minimal damage to two of the bridges. The third was armed differently as the controlled explosion caused a full detonation and significant damage to the bridge. Even though the operation was not as expected, credit was given to the explosives experts and the police logistical operation. All team members were dressed as road maintenance workers and limited disruption was caused to the traffic flow considering just what might have happened had they not been found in time. The 'Road to Hell' would have been an apt title. The reporting restrictions were not lifted.

Chapter Thirteen

The morning was wet, Roy went for a run before preparing himself for work. Back at home, lost in thought, the lack of news about the bombing assured him that the devices had been found and maybe disarmed. If so, the bomb disposal team would have to be good! He let the thoughts linger and then smiled. As his confidence grew, broke into his whistle.

"Happy this morning my man? Are you seeing Dr O'Brien today or am I mistaken?" Joan pulled her face quizzically.

"What do you mean?" Roy returned sharply, his voice betraying a hint of guilt.

"You worry me, you've been on cloud nine the last seven days, buzzed through a meeting with the psychiatrist and enjoying the thought of the next meeting. This is not the man I thought I knew."

"What do you want, the miserable bastard who felt possibly suicidal, a guy who couldn't motivate himself, his life and his work, a guy who dwelt more on the past than the present or the one you see now?" His voice was not raised but it was sharp and his face lowered intimidatingly. There was that coldness in his eyes that gave no clue as to his real thoughts. He was behaving like a cornered animal and he was dangerous.

"I want the real Roy Hanna, not the facade, the sham. Something is going on Roy and you're not being honest with me. Look at me ... see me. It's Joan, you know, the one you say you love, the one you need, or say you do." She turned and stormed out grabbing her bags, and left for work slamming the door behind her. If he was interested, if he could have seen her face, he would have seen the tears swelling in her eyes and the despair on her face, but he did not. He knew, however, he had to say the right thing.

"Joan please listen," but she had gone. Roy just stared and a grin broke his face. He did not care that he had switched off that part of his life and it was up to her as to whether she wanted him. It did have an effect but he would have denied it, with violence if necessary.

***

His day was hell. He grumbled at everyone. Nobody did anything right and by the time of his appointment his mood was black. He considered cancelling, just going home, getting a bottle but that was not to be.

He parked the car and walked slowly to the clinic trying to clear the swirling mists that clogged the clarity of his thoughts. It was like driving in the dark in fog without lights. He walked in.

"Mr Hanna?"

"Yes, Roy Hanna. I have an appointment."

A buzzer sounded and Roy pushed the door aggressively.

"Please take a seat in the waiting room, Dr O'Brien will be with you shortly. May I get you a coffee?"

Roy in his rudeness simply indicated a very positive no. The room was bright. Modern prints broke the white walls like windows looking into strange colourful minds. Roy's attention was drawn to one comprising blues and yellows. The longer he looked the more soothing was the picture; it was as if his anger was being leached.

Bill had heard from his receptionist that the next client was rather tetchy to the point of rudeness and so had allowed him to linger a while. He had hoped to annoy him more, possibly break the barriers further without giving him the desire to storm out and leave. However, he failed to realise that his choice of art was having the opposite effect and by the time he walked into the waiting room to greet him, Roy was feeling much calmer.

"Roy, I'm sorry to have kept you waiting. I've been reading some details from my colleague in America; they were faxed this morning and I've managed to glean some interesting information on which to build our programme."

"I love your choice of pictures, Bill. Particularly the blue one there." He walked a little closer to it and Bill followed instinctively. "I don't remember seeing them on my previous visit, but then I didn't wait in here."

"I'm flattered you like them as I'm embarrassed to say they are my simple efforts. I've always had a desire to be an artist, it's such a good way to release the stresses and strains of the job. This one I painted after a holiday in Luxor. The light is so pure there, and the sand and sun. I was absolutely mesmerised by the sunsets and can certainly appreciate Turner's fascination for them as a subject. You must take this one, I have many and it is unusual to have people make positive comments. A woman the other day was overheard to say that the pictures would be fine once they were finished. It hurt, strangely enough, so I'd be grateful if you'd accept this from me."

Roy looked at the picture and at Bill and put out his hand. "Thank you, you've made what was a bad day good. I know just where it will go."

Bill led his client through into his office. "Coffee?"

"I think I will now, thank you. Please apologise to your receptionist for me, I was rather rude earlier."

They sat down with the coffee and after general discussion on physical well-being Bill produced the faxed information.

"It appears that our American cousins are beginning to accept more and more that there may be something in the complaints servicemen are presenting regarding their health after their Gulf War service. The Pentagon is still bleating that there is no conclusive evidence on the one hand yet on the other they are down on record as saying not that it isn't there, only that they haven't found it yet. I would suppose that is about as much as we're going to get at this stage. To be fair, it's closer than this Government is prepared to say. Now, it's interesting that most of the scientific tests on nerve gasses prove that exposure in the field of battle is usually sporadic and episodic. From this type of contamination, the overwhelming evidence suggests there to be no extended effects; even with long-term dosage there is little evidence to support the problems you and the nineteen thousand other troops face. Did you use DEET whilst in the Gulf?"

"Yes, it was in most of the insect repellents issued. I suffered quite badly if bitten and so I would often wear DEET soaked wrist and ankle bands. Why? You can buy DEET based products in any high street chemist."

"I'd like to know what was in the tablets issued to you that you were instructed to take with your tea every day. If it were Pyridostigmine Bromide, the drug to counteract and protect against nerve gas, then there is a hypothesis that it would react with the DEET and in certain individuals cause ill health. I presume some of the symptoms to be lethargy and memory loss. There is again doubt, however, as clinical trials are yet to be conclusive."

"Strangely enough, they would fumigate tents regularly; spraying with almost gay abandon irrespective of what was going on. Sometimes you would be eating and in would come the insecticide guns blowing smoke everywhere. It would happen every morning, as a large tanker would spray everything to keep down mosquitoes. We were often covered in the stuff. We also used it in the Warrior; mosquitoes loved the cosy, confined spaces and so we smoked them out. Nobody wore a mask, nor washed their hands after touching the sprayed equipment as water was at a premium. It was also rumoured that the pesticides were bought locally, so quite honestly they could have contained just about anything."

All the while Bill made notes, looking up occasionally and shaking his head in disbelief.

"God only knows what we took. Sometimes the dosage was changed depending on the situation, the colour of tablets changed too so I've no way of knowing. If you recall, my military medical records of that period in the desert and beyond have gone AWOL. Some crappy computer error they'd like us to believe, so I've no idea what was injected or given during that time. It's my guess too that they don't know either. Some of the lads used to say, apocryphal it may be, that we were the guinea pigs for the chemical companies."

"There may be more truth there than you think, Roy. The report also mentions two vaccines, botulinum toxoid and anthrax. It has been postulated that their combination might be suspect. Mix all of these with the fires of six hundred and five burning oil wells, the fumes of which were supposed to rise away – I believe that the inclement weather brought rain that resembled tar – and then for good measure microwaves; I'm sure you're aware of the number of microwave systems in the area, some no doubt damaged. I often wonder if that might not be the hidden ingredient, the one responsible for many of the problems. Quite a heady cocktail and really one that cannot be brushed under the carpet as easily as they've done."

"The burning wells were just amazing. The sky was the colour of night; one commander spoke of it like the beginning of a nuclear winter. The weather was terrible and the rain brought down the clouds and a glutinous rain like I'd never seen before. It was amazing, special sometimes too as the amalgam of smoke and cloud swirled almost like evil over the desert."

"Tell me about the missile hit, Roy."

"We'd been despatched to sort out an ammunition dump and although separated from the group, we were within the line. Our exact position noted from the GPS was transmitted coded to HQ. There was so much going on, Desert Sabre had only just begun in earnest, enthusiasm was high and fingers were twitchy. We'd no idea at this stage that it would last about one hundred hours for us, however, we never saw that! All to end in a home goal. We'd settled in and before we knew where we were both Warriors had suffered a direct hit by Maverick missiles. Strange thing was, we were flying huge flags from every aerial. The fucking machine was covered with large inverted 'V's on luminous panels, but still the blind bastards couldn't tell we were friendly. Gung Ho! They'd shoot anything that looked slightly hostile. The missiles go right in, they bore a neat little hole and they destroy what's inside, like putting a ferret in a sealed burrow; nothing comes out but blood, guts and the scent of death. I remembered a strange smell, it lingered as I passed in and out of consciousness. Couldn't get rid of it for days. It was only later, whilst in hospital, that I realised what the smell was ..." He paused as if recalling the exact moment of dawning. "It was singed hair and flesh!"

Bill sensed the depth of Roy's anguish, his face was down and his good hand was propping up his head. He was in tears. Bill stood and walked to his desk and lifted the phone. He ordered more coffee.

"Sorry, Bill. Sometimes I become frustrated, it gnaws at me when I remember, the tears are not for me, you understand, they're for the lads. Some were still in their sleeping bags when the missiles struck; they never knew what hit them. I feel a kind of guilt as I should have been one of the fatalities. Looking back, it might have been better, the way I feel now."

There was a small tap on the door and Bill went to get the coffee. He put the tray down on the table between them and poured Roy a cup. Lifting it into his hand, Roy sipped it.

"Thanks."

"What happened after you were blown clear?"

"It appeared, although I didn't really know what was going on, that some troops who came to help were also injured by the blasts. We were all helicoptered out and treated. It was only when I realised the significance of the smell in my nostrils that I requested a mirror. My hair was badly singed and my face burned. I was just pleased to be able to answer the nagging question, to know my memory of the event was not totally lost."

"And the hand?"

"As you can see, pretty useless. The surgeon believed it couldn't be saved but they gave it a try. It needed a number of operations and some tendon grafts but the movement never really returned. There was a great deal of scar tissue inside the sheaths that prevented the free movement of the tendons, and most of the nerves are totally shot at. I can feel sensations rather than feel if that makes any sense, but it's something you learn to live with."

Roy was very much aware of where Bill was trying to lead him and to bring out any anger that might be bottled up but to Roy the hand was not his concern. He had been a paid soldier and he went to the Gulf to fight, if that meant injury then that was part of the risk; home goals too were part of the risk he took. It was a war; although initially there was a frustration that too had faded with time. What he really could not get to grips with was the illness he now believed was conceived by the coming together of God only knew what and the fact that nobody was prepared to help. Strangely enough he felt he owed a responsibility to friends who were out there, with some who were now suffering more greatly than he.

"Listen Bill, a friend of mine who was in the Gulf never suffered a scratch, went through the whole thing, even managed to get into Kuwait. Unluckily he was one of the few who went through the headquarters of the Estikhbarat, Iraq's Military Intelligence Service and the Amn State Internal Security. He witnessed the immediate scenes of the aftermath of torture and death: the bloodstains, the tools of evil, there was even a swimming pool, covered green with algae, which contained the bodies of those who were raped, tortured and killed for what were supposedly crimes against Saddam. Ask me what he's doing now?"

There was a long pause, Bill made no reply to Roy's rhetorical question.

"He came home, celebrated and married the girl he loved. Two disabled children followed later and a brain tumour for himself as his reward. His whole world is in the same state as Kuwait was ... totally fucked and now you can ask me why?

Because he suffered from the same as me. He may have had a different combination of drugs in him but the end result is the same, we are changed. We are mutants. We didn't join up for this, no fighting man deserves to die this way, slowly like some freak, and it's because of these men, men I fully trusted, men I laughed with, men I trembled with, men I commanded – it is for these men that I must fight."

"Who must you fight, Roy?" Bill sat back as if to relax, moved the pencil to his mouth and studied Roy's body language.

Immediately Roy realised the potential implications of what he had said and backed off, he knew too that Bill would be analysing his words, his expressions and his posture. He looked Bill squarely in the eye. "Myself, Bill, that's who, myself. I can't just give in. I've got to find the answers no matter what it takes."

He was careful not to overstate his point and it was his turn to watch how Bill responded, he felt that this meeting could, if not controlled get to be a cat and mouse game. "It may be of interest to you that Joan has clearly seen an improvement in my overall attitude, but funnily enough this seems to be causing tensions of its own. I now need to control the amount of change so that I fluctuate less fully from one extreme to the other, but I wanted you to know that I'm getting there, at least I think I am."

"Good. How is your relationship with Joan?" Bill studied Roy carefully, half looking at his notes. "Please tell me about her."

"Joan's a teacher, and as you know we're not married but I think our relationship is strong. She's been a tremendous help to me; she's a good listener and fun to be with."

"What about children? You mentioned the anxieties that friends had about having a family when suffering from the Syndrome. When the time comes for you to have a family will that cause you concern? Is it something you've discussed? What are your feelings?" From the expression on Roy's face he knew he had struck a nerve, he had rippled Roy once today but here he had found the quick. Just how far could he make Roy hurt?

"I know Joan would love a family when the time's right, but I am not too sure. What future do I really have? Funnily when I was in the forces I had this Utopian dream of a wife and family, a family who would travel and experience all the good things but now ... If this problem is solved then who knows? All I can say is that if I were to have a family, Joan is the person with whom I'd like to share the experience and the challenge." He knew he had just answered Bill's sensitive question if not honestly, certainly convincingly. Right now, kids were totally out of the equation and to some degree Joan was having to be placed further away in the scheme of things. "All I know is that I love her and I believe that she loves me."

"What about sex, how would you compare your sex life before and after the Gulf?"

"Is this relevant?"

"I wanted to know if there had been any psychological changes, any impotence or lack of drive? I don't want to pry into every facet."

"Before the Gulf, regular sex depended on the type of relationship; whether there was one or not. I was never one for looking for a different partner every night. I enjoyed sex within intimacy. Don't get me wrong, I have had my moments, but I think we're talking preferences here. After the Gulf there was the trauma with my hand. I felt very self-conscious and convinced that a cold, almost useless hand would be rather a turn off. Strangely I was wrong, I've had a couple of strong relationships since and my sex life has been fine; no complaints as they say!"

"Where's your future then, Roy? You're obviously concerned that Drew should find somebody else to take your place, otherwise you wouldn't be sitting here right now and I know Drew doesn't want to lose you. So, let's say five years to the day you called in to see me, what would you be doing?"

Roy stared at Bill, amazed by the naivety of the scenario. He did not rush his answer. His eyes never faltered from Bill's and he waited. His mind flashed up pictures of bombs, money and blackness. "I'll be dead in five years. If I grow much worse there will be nothing to live for. I'm not going to be a burden to anybody and I'm not going the way of some of the lads, that's for sure. I've had enough of the questions and answers, Bill."

"I know it's hard on you but I need to develop a picture out of this jigsaw and these questions are my only way forward, I'm sorry if they cause you distress. Would you be prepared to allow me to hypnotise you? It certainly wouldn't be as traumatic and you would relax more, there wouldn't be the concern about answering something incorrectly."

"You really know how to shock a man," answered Roy, almost breaking into a laugh whilst at the same time cringing, "I'll really have to think about this one. I just can't cope with surprises at this time of the day." Roy stood up and reached out to thank Bill with a handshake. He looked at his watch. It was 18.20. "My, how the time flies when you're having fun! Could I ring Joan, she wasn't expecting me to be so late?"

He called Joan using the telephone on Bill's desk. Bill moved away to the other side of the room and placed the notes he had made into a plastic folder. They would be typed and filed on the computer system.

"I was worried about you," Joan's voice trembled. "I'm sorry about this morning. Did everything go well? Where are you now?"

"I'm just about to leave the clinic so I shouldn't be long. Don't cook, we'll eat out." He hung up. When he looked at Bill he was standing with the painting he had so admired.

"Make sure it's well looked after. Enjoy it, I'm sure you will."

"Are you sure? It's lovely. I appreciate this." He took the picture and moved to leave.

"Another appointment soon, Roy. Don't forget."

Roy moved out of the clinic and negotiated the picture through the busy streets. Hope it fits in the car, he thought. Fortunately, with a little manoeuvring, he managed.

***

"Wow it's fabulous!" Joan could enthuse about art like no other. She bounced in front of it cocking her head backwards and forwards. "Give us a clue?" Her eyes glittered as her face creased into a broad grin. It was contagious. She turned around, bent and studied from the gap between her parted legs. "That's it … you're holding it the wrong way up!"

"Philistine! Come on, let's go and eat. I think it's got real depth. You need educating, my girl."

There was a comfort felt by both that evening. Roy was aware of his ordeal with Bill, the need to appear 'normal', not giving any clue as to his present practice and yet seeking help and guidance. Joan too felt bad, it was unlike her to walk away and break down. She knew Roy could be difficult and she knew she had stoked the fires. However, there was warmth. They walked back from the small restaurant arm in arm. Soon they would show their true feelings between the sheets. Joan's lovemaking was adventurous and this night she did not disappoint. "I'm sorry for my attitude this morning Roy. I should have been stronger."

He just kissed her mouth softly. She knew he was all right.

Chapter Fourteen

Saturday was certainly cold and autumnal. It would not be long before the bright days grew into their usual winter grey, a darkness that brought with it a depression and gloom. It was strange how Roy had quickly adapted to the warmth of the Cyprus winters, winters which still included the sun. The dark, sunless English season did not inspire him. It was time to reflect before moving on to the next step of the ladder. He lifted the lid of his palmtop. Joan had met a friend in Leeds, he was to expect her in the late afternoon. He needed this time. The thought of the next message dominated his mind. He was certain that investigations leading to him as a suspect could be well in hand. He heard that officers had been asking questions of Gulf Veteran Associations, nothing too deep but enough to cause ripples of concern. He was neither a member nor did he become involved in their activities directly, he often just worked with friends. However, they knew he was out there.

The agenda showed that he should send the demand on Sunday. This would be less than a week since the previous note. There would be a new delivery point. From now on he did not need to use the same contact; the word GULF was the key. The wording for the next note was clear. He removed the labeller from the locked filing cabinet and carefully typed in the details, making sure that the tape was wiped clean. He wore tight surgical rubber gloves. Once sealed he left the envelope propped up against the light on the desk and cleared away all the evidence of his activities.

At the same moment, Joan sat with her friend in the coffee lounge in the Leeds Hilton Hotel. They always met there before their shopping spree. It was close enough to the station next door, yet within the city centre.

"I'm really concerned, Louise. He's growing so preoccupied. It's as if he's feeding off something and I really can't put my finger on it."

Louise had known Joan since school. They had always been close. Both in their way had been successful but it was Louise who had been the sharper of the two. She had a first- class brain and academic life had been easy for her. At university she played the boys with tremendous dexterity. Her appetite was extraordinary. Where others would spend hours working, revising texts, she had the ability to read once and retain, verbatim. This left her with a great deal of free time, time she filled carnally. She had never married, like Joan she was in a long-term, stable relationship. She was also one of the most callous girls Joan had known; often she would treat her men like dirt, but because of her propensity for sex she would always find them waiting. She was Joan's opposite, and this was probably the reason they were still friends. She had qualified with a first in law and now worked as a partner in a large firm of solicitors.

"Is he seeing someone else?" she asked matter-of-factly, sipping the froth from her Cappuccino.

"I really can't see that. He's away travelling but always returns home or rings." She broke off in thought. "No, his habits haven't changed. Usually the aftershave changes and the breath freshener is all important. No, he's just the same that way. It's really difficult to put your finger on it. I guess he's just cold and short tempered."

"Sounds like a typical man. Look, I can see you're upset by it all. Come round with Roy next week and I'll cook. My man would love to see Roy again. Maybe something might come out when the boys get together. It's probably something and nothing. Is he still getting his periods of anguish?"

"He was. His boss, Drew, was concerned after a pretty bad depression and he booked him to see a shrink friend of his. He's had two sessions with him. He too believes in the Syndrome so Roy thinks he may have found a powerful ally, in fact he started to change after that first meeting, about the time of that terrible bombing."

"You bring him round next week, say, Friday at seven and we'll see."

They drank their coffee and took the escalator to the main entrance. The Concierge opened the door and tipped his hat as they left.

***

The telephone on Sam's desk rang. He was studying an ordinance survey map of the M6 north of Birmingham and asking himself the question, "Where next?" He picked up the receiver. "Phelps."

"Sam, it's Carl Howarth, Forensic." His voice was friendly.

"Hi! How are you? Anything from the bomb that killed Mike?"

"It's interesting really. Unfortunately, unlike the other explosives used, the last one showed no traces of taggants. We've analysed the origins, dates of manufacture and purchase of the other taggants and they're a really mixed bag. Traces show the explosives were all stolen from their original source or sold to companies abroad; one has come from as far away as Australia. Our guy has obviously bought a mixed bag."

"I thought we'd narrowed the availability of this stuff right down by using taggants. Let's say he's targeted twenty bridges with an average of 10kg per bridge, that's one hell of a lot of plastic. The more I look at this scenario the more I'm convinced we are dealing with some political group. Only they could get hold of that amount let alone bring it into the country."

"As you know, Sam, money talks and if you've the right money and know the correct people you can buy just about anything you like. You can even get it delivered to your door. Times are changing and speaking of change, I believe

MI5 are mixing it with SO13. That should be interesting to watch."

"Hopefully full co-operation this time. A number of knowns have been brought in for questioning but nothing as yet. If you find anything else, I'd appreciate a call. With luck we'll not see you professionally for a while." Sam hung up and moved back to the map.

***

The search continued on more than one front. It was amazing just how many motorway bridges there were, some only small carrying pedestrians over the road system, others carrying roads over roads. 'Spaghetti Junction' had been checked and double-checked although some wit on the team suggested it needed a bomb under it to get the traffic moving!

In a small office, tucked away in a building that was the pride of the sixties, sat an investigating officer. The building, all concrete, square and without an ounce of character, was the main police station for Wigan and surrounding districts. Large, white letters pronounced the word 'Police' and a small, ancient blue light from some long since demolished Victorian building hung above the main door. It was here that the first clue should have come to light. The investigating officer had checked the manufacturer of the type of palmtop that met the description of the unit seen by Sam Phelps and to his amazement the bomber had used one of the most expensive organisers available. He had checked with the producer to find their distributors and then contacted them directly. There was a remarkable number of organisers sold in any one year and to make matters worse they were produced under two names; one was primarily aimed at the schools market whilst the other for the punter in the street. They also made a number of variants.

He telephoned each of the largest distributors requesting lists of sales and where possible, names and addresses of purchasers; this was not as difficult as one would imagine as most people paid by credit card and the invoice was linked with a specific unit, also the larger companies would seek the customers' details for future mail shots. However, this type of research did not take into consideration the purchasers who paid cash and refused to give their personal details, or the machines that were stolen from shops and from individuals. It surprised the officer just how many were stolen. There was a third facet to the equation: companies giving them to clients as gifts rarely kept accurate records.

The manufacturer faxed through a list of those purchasers who had returned their guarantee registration cards but this was far short of the number sold. To compound matters, the identical machine could be bought in America more cheaply and with the number of computer mailing firms, their ability to track down those numbers was a little like finding a needle in a haystack. However, the clue was there, sitting amongst the numbers' information already on the desk, all he had to do was search. It would be just down to good police work but when something is staring you in the face it is often blurred and to the officer, the numbers he studied might well have been written in Arabic. His job was simple: collate and enter the information into the Police National Computer (PNC) terminal that would link the station to the main computer terminal at Hendon and from there to the crime analysis computer at New Scotland Yard. This computer, known as CRIS (Crime Report Information System), was new in itself. The police hoped that it would build up a picture of the bombings by searching for a pattern of time, location and type of explosive. This latest computer was linked also to the HOLMES (Home Office Large Major Enquiry System) where thousands of snippets of information could be filed and cross-referenced in seconds. HOLMES had in its data banks all the details of mainland bombings and the relevant forensic information that could, when matched, pinpoint the bomber. The modem went on line and the clue disappeared. It would be found, but only much later.

Chapter Fifteen

Roy packed away the items he had used to prepare the next note and went to the car. He needed to call at the office; it would be open until noon, one of the lads was always on site. Only one car was in the car park, the company logo clearly marked on the side and boot. He parked near the door, punching his code into the combination lock. He shouted on entering so as not to cause concern to anyone inside. He moved to his office.

"Is that you Roy?" It was Emma.

"Yes, in my office. Didn't expect to see you today, you don't work Saturdays."

"No, I needed to collect some things I left last night but I'm going now. Callum's in the back until dinner."

"I've just come to collect these notes and then I'm going for a drive."

Emma had always had a soft spot for Roy. "Mmm that sounds lovely. Where are you thinking of going?" she asked as they made their way to the car park.

"Through the Dales, maybe. Long time since I've seen some of the more lovely parts of this country of ours."

"Wouldn't be room for a small one would there? I've nothing planned for today."

Roy wished he had not said anything but nodded and held open the door. "It would be my pleasure."

Roy drove quickly, enjoying the freedom of the open road. The sheer grunt of the Subaru brought a tingle to his neck; he whistled to himself and gunned the motor harder. Emma sat almost tense, her tight blue jeans highlighting her slim thighs, her hands on the edge of the seat. The hedgerows buzzed past, as he negotiated the tight lanes. Leaves that had already turned brown were blown as the car whispered past.

"Where are we going, Roy? You do drive very fast."

Roy slowed the car realising Emma was not enjoying the drive and immediately her body sagged and relaxed. Her hands moved from the edge of her seat and she turned and smiled at him. She had a lovely smile.

From Ripley, the car turned left at the roundabout and trundled down the lanes eventually turning into Studley Royal. The gates to the hall were imposing as they drove through. The long elegant driveway was bordered by parkland and many deer roamed freely.

"Look at the deer, Roy!" Emma's face became totally animated as her eyes darted to both sides of the car.

Roy smiled and dropped his hand onto hers. She was shocked at first by its coldness but made no attempt to remove it.

The car park was almost deserted. Roy climbed out and took two fleece jackets from the boot, tossing one to Emma. "Might be a bit big but it'll keep out the cold." She slipped it on and zipped it tightly to her neck. She could smell him and she liked that. It was far too big but it was warm. Roy dragged out his bag, the same one he had used in his bomb setting expeditions only this time it contained nothing more dangerous than his coffee. They moved towards the gates. Roy bought two tickets and they walked through.

Roy enjoyed the country and he had a particular love of this area, the organisation of the garden set against the natural background of the countryside thrilled him. He admired the designers, men of outstanding vision, men who often never saw the results of their labours except in their mind's eye. They crossed over the stepping stones that led across the top of the small, man-made waterfall and then walked along its banks. The grounds were full of many follies and buildings. Roy turned her left up a small pathway that led to a tunnel.

"Looks rather dark in there," Emma giggled. "Will I be safe?"

"Your honour is safe with me ma'am." He could see that she registered a degree of disappointment. It stirred him.

They moved upwards through the tunnel made from huge stones and came out high on the valley side in woodland. Roy took Emma's hand to assist her, releasing it as they walked along the path. Occasionally the trees gapped affording them spectacular views of the ornamental lakes and gardens.

"This is beautiful, Roy." She grabbed him by the arm to stop him and direct his attention to the distant view. As they walked on her arm linked his. The pathway continued to follow the contour of the hill. After about twenty minutes Roy turned as if heading down the valley side, and there in the trees was a small, black wooden shelter. Before it was a gap in the trees. The view that it afforded was beautiful. Down in the distance were the ruins of Fountains Abbey, proud in their isolation. People like ants walked round it. Roy and Emma settled on the bench. He opened his bag and removed his thermos. He poured two drinks. Emma cupped the small beaker in her hands, warming them, sipping the coffee and marvelling at the view.

"I didn't think the youth of today enjoyed things like this, thought they were more into drugs and rave."

"It's lovely Roy, it really is. Thank you for bringing me." She moved and kissed his cheek. They looked at each other. Roy put his cup down and took hers from her hands. He stood up, lifting her to her feet. He held her and lowered his mouth to hers. Their kiss was deep. Emma's hands wandered around Roy's back, neck and buttocks. Her tongue slid between his teeth and he felt himself stiffen; Emma too felt it, rubbing herself harder against him. He broke away and looked down at the young lady standing slightly breathless before him. He knew he could not carry on even though he wanted to.

"The coffee will be cold but the view will still be beautiful." Emma leaned against him, feet on the bench.

Roy said nothing. He felt nothing. "More coffee?"

He checked his watch, the afternoon was drawing on. "We must make a move." They ran down the hillside kicking leaves and laughing, stopping occasionally to look at the mushrooms that grew in profusion, their red caps bright. She ran off and Roy played the game chasing her. The day had certainly blown away the cobwebs.

Roy dropped Emma at home. She leaned across and purposely kissed his cheek, refusing his lips. "It was just a perfect day, Roy, thank you." She climbed out and closed the door. He drove away.

Opening the glove box he took out the brown envelope, throwing it onto the warm seat that Emma had left moments earlier; it would not be there long. Soon it would find its way into the hands of the press and the whole ball would start rolling again.

'GULF, GULF, GULF. FOUND THE PREVIOUS BUNDLES, WELL DONE! YOU NEVER KNOW WHAT THE NEXT SURPRISE MIGHT BE. HERE ARE THE FOLLOWING THREE DUE TO BLOW. I DO HOPE YOU APPRECIATE MY KINDNESS. THE £2,000,000 TO BE IN USED NOTES. £1,000,000 IN STERLING, £1,000,000 IN AMERICAN DOLLARS. PLACE OF HIDING TO FOLLOW WITH DATE AND TIME. DON'T DISAPPOINT. LET ME KNOW YOU APPROVE. PLACE AD IN PERSONAL COLUMN, DAILY TELEGRAPH. 24 HOURS NO LONGER. STATE IF YOU CAN THAT YOU'VE MANAGED TO BRIDGE THE GULF.'

The nominated newspaper faxed the details to Scotland Yard and a meeting was swiftly organised. Bomb Disposal was sent to the three references that showed their position using GPS co-ordinates as per instructions. There was a great deal of caution and circumspection but they were beginning to know their man. Two of the three bombs turned out to be nothing more than plasticine wrapped in a thin film of Semtex then coated with grease. This gave the general appearance to the detectors that the total package was explosive. However, on these dummy bombs, GULF had wired a small anti-personnel charge to the TPU. It was felt safer to use controlled charges on all three. On this occasion it worked, there was little damage and no casualties.

The Home Secretary had received clearance for the money to be readied from the Defence Select Committee. Used notes in the denominations specified were packed and stored in readiness for a further communication. It took just twenty-four hours from their receiving the labelled message. The advert was placed, 'The Gulf is bridged. Cross when ready'.

Roy had, however, planned a surprise, a fourth device that was to explode without warning just before one of the peak commuter times. He was sure that there would be a press release to say that the police and army bomb disposal teams had secured another three bombs and that the battle against the terrorist was truly won. He had allowed a respectable lapse of time to ensure the news had gone to press so that the explosion would coincide with the early papers and hopefully their coverage.

He had not chosen his usual target; he had carefully put his explosive charges on the Pennine Way footbridge that crossed the M62 west of the Scammonden Dam. He had walked the bridge often, marvelling at the view. From its span on a clear day the West coast of Liverpool was visible along with the Welsh Mountains and Winter Hill, to the East Halifax and Brighouse. It was the highest part of the Trans-Pennine route, almost the border between Lancashire and Yorkshire, clearly marked by two pyramid-shaped pieces of dirty concrete decorated with a white and a red rose. The plan was to bring the single spanned bridge down onto the carriageway below.

The bridge where Mike had been killed was two miles west. This had brought the motorway to a standstill. Engineers assessed the damage and calculated that with metal plating and supports, one lane of vehicles in each direction could safely use the bridge providing a 30mph speed limit was enforced. This was better than originally predicted. It was at first felt that like the previous two blown spans, the heavy goods vehicles would have to detour, the worst possible nightmare for this area of the country. Within two days, traffic was again moving, albeit slowly across this section. It was, though, a long delay and the traffic stretched away up the hill and under the new target. Some were going to be in for a rude awakening as the bridge fell.

The early October mist was thick at the summit of the moors. Dismal at most times of the year, as winter drew in its unwelcoming arms, the M62, particularly there, was capricious and very brutal. The orange motorway lights swayed in the slight breeze. Traffic was building, the three lanes channelled into one, their exhaust gasses mixing with the morning mist. Many vehicles crept to the hard shoulder to leave the motorway along the A672 which would take them into Oldham. From there they would be able to pick up the A627M and the M62. Some thought that this was the better option. Sitting for twenty to thirty minutes hardly moving was wasting valuable time.

The police patrolled the outside two lanes ensuring that the vehicles remained in line. Breakdown vehicles stood by, waiting sentinels, ready to remove any that were to falter. The media too had played their part as the broadcasts and news items painted the grimmest picture of travelling this route over the Pennines, but still they came, probably thinking all the rest would heed the advice and the motorway would be empty. Strange how the human race can justify the most irrational of moves.

David King drove this same route daily. Promotion with ICI had taken him from the Agro-chemicals division based in Huddersfield, to Blakeley in Manchester for part of the week. He had worked with the company abroad, once in Japan and for three months in Holland. He loved his job. Fortunately, his home in Stainland was ideally placed for commuting either to Manchester or Huddersfield. He preferred Huddersfield but every Wednesday and Friday he had meetings in Blakeley. He liked to be in work as early as possible and could have taken any number of routes to Manchester. A friend had told him that although the motorway was down to single lanes, the traffic was lighter than expected, the other roads taking the traffic. It had been a toss-up between the A58 and the motorway; the motorway won. He had never played Russian roulette before and he never would again.

Chapter Sixteen

Roy was awake early and out running, the mornings were noticeably colder of late and he wore a full tracksuit. He ran down towards Peel Park. Turning in at the gates brought him to the boating lake, deserted and eerie. A few roosting fowl splashed and scooted hurriedly across the mirror-like pond. He ran round passing the toilets and up the hill towards the bowling green. A fellow runner approached from the opposite direction, hot breath clouding in lungfuls from his mouth. He lifted his hand and bid Roy good morning. Ahead of Roy were some stone steps that took him onto the tarmac driveway. He took them two at a time. He checked his watch. 07.25.

***

David reversed the Audi A4 out of the garage and pressed the control on the dashboard; the garage door began to close. He had purchased the automatic doors not as a sign of ostentation but to keep his wife safe. There were few streetlights in the village and he was concerned about her leaving the car in the dark to open the garage door. He had realised its worth during a bad storm when normally he would end up fumbling with the lock and getting soaked, now a press of a button ended that misery.

He joined the motorway at junction 23 and to his surprise the traffic, now two lanes, was moving slowly west, but it was moving. He flicked on the radio. It was 07.30. The flashing blue lights ahead warned that traffic would be filtering into one lane and although there was a slowing, the filter process was very efficient and the traffic crawled on. On descending the hill, Scammonden Dam came into view, almost empty after a dry summer. The Yorkshire Water Authority still imposed water limits to customers in the form of hose pipe bans, and a number of local people felt that the Authority kept this reservoir unnaturally low to justify their bans. Many of the other reservoirs out of the general public's view were brimming over. He smiled and nodded to himself as he viewed the extended slipways that ran to the dregs of water in the hollow just out of view. There would be no sailing here for some time. His phone rang.

"How is it?" a sleepy voice asked. It was his wife who had been woken as he left but who had curled back under the warmth of the quilt.

"It's fine darling. Slight mist but nothing serious. Just by the reservoir. Traffic's slow but we're still moving. I'll ring you when I'm in work. Don't go back to bed." He joked with her and pulled her leg. They had been married for six years, there were no children. "Love you."

He switched off the phone and threw it on the leather passenger seat. The traffic moved like a giant red eel up out of the gorge and onto the exposed part of the moor. Mist hung in tendrils from a heavy sky, broken by the orange motorway lights. It was there that the motorway separated to miss a solitary farmhouse before joining again at the top of the hill. It was there too that the bomb waited, biding its time, electronically ticking ... waiting.

***

Roy rounded the bandstand and carried on up the hill, his breathing was unsteady and he felt positively unwell. His head began to swim and he stopped, propping himself against a lamppost. He inhaled deeply, trying to control his erratic gasping. "Overdone things this time," he muttered out loud between gasps. He flopped forwards, putting his hands on his knees before stretching up again. He had a stitch in his side. The time was 07.46. He started walking, gently at first until he felt he was more in control of his breathing then picked up the pace, he was now simply walking rather than running. "You're gonna have to slow down, stop this foolish running, my lad," he chastised himself. He never did like the cold. Soon this would be behind him and the warmth of the Mediterranean would be his.

***

David saw the foot of the giant telecommunications mast appear out of the mist to his left. He knew he only had a mile of crawling left before the motorway would open again to three lanes. The red fog hazard light of the vehicle in front was bright and dazzling but essential in this weather. The car in front stopped. Above he could see the footbridge swathed in the mist. The middle of the span from the centre of the motorway was about twenty metres high. He was not directly under it. Suddenly there was a large white flash and an instantaneous bang which seemed to shake the car, followed by a second from the other side, then a third and a fourth. The brightness cut through the mist like a flashing blade and caused David to turn away. Small pieces of concrete rattled the bonnet of the car, cracking the windscreen. He shook his head and blinked, trying to clear the flash from his eyes.

***

Roy slowed again, his heart was beating in an irregular pattern and he began to sweat profusely. He staggered to the gate, the back entrance to the park. He gasped for air and held his chest. Pain tore through his chest wall and everything went black.

***

The span had been detached by the series of timed explosions at either side, and the arch turned onto its side and hung in the air, tethered by three reinforcement bars that were attached to one side and two to the other. They were no match for the huge weight of the bridge, they simply turned like florists' wire, twisting around themselves before snapping as the tumbling concrete span crashed onto the vehicles below, crushing them with ease. The only visible part of the Audi was the boot which stuck into the air. Strangely its rear lights were still on. The bonnet and front seats were totally flattened. David never felt a thing; one minute he was alive rubbing his eyes, the next minute crushed and lifeless. His phone, trapped between the backrest and the seat started to ring and ring. It would never be answered. It was 07.52.

***

It was an old lady who found Roy; she had been exercising her dog in the park as she always did. At first she thought it was a tramp until she noticed his running shoes and watch. She bent near, not touching him and spoke.

"Are you all right? Hello." She bravely moved her hand to his shoulder and gently shook him. He collapsed sideways giving out a breath as he did so. The lady jumped and her dog barked as it darted away to hide behind her legs, more timid than its owner. Quickly she moved out of the park and onto the road. The first few cars ignored her frantic attention seeking but a lorry driver stopped. He dashed round to Roy and felt for a pulse on his neck. There it was.

"He's not dead, probably overdone his running, silly sod, looks like a heart problem."

The driver ran back to his lorry and dialled 999 on his mobile. By now a group of people had gathered round but the old lady was having none of it.

"There's nothing to see, clear off or I'll set the dog on ya. He's going to be alright, we've phoned for an ambulance". The dog barked more out of fear and uncertainty than aggression.

***

The A&E unit of the Bradford Royal Infirmary was quiet at that time of the morning. Roy had come round in the ambulance and was breathing oxygen. The casualty doctor wired up the ECG and monitored the results. Owing to his age he would be taken to coronary care for twenty-four-hour observation. Roy still felt tightness in his chest as the doctor worked around him.

"Run far?"

"My usual distance but a new route. I feel bloody awful." He spoke, removing the oxygen mask briefly.

"What's your name and address, please?" A nurse wrote down the details and left to check them on file.

Roy had to think for a minute and then answered. "I've been out of sorts really, probably getting too cocky and pushing the hills a bit much."

The doctor carried on taking his blood pressure and tried again with the ECG. "Has anything like this happened to you before?"

"No, but I've had trouble since returning from the Gulf War. I've had all the tests but they say there's nothing traceable, probably psychosomatic."

The doctor looked at Roy's hand. "This, a souvenir of the conflict?" Their eyes met and Roy nodded.

"I was the lucky one. Everyone else paid the ultimate price of freedom."

"I want the Registrar to take a look at you and we're going to find you a bed, just so we can monitor things for twenty-four hours. I believe it to be a muscle pain and we can treat that with drugs. Who can we call to say you're here?" Roy gave the doctor his home number. Roy was exactly where he wanted to be. He was a better actor than he thought.

***

The emergency services took no time at all to arrive at the scene of devastation. The closed lanes allowed swift travel. Luckily there were only two vehicles that took a direct hit from the collapsing span: the Audi, now only partly visible and a

Transit van. The van had been crushed directly behind the cab and luckily the driver and passenger had only been treated for shock. The dilemma was the Audi. The front of the vehicle was totally hidden under the structure and the police had no way of knowing how many people were in the car. The traffic police requested computer details from the car registration number to find the owner. The vehicle was registered to ICI. It was some time before they received the driver's details and a call could be made to his house in Stainland.

***

The police vehicle pulled up outside the house an hour after the explosion. The curtains were still closed. Penny, David's wife, had taken his advice and left the comfort of the quilt, showered and was just about to tidy away the breakfast things. She had been concerned about David and had telephoned again to say she was up, but he had not answered her call. She waited for his response from the office with growing anxiety. The doorbell rang, instinctively she moved to the phone before realising the error.

She was surprised to find the police at the door and her face registered that surprise rather than shock. WPC Higginson had been in the force some years and this was not the first bad news call she had made in that time. She introduced herself and her colleague and showed her their ID.

"May we come in Mrs King?" The way the question was asked gave her little time to dawdle, the two officers were moving forwards. She instinctively showed them to the lounge. "Mrs King please sit down. We need some information about your husband, David."

Penny put her hands to her head and tears grew in her eyes that were wide and staring. "Is he all right? Has there been an accident? He didn't answer the phone. I knew there was something wrong, I just knew it. What's happened?"

The WPC nodded to her male colleague to put the kettle on as she moved across to the settee and put a

114

comforting arm around the now weeping woman. "There's been an accident but I'm afraid we can't get to the driver in the car. Mrs King, was your husband alone this morning, driving to work?" She simply nodded. "The emergency services are there at present but I'm sorry to say they feel there is little hope of finding David alive."

Penny let out a wail like an injured animal and beat at the chest of the officer until she grew weak. "It can't be David, it can't be. Please God no, not David." She broke down and began to cry.

The officer in the kitchen had heard everything and called control to inform those at the scene that there was only one person in the vehicle. It would be eight hours before the body was freed and eighteen before the motorway was running again.

***

Joan was just leaving the house when the phone rang. She dashed to it thinking it was Roy. She had been worried. He was never usually so long on his runs. The hospital explained the situation and she put the phone down before lifting it to ring school. She would not be in for a couple of days.

***

The news of the blast had sent shock waves throughout all participating police authorities and the ripples did not stop until they were knocking on the door of Number 10. The Home Secretary wanted urgent clarification of the situation after the securing of the agreement to meet the demands. There was total confusion as to whether this was one of GULF'S or whether copycat bombings were starting. They needed to convene urgently.

The Assistant Commissioner, Special Operations (ACSO), The Director General of the Security Services, Robin Carey and Alexander Smythe Commander of the Anti-terrorist

Branch of Scotland Yard met with the Home Secretary to discuss the future planning and to assess their position in the ever-changing game.

"Just what on earth is going on? I thought that agreement would be posted in the 'Telegraph' to meet the needs of GULF, only to find that another bridge has been targeted and the newspapers are making a total meal of the situation. This is not good. I thought we had this thing sewn up tightly."

"My guess is he's playing with us letting us know that we can't relax with him. He wants us to know he's in control and not, as we thought, the other way round." Alexander Smythe's, assumption was right. GULF didn't want them to think it would be over so easily.

"The press are baying at our doors wanting to know what's going on and they are prepared to play along, providing the latest on the M62 bomb is released."

"Right," frowned the Home Secretary. "Arrange a news conference for tomorrow. I want a story for them. I want it clearly understood that on no account must payment be mentioned, only that very positive steps have been made and an end to the problem is imminent. I want it as open as that, seeing this character is as unpredictable as a cornered rat."

Chapter Seventeen

The seven words were clearly printed in the personal column as arranged but Roy was having difficulty in getting a copy. He had made a number of requests but there was little response as other nursing tasks were the priority. At last the news trolley came into the ward and Roy eagerly requested a copy to find that he had no money; he never ran with any. The sister, however, seeing his great eagerness for a paper, thought unless she bought it for him his blood pressure would rise. There it was, clear as day. He smiled and sank back into the pillows letting the paper rest on the bed. "Yes!" he said triumphantly to himself. His thoughts were disturbed by talk of another bomb; a number of nurses had seen it on the morning news.

"Nurse!" he shouted. "What's this about another bombing?" He knew all the details but he had no idea of whether it had been a success.

The nurse told Roy all she had seen on the news and cursed the callousness and cowardly actions of these people. Roy made all the right sounds, agreeing with her character assassination. From the corner of his eye he saw Joan appearing through the doors at the bottom of the ward. She was obviously flustered. The sister intercepted her and informed her of his condition. She pointed to him and walked with her up the ward.

"Visitor for you, Roy." She quickly noted the responses on the electronic wizardry that were placed on either side of the bed before turning to Joan. "You may be able to collect him tomorrow if all proves well. Will you be calling in this afternoon or tonight?"

"Both, I hope. Thank you for looking after him," she said as the sister moved away. "Brought you some water and some grapes but I really didn't know what to expect." She bent over the bed and kissed him. "Watch my blood pressure. We don't want to give any false readings do we now? It's good to see you. I really must pack this jogging game in and accept that I'm not as fit as I used to be."

"The sister tells me they think it's some kind of muscle problem and drugs should see you out of here by tomorrow. Let's hope the Registrar thinks so when he sees you later this morning." She looked up at the monitors and the wires leading to various parts of his anatomy. "Do you need anything?"

The sister moved towards the bed and asked Joan to leave as the doctor would be commencing his rounds shortly.

She left money and his wallet before leaving. She was going to call into school to have a word with the Head to organise some time to be with Roy on his release.

The Registrar agreed with the original diagnosis and cleared it so that Roy would leave the following morning after his rounds. Roy settled back with his paper and read. He kept retuning to the personal ads, reading the seven words over and over again, 'The GULF is bridged, cross when ready'. He was winning the battle, but could he win the war?

***

The mist hung in mourning as the rescue crews struggled with the wreckage of bridge and vehicles. The police were fortunate to be in a position to divert all the westbound traffic away from the scene, but the east bound were not so lucky as the bridge had blocked their route to the exit lane. The closing of the three lanes into one allowed the vehicles trapped within the single lane system between the last turn off and the broken bridge, a distance of some three and a half miles, to negotiate an escape route. They simply turned and ran down the fast lane in the wrong direction, eventually turning along the slip road that usually fed cars onto the motorway, only to become snarled up in the traffic leaving down the other. It was clearly chaotic but it was the best they could do under the circumstances. The only vehicles directed towards the bridge were the number of heavy lift cranes and wagons needed to remove it, a task that proved difficult and frustrating for all concerned.

It was amazing too how the press could get where dirt could not, and despite the misty conditions, helicopters hovered photographing what they could of the tragedy. From the direction of Manchester drove a white Land Rover Discovery, headed by a police motorcycle. It cut through the traffic using the hard shoulder before squeezing through the queuing lines. Once clear it picked up speed heading for the summit of the hill and the fallen bridge. Inside were Carl Howarth and two colleagues from the Forensic Team. In his mind he hoped that this bomb would reveal the same hallmark of GULF, it would then allay fears of copycat bombings.

Carl was amazed that there had not been more casualties. The injuries to those who had collided into the bridge and the vehicles in front were superficial, more than could be said for the damage to the vehicles. He clipped on his ID badge and dressed in disposable blue overalls. The team set to work sifting for clues. David King's body would have to wait.

***

The news conference was packed as expected. The Commissioner, flanked by Commanders from the relevant Special Operations' groups, presented a very flattering assessment of the state of affairs which offered little in the way of new information. She spoke of the complexities and the difficulties faced but weighed heavily on the success, particularly the continued co-operation of the various teams.

"With this teamwork and the vital leads that we are now investigating, we hope to see a swift end to this campaign of terror. I should hope that we are all, ladies and gentlemen, nothing if not vigilant."

There was also a great deal of support for the media's co-operation in keeping the situation away from the public; the Commissioner hoped that they would continue with that support. However, there was a clear statement that should make headlines the next day and hopefully contrast the news of the latest bombing. Many questions were hurled, some disrespectfully, at Sheila Dewar, but she was more than a match for them and the meeting ended on a positive note. The camera stopped filming as the group left and reporters, cameramen and technicians huddled in small groups discussing the situation.

***

The investigations were going on at a pace. All information was channelled through ACPO, and a number of leads thrown up from CRIS, the computer system, were showing promise. It had been decided to look closely at all the Gulf veterans who had received help for ailments, believed to be caused by their war service. The missing MOD Gulf War medical records were swiftly located from the 'Lost' file; the Government had maintained its magician's tricks and these files would form the foundation of the investigations. The HOLMES computer did the rest as it cross referenced the areas where the phone calls had been made and the area of the bombings with veterans' addresses in order to narrow the field. Those that were then thrown up by the computer could be watched carefully and their past investigated in greater detail.

The computer identified fourteen hundred names, all Gulf Veterans, all at one time had been treated for symptoms linked with their time in the Gulf. Of these, one hundred and twenty-five had shown some strong political bias which might have generated enough resentment to blackmail the Government. One hundred and seventeen had connections with computing and might have access to computers as well as the means to travel about the country; nine displayed mental instability, frequently visiting psychiatric clinics for both domestic and street violence. Six of these nine had clean police records before their time in the Gulf; clearly their mental state had been affected by their experiences, but did they have the ability to design bombs? Sadly, there were twelve recorded as suicides. The significance of these could not be ruled out as family resentment might be strong and revenge sought.

Small teams of liaison officers from MI5 were to be allocated as watchers to forces around the areas where the suspects were living and the individuals would be put under close surveillance until their innocence was proved without doubt. It might be demanding on manpower but it generated results. Other clues found would also narrow the field down considerably; the Wigan clue brought a number of names into a group, Roy's name was in one of these; he fitted a number of strands of the pattern and he would be allocated a watch team if preliminary checks proved positive.

Two officers from CID were allocated to make preliminary investigations into Roy's past. Once the pieces of the jigsaw fell into place, it would not be long before he would be watched with a greater degree of vigilance.

They spread the information recently retrieved from the central computer in front of them and started to understand a little of their subject. It was becoming clearer that here was a man, injured in the course of his duty by friendly fire, giving reason enough to make the strongest man angry. Returning home, he had suffered from a number of the Gulf War Syndrome symptoms. However, he was not connected with any of the Gulf Veteran Societies.

His army record was exemplary, rising through the ranks, always keen and well disciplined; a good leader of men. It was reported that he was also a loner, tended to keep himself to himself when off duty, he had a liking for aesthetics rather than the wild times. He was never reported throughout his career and was deeply saddened to leave the forces after the war.

"Sounds like a pretty good egg to me. What does he do now?" mumbled Gary Barlow, the elder of the two officers.

"He's working for an office supply firm in Bradford, travels a good deal selling everything an office needs, drives a grey Subaru, registered to the company and lives in West Street with a Joan Johnson, a teacher. She teaches ..."

"Bloody hell, Lee, hold on. Strange car for a rep. Must be into rallying. I always fancied one of those ... blue one with gold wheels. Go like shit off a shovel." He looked up at Lee who was staring at him with an expression that was a mix of boredom and surprise.

"You never cease to amaze me, my friend. We're supposed to be clue hunting, not dreaming about some fucking car. Can we get on?"

"Interestingly too he lost both parents early on in life, motor accident, on a motorway. No other close relatives from what it says here. He also travels to Cyprus quite a bit, probably as he was posted there for a couple of years; may have friends there."

Both men failed to take into consideration that Cyprus was split and it was to the northern part of Cyprus, the side occupied by the Turks that Roy had travelled; if they had, and had brought a greater degree of lateral thinking to the equation, they might have saved time and lives and they had precious little of either to spare.

Looking at paper and old photographic records did not really give them any feeling for the man and they both thought that a journey to Bradford and the buildings mentioned might give them a closer understanding of their quarry. A bobby's nose could usually tell a good 'n from a bad 'n.

The day was fine and the unmarked light blue Ford Sierra pulled into the traffic. The age of the car and its general appearance helped it blend into some of the more salubrious parts of their catchment area. In fact, there was nothing that said 'Police' about the car. Each officer carried a radio and one a mobile telephone.

Chapter Eighteen

The morning seemed to drag. Roy had read the paper by 10.30 and worn the print from the corners of the personal column. He would be going home the next day and with luck he would soon be flying out to Cyprus. He would then stay there for as long as it took to get sorted, Joan could follow during her half-term break. He listened to the hospital radio collecting the odd news item but he longed for the television news at lunchtime. The main ECG and monitors had now been switched off and he could move freely about the ward. He did not feel like talking and most of the other patients were quite poorly. The hospital brought back myriad memories, some good, some bad, but they were predominantly clouded by the image of his mother, small and fragile in the large hospital bed.

"Coffee, Roy?" chirped a pretty nurse from down the ward. "Cheer up, you'll be out tonight if all's well. Is that silence a yes or a no?"

"Sorry, yes, yes I'd love one."

He took his coffee through to the day room and sat with his feet up on one of the coffee tables. One other patient was in watching the television. From the volume of the programme it was clear that hearts were not the only organ in need of help. He picked up an out of date magazine and started reading.

The television programme ended and the elderly, deaf gentleman moved out mumbling to himself. Roy took the opportunity to turn down the sound, he also flicked channels; a habit that aggravated Joan. There was nothing of any interest so he turned the sound fully down keeping an eye out for any news that might come on.

The nurse who had made his coffee pushed her head around the door, "You've two visitors Roy, they're by your bed. I didn't know you were friends with Dr O'Brien."

Roy jumped up and walked at a brisk pace to the door. The nurse watched the invalid, and tutted.

"Death's door yesterday, fit as a fiddle today and they call the Health Service!" the nurse was grinning. "You need to remember you are not one hundred per cent yet, slow down. They'll not go without seeing you."

Roy actually blushed and apologised before slowing his pace. He could see that his two visitors were Drew and Bill. They both stood as they saw him strolling down the ward, his Health Service dressing gown wrapped tightly round his figure. He held out his hand in greeting.

"Welcome, it's lovely to see healthy faces," he beamed, genuinely pleased to see them both.

"What the bloody hell have you been doing? I buy you a company car so you don't have to walk and get buses and here you are trying to kill yourself by running at ridiculous times of the day," jested Drew. "You look better than I thought you would, my friend."

"I'm actually feeling well, just bored out of my box. Luckily I'm home tonight."

"You'd be more bored on the road. There's been another bomb and it's caused chaos again. One of the lads spent four hours sitting in a queue."

It was Roy's facial expression, the immediate interest and the slight smile that alerted Bill; it was a strange response to such a serious problem, as if he were feeding off Drew's every word. He filed his thoughts away for future consideration. It was strange too that Roy neither asked the place nor the time of the bomb, it was as if he already knew all the details.

"You may be interested Roy that there's been a breakthrough in the Gulf Syndrome problem. Apparently they've started to realise what you'd said to me, that the spraying of Organophosphates (OP's) was carried out without real safety arrangements and they're linking some symptoms with those faced by some of the four thousand sick servicemen and women. The Defence Select Committee's report of August '95 suggested that the Government was not addressing the problems, that they were not working closely with the Americans in their research. The survey to compare samples of people who were in the Gulf and those who have never been near has never got off the ground."

"It's always the same, it's a bloody big cover-up. Something's wrong and they'll not admit to anything."

"They've said again that they're going to look at the one hundred and eight different symptoms diagnosed by Gulf Vets and then do some contrasting study. They say the MOD is committing itself to finding the answer to the problem." Bill's voice faded as if even he felt that whatever was done was not enough, and for many would come too late. "At least they say they're doing something."

"They want to start by compensating the families of those who have died so far, then we might believe there's a commitment. It's all well and good playing with figures and moving missing medical reports around but that's not going to solve the problems of the servicemen who are suffering, and it ain't helping me." Roy's voice had grown and seemed to echo through the ward.

The Sister moved towards them. "Mr Hanna, you really should be taking things more easily. Could I please ask you to keep your voice down, there are very sick people here." She gave Bill a hard stare.

That really calmed things down. They chatted quietly for another fifteen minutes and prepared to leave. Roy had set the agenda for a holiday of indefinite length and Drew agreed without batting an eyelid.

Roy walked with them to the door and into the corridor.

"God! Nearly forgot to give you this." Drew delved into his inside pocket and took out an envelope. "Emma says she's missing you and to get back to work quickly." Drew then winked at Bill and ridiculously Roy felt himself redden.

He quickly thanked them for coming and went back into the day room. He was determined to watch the television news. He opened the envelope and there was a card. The cover was of Fountains Abbey and the note read:

This view always cheers me up, hope it does the same for you. Get well soon. Love, Emma.

He simply shook his head and turned on the television.

***

West Street was not how they had imagined, it was not at its best, but you could not judge a book by its cover. The grey Subaru was parked outside the house.

"Hope he's got a good alarm on that thing."

"Doesn't look very special to me," muttered Lee.

"Wolf in sheep's clothing, mate. Top speeds about 140 with a 0 to 60 somewhere in the region of 6.5 seconds."

"Thank you, Murray Walker. Can we get on? Do you think he's at home?"

Gary opened the door and trotted across the street. He took a long sideways glance at the car before moving to the door. He turned to look at Lee who had removed a camera with telephoto lens from the rear seat. He knocked loudly and waited. There was no response. He knocked again. Moving back towards the parked car he noticed the lace curtains of the house opposite move so he made straight for the door and knocked there. An elderly Asian gentleman came to the door. A strong smell of spiced cooking escaped, filling Gary's nostrils. He instinctively stood back a bit where the air was fresher, suddenly feeling hungry.

"You looking for Mr Hanna?"

"Who? No, just knocked on the first door I came to. Could you direct me to Undercliffe Road, please?"

"Certainly, certainly." The old man moved down the two steps to the pavement and pointed to the end of the street.

The smell seemed to surround him totally. "You turn right, yes right and then follow road to traffic lights. Go straight, straight and Undercliffe Road you will be on I'm sure."

Gary thanked the old man and started walking to the end of the street before turning as instructed. The old man shuffled back inside, closing the door and trapping with him his aroma. Lee started the car and followed, collecting Gary who was now a few hundred yards up the road.

"Didn't want the old guy saying Hanna had had a visitor."

Lee just nodded and sniffed loudly. "Very funny."

They moved off using the A to Z and stopped outside D.M. Business Machines. The building was quite large with an attractive facade and warehousing to the rear. Two cars were parked in front and a large box van belonging to the firm was to the side. Gary wrote down all the numbers and radioed them for checking, maybe they had been seen near the explosions. It was a long shot but certainly worth trying.

***

Joan had left for the hospital minutes before the blue Sierra turned onto West Street. Across the back seat she had Roy's clothes. Finding a parking space at the hospital was always difficult, particularly as she wanted to be as close to the door as possible for Roy.

The ward was quite busy and Roy was eagerly awaiting her arrival. He walked up the ward to greet her. His kiss said everything to her. He took his clothes and drew the curtains around his bed. It felt good to be on his way home. Joan had slipped off to speak with the nurse, she wanted to be sure that Roy only did what was best for him. She came away with a list of Do's and one Don't. She knew he was going to be hell to live with under this regime.

Roy thanked everyone and they left hand in hand.

"Missed you." He leaned across and kissed her cheek.

"Roy," called the nurse, "you've forgotten your card."

She walked up and handed Emma's card to him. He had hoped to leave it in the bedside cabinet.

The cold air of the car park was in direct contrast to the warmth of the ward and he shivered, even though it was mid- afternoon. Once in the car he felt more relaxed and whistled to himself.

"Let's get you home and into bed," said Joan firmly.

"This trip's getting better by the minute and that sounds to me just the tonic I need." His cheeky grin said it all. "Love to see you in a nurse's outfit."

"Pervert!"

The car turned into West Street and parked. Neither noticed the two men in the blue Sierra, nor did they see the camera. Joan walked with Roy to the door and opened it before returning to lock the car. She glanced down the road to where the Sierra was parked but thought nothing of it, after all, why should she?

Joan's registration number was recorded and processed as had been all the others that were connected in any way to Roy. The Sierra was started and they returned to the office, dropping the roll of film off in the lab on their way. There had been no positive identification on any of the car number plates although there had been a report of a sighting of a grey car near a hotel days before one of the bombings, but as it was going dark the observer could only give a brief description; at least it was something to go on. They would contact him and show him a photograph of the Subaru, it might just jog his memory.

Chapter Nineteen

The next twenty-four hours were the worst he had suffered; he was totally mothered and smothered by Joan. She protected him from all that life could throw at him. His paper was brought to him in the morning and she generally fussed like a mother hen. He was completely hemmed in. When she went out shopping he took the opportunity to telephone the agent who usually handled his flight arrangements for Cyprus and booked to fly the following Monday. He gave his credit card number and the booking was made; his ticket would arrive the next day. He had deliberately left his return flight open as he might never be coming back.

Joan was shocked when he told her over the meal that he had booked his flight and the rest of the meal was eaten in silence; that was the calm before the storm. Roy moved the dinner things into the kitchen and loaded the dishwasher.

"And what will happen if you become ill again, am I supposed to come hot-foot to collect you? You really can be the most selfish person I know. Why don't you give yourself a little time, we'll both go out in October when I'm on half-term. The doctor did say you should take things easy for a while."

"That's exactly what I intend to do. Sitting on the beach at Beddis or Salamis in the warmth would do me more good than sitting round here, besides if I'm here I'll just be itching to get into work. Over there I can do nothing but relax. You'll be out before too long and I'll feel much better."

Joan could see both sides of the argument and she was not about to get into a slanging match. She needed to get back to school too. "Maybe you're right, maybe some time apart might do us both some good." She drifted into the lounge and moved towards the window. The streetlight, which had just come on was showing pink; as it warmed it would turn to orange and cast its light into the recesses and dark places of the street. Her eyes were drawn to a parked car, its colour masked by the sodium light, in which sat a solitary figure. It made her feel as if she were being watched. She drew the curtains.

The following day Joan returned to work. Roy had said that he too would call into the office, if only to sort things out before he left. He had written his resignation many months ago when he was planning everything, he knew it would come to this but he realised he could not leave Drew hanging on any longer. He had supported him long enough. Shortly he would receive a salary from elsewhere, a salary that he planned to use to help fight the cause.

From his palmtop he retrieved his next note. This would be the final communication he would make in this format. He would post it from Heathrow as he left on Monday. He took the labeller from the drawer and began typing the message which gave very precise instructions for the deposit of the money. To make things more clear he included a photocopy of a plan of the drop area and even the GPS co-ordinates. He checked that the message read correctly and, as he had done previously, carefully wiped the tape and placed it into the envelope with the map. He addressed it to the editor of the 'Daily Telegraph'. He collected up the label-making machine, his letter of resignation and slipped downstairs. The Subaru car keys were on the table. He would be really sorry to see the car go. He opened the front door, pressed the key fob and the alarm blipped. It was like music to Gary's ears. He sat up and watched. Gary had changed cars, today he was in a white Fiesta van. The Subaru fired first time and moved away from the kerb, purring lightly. A thin plume of white exhaust curled animal-like behind. The Fiesta neither started first time nor purred; the diesel motor rattled into life and followed. Gary assumed correctly that Roy was heading for work. In his mirror Roy noticed the Fiesta pull out behind him and follow him to the traffic lights; his senses told him everything. He stuck exactly to the speed limit and watched. Instead of driving on through the lights he turned right, he knew a long route to work, a route not taken by someone trying to get to that part of Undercliffe, after all why do ten miles when you only have to do three? As he thought, the Fiesta stayed close by.

Gary should have followed his assumption that Roy was heading for work. He would have been there when he arrived and Roy would not have been any the wiser. He was bored. Watching nothing all day tended to make you overreact and he had, unbeknown to himself, done just that. He had been careless.

Roy turned into the car park and drove the Subaru next to Drew's car. He went around to the boot and took out the bag containing the letter of resignation and the labeller.

Emma beamed when she saw him enter. She moved from her desk and kissed his cheek. "I was really worried about you. Did you like my card?" She seemed so young.

"I thought it was lovely. You really know how to cheer a man up. It's a good job they weren't monitoring my blood pressure."

"Can we drive out again sometime, Roy?"

Roy just lifted his shoulders and smiled at her. "Is Drew about?" She pointed to his office.

***

Joan rang Louise from school during her free period. She was concerned that Roy should plan to go abroad without discussing things, particularly after his hospitalisation but she was also upset; although she would not let Roy know, she had seen the card from Emma. If he had not tried to disown it, she would not have felt suspicious. She was convincing herself that he was having an affair.

"You're still okay for the evening with us? We'll sort things out there. Stop worrying."

That was easier said than done. She had invested a lot of herself in Roy; she knew that she still loved him a great deal and that he was worth fighting for. If it were another woman she could face that challenge, it was the unknown that she feared more than anything, his distant coldness, his callous, selfish attitude that she found so distasteful.

Meanwhile, Drew was pleased to see Roy back with him and they discussed the holiday. It came as a shock when Roy handed him the envelope containing a neatly handwritten resignation. Drew simply tore it up. He was not prepared to give up on Roy now, he had fought hard with him, he was a friend and friends do not give in.

"I might never want to leave Cyprus. I can't say when I'll be back and businesses just don't function like that; you need the stability I can't give. I thank you for the friendship we have and pray to God that it'll shine through any eventuality, but you've got to see this beyond the role of friendship. Please, for me, let me go. You can get salesmen better than me tomorrow at the drop of a hat. If I return feeling better, then I'll hope there'll be something here for me." He held out his right hand and Drew gripped it. "You've been like a father to me, Drew. Thank you."

"When do you fly out?" Drew moved to his desk and removed two tumblers. He poured two malt whiskeys. "Here's to you, my friend. Keep fighting."

"I'm doing that, of that you have no fear, no fear at all." He tossed the car keys onto the desk. "Callum in the warehouse would kill for those. I'll go through to say goodbye to the lads and leave through the warehouse door, the walk home will do me good. Say goodbye to Emma for me, we know what she's like!" This time it was Roy's turn to wink at Drew. Before he left the office Drew arranged to take him to the airport. Roy eventually left via the back door in the knowledge that his follower was somewhere out front. He took the footpath to the main road and walked home whistling.

Gary moved the Fiesta away from the company building, far enough not to be seen but close enough to move should Roy leave. He listened to the radio and drank coffee from a polystyrene cup. "Join the police and see the world," he said to himself. The Fiesta was still there an hour later.

Chapter Twenty

The dinner party went well, both Roy and Joan relaxed. There was a great deal of laughter; Louise could tell a good joke. Roy to the outside seemed fine and that confused Joan even more but she was thankful that he was happy. They kissed in the taxi home and made love twice when they arrived home, once aggressively behind the front door soon after it was slammed and the second time more slowly in bed. Thoughts of Emma danced through Roy's mind as they coupled. He must get a grip of himself.

The Saturday morning was overcast. Joan remained curled in bed as Roy, dressed in some old clothes went into the cellar; there was a good deal of tidying up to be done. All the work on the bombs had been carried out there and he wanted to ensure that no clues remained. The telephone rang.

"Mr Hanna, is that you? It is Mr Singh from across the road. I'm sorry to be troubling you but I'm worried. For a few days now there have been cars parked on the road and men have been sitting, waiting in them. I wonder if you think we should call the police?"

"Funny you should say that Mr Singh, I noticed one yesterday." He moved to the window and looked down the road. There it was, a blue Sierra.

"Leave it with me, I'll sort it out."

Roy found the number of the local police station and telephoned. He gave his name and address and explained as part of Neighbourhood Watch he would like to report a suspicious car. He gave the registration number and waited a while. He was thanked and informed that they would put someone onto it. Within ten minutes the car had gone.

He returned to the cellar. Most of the old wire, connectors and paper he threw into his bin in the yard. He swept everything before washing down the work surfaces with bleach. He took from the hook the case containing the night sights and put them on after turning off the light. They worked perfectly. He would need these in Cyprus. He switched on the light and checked the room one last time.

His next task was his study. He cleared everything away carefully and checked his palmtop, that too would go with him; an identical one would stay but it would contain nothing. It would remain on his desk as his had always done. It might give Joan hope that things were as normal.

The Sunday was strained. They breakfasted late before walking in the local woods. Joan kicked the dry leaves. They chatted and laughed but it was not easy for either. Joan had planned a meal just for the two of them at home, it was a time for re-establishing a foundation, ground rules and confirming their love for each other. That night Roy's mind raced. He loved the woman who was opposite him, illuminated by candlelight, who kissed his hands with true affection; he loved her sensitivity and her strength. Maybe he should simply send the list of remaining bombs to the newspaper, get on with his life, take things less seriously, forget all about trying to get faceless people to understand the invisible problems that he and many others faced. Why should it be up to him? There were surely others far stronger than he, with greater financial and physical resources who could bring this irresponsible government to task, re-dress the balance. He moved to the window. A large white transit van was parked. They were watching him he knew that. They were not sure, otherwise the knock on the door with great force would have come in the night, sniffer dogs and armed police would have swarmed over the place like ants around a nest. They were closing in though. He was now after all, no innocent protester, he was a bomber, terrorist, murderer and blackmailer. He must now see it through to the end and pray that good would prevail.

He moved back to bed. Joan's body was silhouetted against the dim light. Tears ran down his cheeks. He loved this girl, though at times he pretended he did not. Tomorrow he might be able to put her to the back of his mind and get on with the job he had to do, but in his heart of hearts, he loved her. His tears ran in streams, they were real and he wept for one person, he wept for himself.

Joan woke first and kissed Roy's mouth sensually. "Promise me you'll look after yourself, promise you'll think of me occasionally and promise me you'll ring and fax. I love you, Roy Hanna, more than you could or will ever know. Remember that."

He took a deep breath and returned the kiss to keep his tears at bay.

Roy helped collect all her things together and walked her to the car. The van was still there, its windows mirrored. It was battered and rusty but he knew it was occupied. The directional microphone was picking up every word and it was being recorded.

Roy turned his back on the van and whispered to Joan, "I'll ring you whenever I can and definitely when I arrive." He slipped his mobile phone into her bag." Keep this with you I could ring anytime. I love you too."

Joan jumped into her car and started to move away. She stalled it and they both laughed releasing some of the tension. Roy waited until she had turned off the street.

The police officer in the van called control. He had a hunch that one of them was going somewhere and asked for back up to follow. Lee organised three officers, two in cars and one on a fast motorcycle to follow. All were in radio contact with each other; they used highly secure back-to-back radios. Lee would remain at base to keep overall control. "Tip off the Airport Police at Leeds and Manchester Airports," he called out to a colleague, "but leave him alone. Check the flights out today, he's probably heading for Cyprus."

An hour later Drew arrived. He was driving the Subaru. Roy was ready. He loaded the cases into the boot and locked the door. Drew tossed the keys to Roy. "Thought you'd like to drive. Don't scare the shit out of me young man, I've a wife and two horses to support, let alone a massive mortgage."

The wheels spun and the car moved off rapidly.

"This is Bravo Two, car, grey Subaru, two people." and he called out the registration. "Heading towards Eccleshill."

"With him, Bravo Two." The motorbike had managed to beat the cars. "He's heading towards the ring road, suggest we have a destination of Leeds Bradford Airport. Position at Apperley Bridge, Phil." Phil was driving a Post Office van.

Roy spotted the bike instantly, the glowing headlight was noticeable for some distance. "Shit Drew, I've forgotten my wallet. Hang on." He indicated and swung the car right and doubled back. The motorcyclist had to continue.

"Bravo One, Lee, I've just lost him he's turned round heading back towards Bravo Two."

Lee thumped the table with his fist. "He may have forgotten something. Stay where you are, Simon. Jenny, go to position of Bravo Two. See if he turns up there." He then called Traffic, giving information on the car. "Call if your chaps get any sighting, these cars are as rare as hen's teeth so someone should spot it!"

"Just check the pocket of my jacket, please Drew, my wallet might be there?"

Drew leaned into the back and felt the inside pocket of the jacket. He felt the wallet. He put his hand in and pulled it out. "It's here, false alarm!"

Roy had no intention of returning home. He flicked the car through a number of side streets and was soon heading down the M606 to pick up the M62 to Leeds. He would take the fast route. The traffic would be easier to hide in but still he watched the mirror and stayed in the outside lane away from any parked police vehicles but he saw none.

They pulled into the short stay car park and Roy let the engine idle as he collected his belongings from the boot, shook Drew's hand and left. "I'll ring you. Give my regards to Bill and look after Joan for me."

Drew waved and climbed into the car. He moved away and turned left to leave the airport. He would go back through Yeadon. The car turned left at the roundabout and the road dropped through the tunnel built to take the road under the main runway. A motorbike passed going in the other direction, obviously in a hurry. It was Simon, Bravo One.

Lee in control received notification that the target had arrived at the airport and cancelled the watch from all other units.

"Simon, how close are you to the airport?"

"It's in sight, Lee. Do I go in?" He stopped the bike in the 'short stay' and walked towards a traffic warden. He showed his ID card. "I'm outside now, shall I just wait?"

"The next flight out is the Heathrow Shuttle. I'm assuming he's on that and according to our computer here he's booked on the 14.30 flight to Istanbul. Just stay and make sure he doesn't leave by any other way."

Simon leaned against the wall, removed his helmet and lit a cigarette. It had not been his best morning.

***

Roy had moved through to the shuttle lounge after checking in his luggage, he would not see it again until Cyprus. He helped himself to a coffee before settling down to read his paper. He glanced round and checked the faces of his fellow travellers before he relaxed. His flight was called on time and he moved through to the gate. He felt excited, he felt as though he was in the game again.

The flight left on time and was uneventful. Simon waited thirty minutes and then trawled the airport but there was no sign. The Heathrow police would check his debarkation and he would be able to leave. Roy's arrival was confirmed.

Chapter Twenty-One

Bill sat in his office mulling over Roy's case notes. Something had bothered him at the hospital and he had not rested easily since. Why does an ill man take such delight in hearing tragic news of a bombing and why did he not ask the obvious questions? He scanned the notes, reading them over and over again, trying to remember Roy's manner, inflection of voice and concerns. He recalled Roy's words, 'It is for these men I must fight'. He noticed too from the notes that he had made at the time that his answer about his enemy was without conviction. Roy was neither involved in any Veteran's group nor political party as far as he was aware. He moved to his desk and telephoned the hospital. "Doctor O'Brien speaking, could you put me through to the Registrar, please?" There was a pause before the earpiece was filled with soft music.

"Doctor Patel speaking. How may I help?"

"Good morning, Doctor, it's Bill O'Brien from Psychiatry." They exchanged greetings and chatted briefly about the hospital's shortcomings before Bill got to the point. "I wonder if you could help me unofficially for the moment? You had a chap brought in the other morning, suspected heart attack whilst jogging, by the name of Roy Hanna; he's one of my private patients. Could you give me some information about your findings? It could be important."

Dr Patel briefly told Bill the treatment he had received but stressed that the initial ECG showed no abnormality, blood pressure was within limits and remained so throughout the monitoring period. He felt it may have been a combination of muscle spasm and stress. Other than his hand deformity he thought Roy was reasonably fit.

Bill thanked the doctor and assured confidentiality. He walked through to his Secretary. "Could you telephone Drew

McKenna? The number is in the book. Arrange an appointment for me to see him later today. I've appointments at the hospital until two. Call me on the mobile." Bill left the clinic. His Secretary managed to secure an appointment with Drew for three that afternoon.

***

Roy purchased some whisky from duty free before looking at the electrical goods. In a glass cabinet sat a palmtop, identical to the ones he had used. He asked the assistant to let him see the new model. She unlocked the cabinet and put it in front of him. She was distracted by another customer. How easy it would be to slip a hard disc into the port, a hard disc that contained Semtex. It could sit there until another enquiry brought it to life, the disc would activate and the bomb would explode. The act of leaving the device, to the time of detonation would vary. He shuddered. He was getting carried away by this terrorism. It was strange to think of all the opportunities to terrorise one's fellow man. He thanked the assistant and tapped the case closed. "I'll leave it this time, thanks."

The airport security officer noted his interest in the computer and continued to follow Roy. Like Roy, the officer carried a flight bag and paper, he also had a duty-free bag. Roy's flight, although slightly delayed in arriving, was called on time. He checked the screen and found his gate number and moved to collect his things. He followed the signs that directed him through the labyrinth of passageways and travelators to his gate. He stopped three times, once at the toilet where he brushed his hair after splashing his face with water, secondly to drop an envelope in the post box and finally to call Joan, he hoped she would be on her break. She was embarrassed when the mobile phone rang, she was on playground duty but delighted that he had called. He walked to his gate with the other passengers until it was time to board.

The security officer immediately contacted his control. "It's Ian. Suspect on the plane. Seemed fine, didn't leave anything anywhere other than a letter in the post box on passageway B".

"Stay with him, Ian, until the gate's closed, then back here for debrief. We have a chap from SO13 who wants a word."

Once on board, Roy moved down to the front of the plane. He had noticed the service air attendant enter the flight deck and he waited until the cabin door opened.

"Excuse me, I've forgotten to post this and I wonder if you'd mind collecting a stamp and posting it when you can? It's most important. I'm getting so forgetful." Roy handed the man the envelope and a pound coin. "First Class, if you could."

"Not a problem, I'm passing the post office in the main hall on my way back," said the man, who smiled at the stewardess and left the plane.

Roy knew he was taking a risk, the guy might forget or lose it but he was prepared to take the risk. He could not risk posting it for fear of still being followed. Should they realise that he was the bomber they could forward instructions to hold him at Istanbul and then all would be lost. Handing over the envelope was a small risk to take for his own security. This way the letter would be posted in a different box from Joan's.

***

The officer from SO13 was waiting for the security officer in what appeared to be a conference room, the triple glazing kept the aircraft noise to a minimum. Ian's senior introduced him to Colin Tagholm. They shook hands.

"Just tell me what he did whilst in the airport."

Ian explained that there was nothing out of the ordinary; he thought the suspect was relaxed and professional. He did mention that he looked at a computer in duty free. Colin looked up from his notes.

"Which one?"

Ian described what he had seen and they sent down for the sales assistant and also requested video footage from the security cameras of that area. Twenty minutes later they watched Roy looking at the palmtop. Colin turned to the assistant.

"Did he ask any details or say anything to you about the computer?"

The assistant thought for a while but really could not remember, it had been so busy that morning. She was allowed to leave.

"We've brought the letters from the post box where you saw Roy drop the envelope. Would you recognise it amongst these?"

There were three. Ian immediately pointed to the brown envelope. Colin picked it up; it was addressed to Joan Johnson, Bradford.

On his return to HQ Colin called his Inspector. A call was then linked through to Commander Jonathan Keen. It was he who started the ball rolling to involve MI5.

***

It was just after three when Bill's Porsche pulled on to the car park of D.M. Business Machines. He walked in and smiled at Emma. "Bill to see Drew I have an appointment at three." He looked at the clock on the office wall. "Bit late I'm afraid."

Drew had heard the Porsche and came to meet him.

"Come this way Bill, coffee?" Drew turned to Emma. "Two coffees, Emma, when you can please, love. Come through Bill. Now what can I do for you?"

Bill explained carefully that he was concerned by the way Roy had acted and responded during the second of their meetings; he was also concerned about Roy's fascination with the bombings that had been going on. On reflection Drew remembered Roy's curious interest in news on the latest bombing.

"So what are you driving at, Bill?" Drew was growing more intrigued. He treated Roy like a son and for that same reason felt responsible to discover what Bill was insinuating.

"I don't really know myself. What's at the back of my mind is unclear. What I really need is a sounding board. I called the doctor who treated Roy after his hospitalisation. I know most by sight and a few by name at the hospital. Roy was totally free of any abnormality on his ECG or tests, the treatment administered was purely precautionary, litigation being what it is today. When did Roy talk about going abroad to you?"

"Only when we met him together. Listen, I must tell you I don't think it's a holiday he's gone on, I think it's possibly a permanent move; he handed his resignation in to me today. It's there in the bin in pieces. He's mixed up as well you know."

"Of that I'm aware, my friend, but mixed up in what?"

Emma brought the coffee in and put it on the coffee table. The two men stopped talking. She left.

"So what are you saying?" Drew's voice had an air of concern.

"I'm probably way off beam here but I think he may be tied up with these bombings. I know, I know," he repeated anxiously. "It sounds totally ridiculous but I just have this feeling. The problem is I don't know where to go from here. Tell me, do you have a copy of Roy's appointments over the last twelve months? If he's been in the area of the bombings then that might give us a clue."

Drew called Emma and asked her to bring up on the computer all the appointments and expenses Roy had made over the previous two years plus any orders he had made. "Let's be thorough, I don't want you leaving here other than clear in that warped mind of yours that Roy is nothing but a salesman, slightly mixed up I'll grant you that, but a salesman."

There was anger in his tone and Bill knew that he might just have disturbed a hornet's nest.

***

The British Airways 757 landed in Istanbul on time. Roy cleared passport control before moving towards the internal flights' boards. The Cyprus Turkish Airline flight would depart from Gate 7. He checked in and made his way to the seating area near the gate. His flight would depart in forty minutes. He would wait twenty minutes and then ring Joan.

Collection was made of all the post boxes in Heathrow, a brown envelope addressed to the Editor of the 'Daily Telegraph' was swept into the nylon sack with hundreds of others. It was on its way.

Roy had no luck with his call. As he returned to his seat people were beginning to collect around the door leading to departures. He waited until the group had dissipated before joining the line. An old man in front struggled with a plethora of packages and bags, mostly wrapped in black plastic. With a degree of shoving and pushing he managed to fit them onto the x-ray conveyor. How he was going to manage once on the plane only he knew. There seemed to be scant regard for the rule, one piece of hand luggage each. Roy helped and the Turk smiled, his eyes creased into a thousand lines before he was directed to the metal detector.

A security guard sat, bored, waiting for the bleep that never came. The machine was probably switched off to match its operator. Through the window Roy could see the aircraft as he moved steadily towards the gate. He loved the country in which he was about to arrive. No matter what propaganda the Greeks dredged up about it, it was his second home. He had lived amongst both Greeks and Turks and he knew whom he preferred. His preference was now clear to all. He never missed the chance to promote their dilemma, he knew the history of the island and he had not stowed away the facts the Greeks tended to do. The British had granted independence within the Commonwealth on the understanding that they could maintain two sovereign bases, one of which was Roy's home and inspiration for a time. The rest could be run by both Greek and Turks, the Greeks holding the majority, therefore the most power, but they were to guarantee a say and freedom to the Turkish minority. It did not last, with the Greeks reneging on the deal spending a number of years moving the Turks into areas of the country they saw fit, often using violence, whilst at the same time removing any rights they might have in the government of the island.

When Greece's fascist Colonels sent troops to overthrow the government of Cyprus, a government that had been installed by Britain, Turkey became determined to support its neighbouring people, just as Britain should have done. After numerous requests to protect the Turkish inhabitants and just as many excuses from Britain, Turkey sent in twenty-five thousand paratroopers and moved south to the present 'Green Line'. The Republic of Northern Cyprus was born, now unrecognised by everyone but Turkey and the Sudan. There was, however, an advantage: it was as yet unspoiled and beautiful in its emptiness; a place not found by hoards of drunken holidaymakers that were de rigueur in most Greek resorts. The miles of unspoiled beaches were, in Roy's opinion, what the Greeks wanted now; their greed escalated.

Roy showed his passport and entered the aircraft; fortunately, he was seated away from the old man who nodded and grinned every time Roy caught his eye.

***

There was more to look through than either Bill or Drew had imagined but they were at least methodical. Armed with more coffee they began their search. The contrast in enthusiasm was marked. Drew sighed deeply, seeming to lack enthusiasm for the task, whereas Bill studied carefully making copious notes.

"What exactly are you searching for, Bill?"

"We are searching for clues, my friend. The bombs so far have been mainly in the north east and north west, nothing in the borders and some in the south, predictably the M25. The M6 near Wigan was the first target. Any business over that way?"

"Just a minute," interrupted Drew. "There was a large contract in Liverpool. Roy spent a number of days developing a computer system for a group of retail outfits. I vaguely recall that the purchaser knew me from my days in the States. I remember too this was the second order; it wasn't too long ago either."

The two men searched the records until they found what they were looking for.

"Look! Liverpool and Preston, both in the vicinity of the first bombings."

"Don't be ridiculous, Bill. Hundreds of reps travel to these places but it doesn't make them the bomber."

"Hundreds of reps didn't serve in the Gulf, hundreds of reps don't need psychiatric help and hundreds of reps haven't just done a flit to a country that doesn't recognise extradition."

Drew looked up and for the first time realised that Bill's long shot might hold some truth. "Let's keep looking."

***

Gary Barlow and Lee Jennings pulled up outside the hotel close to the site of the second bombing. They walked to the reception and showed their ID to the receptionist. They requested to see John Jones, the waiter who had reported seeing a grey car parked close to the hotel. The receptionist put out a call and within minutes Jones walked towards the two officers. He had been expecting them, since their earlier phone call. Lee introduced himself and his colleague. Gary produced the photographs of the car taken from all angles. The result was immediate. John's face registered instant recognition.

"That's it!" He looked carefully at all the photographs stopping at the one showing the front view. "I'd forgotten about that bulge on the bonnet." He could not remember whether it was days or weeks before the bombing but he clearly remembered the night. "The car was parked over there." He walked the officers to the revolving door. "I'd come out for a smoke at about ten. A bloke dressed mainly in black opened the boot and took out a large shoulder bag before setting off for the bridge up there. Thought he was a fisherman but as I went back inside, I couldn't remember seeing a rod. I came back out just before midnight; we'd just finished clearing away. The car was still there. I walked up the road a bit and there he was. He'd just climbed over the fence by the bridge. I had been right, he didn't have a rod. He walked back to the car and threw the bag in the boot; I noticed it was much lighter and then he drove off. But that's the car all right. What kind is it?"

"Subaru, very fast and very special," chipped in Gary.

Lee just looked at his partner before turning back to Jones. "You've been a great help, Mr Jones. We'll need to see you again sometime in the future."

Chapter Twenty-Two

The aircraft banked slightly and the turbulent air rising from the Girne range of mountains shook the wing tips. The sky was blue apart from the few white cumuli that hung like cotton. Below would be his castle, to the south east Gazimagusa. He could see the green of the mountain foothills give way to the yellow of the plain, heated from the long, hot summer, and then the roads, snaking grey along its length. The runway was below him as the pilot overflew the beacon that had been their guide. He turned left flying east to take up his downwind leg. The seat belt sign flicked on and passengers extinguished their cigarettes; smoking was still very much allowed on these flights. The descent made a child cry as ears adjusted to altitude. Another left turn brought them onto base leg. He could see the runway stretching out ready for their arrival, another turn and then the welcoming clunk of the extending undercarriage. The landing was firm but they were down. Many of the elderly Turks clapped for reasons best known to themselves. In an hour he would be home.

***

The more Drew and Bill searched, the more they seemed to find. It was the invoices for palmtop computers that puzzled them more than other anomalies; throughout the course of eighteen months the firm had received sixty-two. Twelve had been sold, the rest were in stock. Drew called through to the warehouse to check the stock items. The remaining fifty were missing. Drew wondered whether they had been given as gifts by Roy to established clients. He would speak with him when he could.

"So, you see why I'm concerned, things are just not falling into place as they should do. With your support I want to go to the police. If he is innocent then there's little damage done but if things are what I feel them to be, Roy may be in need of more help than either of us had first considered."

"Let's both go and sleep on it. I'll take these records home and go through them again. Can you meet me tomorrow? We'll meet at 5pm and make the decision about the police then, that way we're sure."

Bill agreed and shook Drew's hand, apologising for raising his suspicions for he knew just how close the two men were. When Bill had gone Drew continued going through the records until late. The longer he looked the more convinced he became that his friend was involved.

***

The taxi dropped Roy outside the flat. From the outside in the late afternoon sun it looked warm. The shadows from the palm trees were long. In forty minutes it would be dark. He opened the door and the cool of the flat rushed to greet him. The closed shutters kept the flat dark and cool. Leaving his cases on the pathway, he skipped up the steps and wound the shutters open, one by one. The sun trickled in. Once he had retrieved his belongings and checked the flat, he poured himself a long drink and pulled a chair onto the balcony to catch the last of the sun. He would try to ring Joan.

The ringing phone was just what she had been waiting for. She found it difficult to concentrate, she had found herself looking at the phone, willing it to ring and now that it had it caused the butterflies in her tummy to crash and tumble.

"Joan, I'm home, sitting on the balcony watching the sun disappear. Missing you. How are you?"

"I've been like a cat on hot bricks, you know how I worry. Thanks for your call earlier. You'll be pleased to know I've booked my flight for half-term and I can't wait."

They chatted for a time. Roy then unpacked and walked into town to find Tongus, he knew just where to find him. He needed a few things, especially a jeep. The dim street lamps gave little light but a feeling of security. He liked the approach to the old town with its curved walls. He stood for a moment and admired the statue in the centre of the roundabout before moving across the road. He entered the old town by crossing the bridge over what once was the moat, squeezing into the wall occasionally to allow the traffic to pass. Once through the towered gate he strolled down the narrow streets, savouring the smells and sounds. In front of him was the once mighty cathedral, now a mosque. He turned down towards the port. On his left was Petek's Bar and sure enough, sitting at a table was Tongus, backgammon board between him and a friend. This was the evening's relaxation. Roy stood and watched the scene for a moment before moving behind Tongus. He signalled to the man facing his friend to say nothing.

"Shit move," he whispered in broken Turkish into Tongus's ear. It had the desired result. He whipped round, anger in his eyes until he saw Roy. His face metamorphosed and a huge cry echoed through the bar. They hugged each other and beer was brought. It was going to be a long night.

***

Although the note arrived early, the letter was not read until 09.15. The scramble after that was intense. The editor faxed the note to New Scotland Yard. Immediately a meeting was called of the heads of the groups. At 11.40, Sheila Dewar addressed the group. It was an open forum. They each had a copy in front of them:

GULF, GULF, GULF. THANK YOU FOR AGREEING TO MY DEMANDS. REMEMBER THERE ARE MANY BRIDGES LIKE THE ONE JUST GONE! THE MONEY NEEDS TO BE BROUGHT THROUGH TO REPUBLIC OF

NORTHERN CYPRUS ON ONE OF THE U.N. TRIPS TO RIZOKARPASSO. YOU NEED TO DEPOSIT CASH AT PLACE MARKED 'X'. PLACE IT IN A BERGEN. IT MUST BE DONE BETWEEN THE HOURS OF 18.00 AND 19.00 0N 14 OCT. THE LANDROVER SHOULD CONTAIN ONLY TWO PEOPLE. INSTRUCTIONS OF WHEN AND WHERE TO COLLECT BOMB DETAILS WILL FOLLOW SUCCESSFUL COLLECTION.

They also had a copy of the castle plan, which showed the 'X' in red and, clearly marked in brackets, the location co-ordinates, alongside a brief history of the Cyprus situation. They also had a faxed copy of the Investigating Officer's report on the eyewitness account of the car sighting. All around the table were convinced that Roy Hanna was their man and all were eager to ensure that he would not enjoy the profits of his deadly labours.

"The only problem I see at present, gentlemen, is organising the money. That's being done as we speak at one of the sovereign bases in Cyprus and I should hear soon whether we will be ready to move on that. To get the U.N. vehicle to the mountain area, which as you can see from the map is a long way from their destined route, will require sensitive handling. The vehicles travel weekly to Rizokarpasso, a Greek enclave since 1974, delivering rations. The whole issue of the UN travelling away from set routes is growing more difficult, particularly in the light of the latest border clashes. As you will have seen on the news, gentlemen, a number of people from both sides have been killed recently.

Three operatives from MI5 will travel to Northern Cyprus tomorrow, two travelling as a husband and wife, the third travelling alone. Their mission will be to track the target at all times. We are fortunate in having four days, we must ensure we use them wisely."

Philip Haslem-Parr, representing MI5, broke in at that moment. "We'll also be closely monitoring Hanna's girlfriend, as well as looking at his last place of work. As soon as we have anything it will be distributed on the network. I trust we'll have the full co-operation of all the services." He looked back at the Commissioner.

"I'll be meeting the Home Secretary in an hour and I'll put the relevant points to him. I know he's brought the matter to the PM's attention so we'll meet again in two days when I can furnish you all with a definite plan of action that's fully sanctioned. Please keep each other very closely informed."

***

Roy had not managed in his attempt to get a black Vitara 4x4. Tongus had one but it was out on rental, he would see if he could get it for him later. Roy had to make do with a blue one; at least it was a dark colour. He had purchased camouflaged hunting clothes, a foil safety blanket and down sleeping bag. His plan for the next two days would be to drive out to St Hilarion Castle combing every part, particularly the 'drop' area and the vantage point that he would use. He would also locate and familiarise himself with the forestry roads in the vicinity that he might use should there be a problem. He wanted to be confident of everything.

***

The SAS three-man team had been on exercise in Cyprus for four days when the call came through with the mission details. They had less than twenty-four hours to plan and would be moving out the following morning.

***

Mr and Mrs Mason disembarked at Ercan Airport and a taxi drove them to the Palm Beach Hotel, probably the best hotel in Gazimagusa. Their twin-bedded room was a superior one. They showered before eating. Bob rang reception to book a hire car for early the following morning. He was assured it would be there for 6am.

They had worked together in the past. They were an excellent team. Bob had been with the service for three years and Pippa, her friends called her Pip, two. They left the hotel and took a taxi to the town centre, a mere two minutes and then walked the mile to Roy's apartment. They wanted to get a feel for the place, to look over their target. There was a light on but the external shutters were almost closed. Bob went to the front door and looked at the lock before joining Pip.

"Looks pretty straight forward to me," said Bob. "I'll do early watch tomorrow."

On returning to their hotel, Pip went down to the Turkish bath. Tall and slender she managed immediately to attract the attention of more than the waiters. Bob rang home leaving the message that they had arrived safely and they would be sightseeing from first light. Jim Bentley would arrive the following day.

In Bradford, another operative of MI5 had watched and waited for Joan to leave the house; he would need five minutes. He moved through the terraced house swiftly and efficiently. Two microphones were placed in both telephones; both were infinity bugs. Once activated they would pick up everything that was said in the room by dialling in a code. Nothing else was disturbed and the operative left the house as he had found it. A minute later the telephone rang twice and stopped; the bugs were active. He then walked down the street, climbed into the waiting police car and they drove to the outskirts of the Industrial estate that contained D.M. Business Machines. Dressed in black, he moved along the footpath taken by Roy earlier, found the window and was in quickly. He moved through the rooms conscious the alarm had been activated. It took him three minutes to place the same devices in telephones in the main offices. A few cupboards were turned over to make the break-in seem like petty theft then he left, walking swiftly to the car. A distant siren could be heard but by the time it arrived he was long gone.

Back in Cyprus, in a small building in the barracks, the SAS team toiled with the planning, the logistics were most important. Toes would ensure he had everything he needed. Dressed as tourists, Stan and Colin would travel through the border at Dekhelia and then on through the Turkish border. Toes, a sobriquet earned by his losing two from his left foot to frostbite in a climbing expedition some years earlier, would be concealed in a compartment of the Land Rover. This was necessary as tourists were only allowed a single day in the north. Toes would be left with his equipment and the others would return to the south. They would collect him when the job was completed. Equipment too would be concealed in every available space in the Land Rover. Once over the border, they would make their way into the hills and locate the castle.

Chapter Twenty-Three

Bob woke just before the alarm and moved to the hotel window, the balcony afforded a breathtaking view out to sea. The light of the morning was painting the sky yellow and the sea reflected its beauty. Behind him the only sound heard was Pippa's gentle, rhythmic breathing. He moved into the bathroom, washed and dressed before collecting the rucksack he had packed the night before. As promised, the dark green Seat was waiting. He signed the forms and took the keys from the Receptionist.

There was little traffic. He drove past the school and onto the dual carriageway that once linked Varosha, the newer suburb of Famagusta. Varosha, however, was now trapped behind wire, deserted, a No Man's Land created with the establishment of a Green Line in 1974. Hundreds of homes, shops, flats and hotels were left empty.

The ancient city walls were to his right and as the car climbed the hill a large, black statue filled the windscreen. He negotiated the roundabout. In two minutes he was there. He parked down the road watching the two flats for any sign of life. There was none. The Vitara sat in the shade of the palm tree, it had not moved. He opened the rucksack removing a small black device; it was a transponder. It worked like a tracker device sending signals to satellites and then bouncing them back to a receiver that would pinpoint the device.

There was a magnet to one side. Bob slipped out of the car and walked past the blue vehicle. He stopped to do up his bootlace and stuck the transponder behind the rear bumper before walking on. He circled the houses before returning to the car. He did not want to remain in the vicinity of the flat longer than necessary. Northern Cyprus is one of those places where everybody knows what everyone else is doing, and if they do not it does not take long for them to find out. Bob's vigil was soon spotted by neighbours and curiosity was aroused. They would find out the identity of this man and the nature of his business. This insularity had its drawbacks but it would certainly be an advantage for Roy. Bob drove the car back to the hotel and ordered breakfast, his morning jaunt had made him hungry.

***

The news of the break-in brought Drew to the office early; he was the first there. A police officer was waiting and they checked the premises together.

"Looks like the alarm scared them off, you've been lucky, Mr McKenna. Please check through and should you find things missing I'd be grateful if you'd call this number. The fingerprint boys will be out later so if you can evacuate this room it might help."

Drew thanked the officer. It certainly was no way as bad as he had thought. The phone rang twice but stopped as he attempted to pick it up. He thought nothing of it. The two MI5 operatives could now hear Drew moving about. They would hear everything that went on in the main rooms. If Roy were to call, they would know instantly.

Joan woke early too. The bed was warm and cosy and her thoughts drifted to Roy, she could almost feel his touch. She leaned over and picked up the phone. The ringing tone in Cyprus was different and it always made it seem millions of miles away. Not a million miles away a tape recorder was activated and the same ringtone was being recorded.

"Good morning, beautiful man. I'm lying here, warm as toast just thinking about you, so I thought I'd just call to say good morning."

"You're full of surprises. I can just imagine that lovely body of yours too. It won't be long before you're here."

"I suppose you've a busy day planned with some floozy by the beach whilst some of us are taming children."

"I'll certainly be on the beach but I'll be alone, I can assure you of that."

"Must go. Remember, I love you."

"I love you, too."

The phone call ended and the listener switched off the recorder. He could, however, still hear everything in the room.

***

The three men had loaded the Land Rover well. Toes climbed into the false floor concealed under the rear seat. They drove towards the British checkpoint, sharing a joke with the soldiers on duty before crossing No Man's Land. To both sides were the ruined houses. The Green Line was no respecter of property, it cut through roads, houses and even the capital Nicosia; this was dead land. They rounded the bend and on the left was the Turkish border post. A red and white barrier barred the road. As their vehicle approached, a policeman and soldier moved to the roadside. The soldier stood to the rear of the vehicle and the policeman smiled.

"Morning." He looked at each of the occupants in turn. "May I see your passport and papers?" He took them into the hut and wrote down the names from the passport and the number from the pass. He handed them back and included some details of the Greek atrocities carried out on the Turks before the invasion; the propaganda war continued. "Enjoy your visit in Turkish Cyprus." He saluted and walked over to lift the barrier.

The Land Rover moved forward and each man waved and smiled. The road ran downhill into Gazimagusa, a road full of potholes. Few people travelled this road apart from the UN and the occasional lost tourist. They were soon well on their way. Reading the map Stan suggested they would be there within the hour. He was a few minutes out in his approximation and was ribbed for it. Toes kept up a constant grumble about the driver knowing every bloody pothole on the northern side but for the most part they simply ignored him.

They had arranged to hide the equipment Toes needed after helping with the first recce. They would also decide on an emergency rendezvous (ERV) should things go wrong.

They stopped in a quiet area of the pine forest and helped Toes from his hole. He stretched and straightened his clothes before moving up the winding path that ended in a small car park overlooking the jousting ground below the castle. They had agreed to look at the castle plan first. They chatted briefly to the attendant at the small tollbooth before walking through the barbican, following the path sharp left, passing ruined buildings until they arrived at a gateway. Stan stopped and removed the copy of the map and a GPS system. They could see they needed to be higher, the co-ordinates were very close. They continued through the remnants of the once magnificent royal living quarters, then the barracks, before breaking out onto the roof of a tall tower. They all stood and marvelled at the view.

"Bingo," muttered Stan. "This is it, 'X' marks the spot."

Roy had arrived twenty minutes before them and was watching their slow progress up the pathway from a higher castellated tower, his binoculars trained on the one with the map. Toes caught a flash from the sunlight reflecting off the lens and his stiffening and his look alerted the others. They then knew they were being watched, perhaps innocently, but they could not take the chance. There had been three cars in the car park. They adopted their tourist mode, each being photographed before descending to the car.

"Bit sloppy lads, if it was our man, he could have seen our interest in the tower. Let's hope not, so early in the game. Well spotted." They both patted Toes on the back.

On leaving they drove back the way they had come and took a forestry road that ran below a ridge. Somewhere near, which was safe and offered a view of the castle, they would leave their man.

Toes had been thorough in his packing. He could be spending five nights in the open. As well as essentials he was equipped with a cryptographic radio that would link him to the many listening stations in the south. The ninety-nine square miles of sovereign bases bristled with antennae, they were the ears of England and the States for communications from the Middle East. He also carried a mobile phone, he just never knew where or what situation or place he might find himself in and the radio might have to be abandoned. He also had for good measure, long-range night vision glasses, his fighting knife, three stun grenades and an HK P7 9mm pistol and suppressor.

"Fuck me, Toes, you've enough here to start a bleeding war. You are here to observe, not solve the Cyprus problem on your ownsome."

"Boy Scouts' motto. As you can see, I'm very prepared."

They covered the stashed equipment with camouflaged netting before driving into Girne. Roy moved through the castle looking carefully at different routes away from his eyrie. He had not suspected the three tourists.

***

Bob woke Pippa with a gentle shake and pointed to the coffee on the bedside table. She smiled and yawned before moving to pick up the cup. The covers fell from her shoulder and the light through the thin nightshirt silhouetted her breasts. Bob looked and then looked away. She was a stunner.

"How did it go this morning? Tracker in place?"

"No problem at all. There's been no signal so I guess he's still asleep. Do you want breakfast?"

Pip shook her head. She tossed the covers back and went onto the balcony. Now her whole body was silhouetted. Bob felt a movement in his groin and had to look away, trying to concentrate on the job in hand and not the obvious distraction.

"You going to slum around all morning?"

Pip turned and walked towards the bathroom. He heard the shower. Just then the bleeper sounded.

"Pip, we're active."

She continued her shower, knowing there was no rush to chase, they would simply track his route and then follow at a safe distance. Jim held the black box. It was no larger than a paperback book. There was a screen showing a green map of the area and below a co-ordinate read out for the moving marker. Controls below could enlarge or reduce the scale of the map on screen. He continued to monitor the screen but busied himself with packing provisions for the day. Pip would need her own. They planned for her to follow the Vitara, note its activity and then plot the journeys on a map; there might be a pattern which could help them later. This information would be phoned home. Bob had some house breaking to do, a tricky operation at the best of times, but here where every neighbour had eyes and ears in every part of their anatomy it would be doubly difficult. They would stay in contact by each using a Magellan GPS pager system. This ensured the absence of a telephone bleep and allowed brief messages to be sent immediately.

Bob exited the room, leaving the pack and key on the bed for Pip, he had no doubt she would be in the shower for some time. He began the walk to Roy's flat. The sun was warm. He planned as he walked.

The Vitara had indeed gone and the road looked empty. An old man turned out from a side road and wished him good morning in Turkish. He waved and smiled as the man wobbled past. It took him only seconds to open the front door, five minutes to search the flat. He noticed the camouflaged clothing and night sights, making a mental note, but there was no computer. The planting of the bugs was easy, one in each of the phones and one in the kitchen, concealed behind the picture. Before leaving he glanced outside through the shutters and then slipped out.

Pippa was climbing the mountain road, both windows were down and her mousy hair blew freely. The GPS showed the Vitara stationary and she would soon be close. The road to the castle was bumpier and she was soon driving past the jousting ground and turning onto the car park. The Vitara was there. She checked her e-mailer and Bob had left a simple message, his task was complete. She typed a congratulatory note and sent it. The things you could do today with satellites never ceased to amaze.

She left the car and entered the ruins, sitting briefly at a vantage point that allowed her the full view of the road she had just used. The sun warmed and she lifted her skirt high on her thighs and stretched back to take full advantage of her brief stay. She could see the Vitara and therefore there was little need to move. It was the tumbling of small pieces of soil and stones that brought her to her senses. She turned sharply and looked up, the dazzling yellow of the sun strained her eyes and for a moment she was blinded.

"I'm sorry, I didn't mean to startle you. I lost my footing. I should really have sensible footwear."

Roy's body blocked the sun from her face and she focused on the apologetic figure.

"There's no harm done. I shouldn't really be soaking up all this sun. I should be exercising my mind and appreciating the wonders of this beautiful relic." Pippa stood up and straightened her skirt. It was then that she noticed Roy's hand.

"I can certainly recommend the view from the seats at the Queen's window. Please allow me to show you."

Reluctantly Pippa allowed herself to be escorted higher, through the bowels of the fortress until they came to the window. It took her breath away. The sheer fall of the cliff face, the view through to the coast and the azure sea and sky that merged without horizon made her agree, this stranger was right.

"My name's Roy, Roy Hanna." He held out his hand.

Pippa did not respond immediately, she let the name sink in before turning with a smile that masked her annoyance at being so foolish. "I'm Pippa. My husband and I are here for a short break. Have you been here long?"

They talked freely as they walked back down. It was hard to believe that this man could be responsible for the bombings but then again, she was aware more than most, that in her line of work, first impressions could be deceptive. She stayed amidst the ruins and thanked Roy for his kindness, expressing the hope that they might bump into each other again as they were both in Gasimagosa. She sat, the dampness under her arms was the tell-tale sign that she had been under pressure, as she watched Roy make his way to the Vitara.

Toes, hidden in a small hollow amongst the cliffs opposite the castle had observed most of the incident; he had particularly enjoyed her legs. He logged the time of the meeting and when Roy left. He would keep an eye on her before making a brew. His location was carefully selected; he was a professional. There was nothing in front but a cliff face that dropped vertically to the jousting ground some three hundred feet below, to his back were pine trees that led to the forestry track. The rocks in which he was sheltered would collect the heat of the sun during the day and release it slowly at night. He was more than pleased with his bivvy.

Chapter Twenty-Four

Bill and Drew had agreed that they must contact the police to discuss their findings; it might be nothing, but it could be important. Their conversation was already recorded and the necessary action was in hand; all they were waiting for was their call. The security forces had agreed to leave Joan alone for the present, if they were to spook her, Roy would soon know. No, they needed to keep that part of Roy's life as uninterrupted as possible. All the bugging devices were in place and they would glean all they wanted to know from those. There was of course, the one doubt: suppose, even by the slightest margin, that Roy was not their man. They dared not dwell on that for too long. Everything pointed that way and the latest findings from Drew McKenna narrowed the odds considerably.

***

Jim Bentley's flight arrived late. A tall, sombre man in his late thirties, he was credited with a distinguished military career, being awarded the Military Medal in the Falklands as a young soldier. He had a steady nerve. His intelligence and bravery were legendary. He was still single and chose to live alone, had few real friends and kept himself to himself. His only real vice was his love of red wines, his palette was expensive but his pockets were deep. He kept in the peak of physical fitness.

He waited for his two small suitcases, both black, both identical. He kept his nose half buried in the book he had started on the plane until his luggage arrived on the carousel. Once through Customs he stopped at the car hire desk to confirm that a car had been booked in his name. He collected the keys and was shown to a new Seat Cabrio.

The drive was longer than he had imagined but the late afternoon was forgiving; the slipstream buffeted his head. He headed for Gazimagusa but turned off the road following the signs for Salamis. His hotel was situated along the main coast road that ran up the 'pan handle', the long-extended strip of land that gives Cyprus its distinctive pan like appearance. He turned off the main road and ran down a track to a small, red-roofed hotel that sat on the beach. The neatly kept gardens gave the hotel a strong Mediterranean feel. He had specifically requested a room overlooking the ancient ruins of Salamis and he was not disappointed. Although Jim knew that Pippa and Bob were already working, he would not meet with them. However, he could receive and send details using the personal hand-held e-mailer should the need arise. His job was to wait; only time would tell whether his services would be required.

He changed quickly and went for a swim. His body was muscular and hard. There were two scars, one to his left shoulder and one to his thigh, both received in close hand fighting in the Falklands.

The water was clear and warm. He swam along the coast, 500m from the sand, there were few waves. Climbing out onto the jetty near Beddis, he lay on the warm wood looking at the sky. In three days he would know if his journey were in vain. The hotel, a mile up the beach, nestled amongst the sand hills and he started to run back. This regime he would keep morning and evening whilst there.

***

Roy had parked his Vitara in Girne and walked to the harbour. He sat at the same table he had shared with Joan in the summer and ordered a beer. The waiter brought his order. He sipped the cold froth from the top and his mind re-ran his day's observations. He was sure now that he could leave the castle by more than three different routes that would link with the parked vehicle. There was an interesting alternative to arriving back at the car that would take him on foot to an old farm building some two miles away from the castle. From there he could walk into Girne but he would use this method only if things went horribly wrong and there was a welcoming party laid on. He felt sure that things would be straightforward. The harbour was calm and he stared at the perfect reflection of the buildings opposite.

Pippa had seen the car and parked some distance away before strolling round the small town. She had in her bag the receiver that would signal the Vitara's movement. She would like to meet Roy again accidentally, to gain his confidence.

The horseshoe harbour was extensive, there were few boats as the summer was ending, only the real sailors who lived on their boats were still sailing. She took countless photographs, using the telephoto lens to scan the people drinking at the many tables that framed the harbour edge. Sitting alone, staring out to sea was the man she had been looking for. Unhurriedly she strolled round.

"Hello again, small island." She smiled at Roy. "I'm having a coffee, may I buy you a beer for your kindness this morning?"

Roy stood and offered her a chair. "Please, allow me. Turkish or Nescafé?"

"I'm afraid the Turkish coffee is a little harsh."

Roy ordered two Nescafés and settled back. The conversation mainly stayed with the history of the island and Roy's affection for it. He recommended a number of places to visit and she made notes in the tourist handbook she produced.

"Does your husband not like to see the sites?"

"My husband travels a great deal with his job and therefore the last thing he likes to do is spend his precious holiday time travelling around. He's far happier with a drink in one hand, a good book in the other and a beach under him. I'll be joining him on my return to the hotel. Tell me, are the waters safe?"

They finished their coffee and Roy walked her round the harbour and reassured her that swimming was safe. They parted as she decided to visit a tourist shop. Within minutes the Vitara was on the move.

In just over the hour, Roy pulled into the garage owned by his friend. A mechanic pointed to a small office as Roy asked for Tongus. He beamed when he saw Roy.

"I have your car my friend, although why you want to bake in a black car I don't know." He took Roy to the parking compound and a large Alsatian dog barked, the hair on its neck raised as it strained at a leash. There was his black Vitara. He tossed Roy the keys. "Look after it, it's the newest I have."

Roy moved to stroke the dog.

"I wouldn't do that, my friend, unless you want another bad hand. He only likes me. He can be very mean."

He moved away from the flashing jaws realising the error of his way. He climbed into his new car, and waved before driving the Vitara out of the compound. The dog growled and barked in a desperate attempt to stretch the leash but without success. It continued to bark as the blue Vitara was brought in. It was parked close to the dog and Tongus patted the animal as it jumped and licked his hand.

"You should like my friend Roy, you stupid dog." He brought a biscuit from his overall pocket and gave it to the dog, who was now playful and quiet. Roy drove back to the flat.

Pippa drove around the area of the strong signal but failed to locate the car. In the end she gave up and travelled to the hotel, they could try later. Bob was not in the room. She moved to the balcony and looked down. He was there, prostrate on a lounger enjoying the late sun. She would join him.

Anyone looking at Bob would have thought he was listening to a personal stereo, the small box by his waist and the lead to his ear certainly gave that impression, yet he was not. He was listening to Roy move about the flat and from that he knew that Pippa would not be long in arriving.

"It's certainly a good life for some." She kicked a little sand at him. "Can you believe I lost him?"

"He's been in the flat for a good half an hour or else he's being burgled as we speak."

"We must check his car tomorrow, he may have thrown the tracker. I could only pinpoint him to an area of town, after that there was no signal."

***

The meeting planned by Sheila Dewar was eagerly awaited, there was a tension in the room as each figure listened intently to the progress made over the previous two days.

"The money is ready and permission for the UN movement to the mountain area has not been the problem we anticipated. I've met with the Home Secretary, the Defence Secretary and the Chief of Defence Staff, who is with us today. We have at present a member of the SAS in the field, who is closely surveilling the drop area. His role is purely a monitoring one, to ensure that it is the suspect who is seen to take the money. Reports to date suggest he has already made a positive ID at the scene. We've two other operatives actively tracking Hanna, they've bugged his apartment and placed a tracking device to his vehicle. One has actually made personal contact, accidentally, I hasten to add, but we feel this could work to our advantage. The third operative at present is dormant; his true role will only be divulged should a problem arise with the return of the bomb details. We are now totally committed to believing that Roy Hanna is our man and although any further information on the bombings is being channelled through the PNC, we feel our attention should remain with this suspect until the 14th. Gentlemen, any questions?"

"Do we have the co-operation of the Turkish Government to monitor the ferries and flights into Turkey should our man make a quick dash?"

"The routes, of which there are few, have been secured and you need have little worry on that score."

The meeting ended and the group dispersed.

***

Toes, wrapped in his sleeping bag and camouflaged webbing, was totally happy with his lot. He was watching the castle and the road to it through the night sights, noting any activity. The Turkish Army post down in the valley was the only thing that showed life apart from the movement of animals, night birds and the shining of lights six miles away in Girne. On the faint wind he could hear the occasional strains of music drift through the mountains. No one came to the castle. It was after two when he slept, waking as the sun broke the cover of his resting place. Nicosia, behind on the plain below, would wait longer for its dawn.

***

Roy slept until late. On the penultimate day he only had one task and that was to check his equipment and relax. As for Pippa, she was annoyed that the marker had not moved again. She jumped in the car and drove to the apartment. The Vitara was there but the colour change angered her.

"Shit! He's changed the car."

The news was not well received.

"We really need to find the tracker or you are just going to have to sit and watch and believe me, doing that here is far too risky; wait just a few minutes outside the flat and the world and his wife will see you. Where was the last place you had a trace?" snapped Bob.

They drove to the location and left the car. Pippa walked down one side of the road and Bob the other. It was Bob who spotted it and that was by sheer luck. A barking dog behind a garage caused him to look and there in the compound was the missing Vitara.

"If you think I'm climbing into the lion's den you can think again, Pip. No."

Pippa shook her head before strolling to the garage. "Hello, do you hire cars? I'd like to hire a Vitara 4x4. Do you have one?"

Tongus was more than thrilled to hire, he had not hoped to rent many more now the summer was almost at an end. "I've a yellow and green one but they're not cheap."

"Would you have a blue one?"

"As a matter of fact, I have."

They negotiated and Tongus drove the Vitara from the compound, accompanied by the dog's enthusiastic barking. Instantly the receiver sensed a move and signalled.

"You clever girl," Bob muttered to himself.

The Vitara passed him and returned to the hotel.

"All you have to do is put the bloody thing back onto Hanna's car, and the sooner, I should add, the better." Pippa's anger showed. She was annoyed at herself as much as anyone.

"He's still not up, there's no radio playing or movement from the flat."

Bob took the hint and went and placed the transmitter, using the same routine.

Chapter Twenty-Five

Jim had been awake at dawn, had swum, run and was enjoying breakfast. In twenty minutes he would walk down the track to the main road. He had an appointment with a convoy; they were expecting him. At the appointed time he was sitting on the roadside and almost to the minute, the daily UN convoy of three vehicles approached. He stood up, waved a greeting and the lead vehicle slowed, before pulling to the edge.

"Good morning. I believe you have a package for me from home?"

The officer in the passenger seat handed a long, rectangular metal box through the open door.

"Good luck," was all he said before closing the door and signalling to the driver to move on.

Jim watched them leave and then walked back to his hotel. Once in his room he put the case on the bed and opened it. It contained a Parker-Hale M-85 7.62 sniper rifle. It was his personal weapon. The case also contained telescopic and passive night-vision sights as well as an LEI-100 Laser sight. He removed the contents from the case and checked them meticulously before building the weapon. Everything he had asked for was there, including the five, ten shot magazines. It was an accurate, high precision weapon designed to give first shot accuracy up to six hundred metres but it could, in the right hands, be accurate to nearly a kilometre; it was in more than capable hands. Jim would need time to zero the sights; he would do that at a later date. With luck he would not have to use it, but if he had to, his accuracy had been tested and proven on many occasions. He stripped the rifle, cleaned it and stored it before walking to the beach.

***

In the hotel room the black receiver blinked and bleeped to signal Roy was on the move and Pippa and Bob both approached the screen. It was 11.30. It was Bob's turn to follow and he quickly grabbed his things and headed for the car. The route was clear and it soon became apparent that Roy was heading up the coast before turning down towards the beach. He parked the Vitara under the trees to give him shade and then retrieved his bag. The wooden jetty stretched out into the calm sea and Roy settled nearby.

Five minutes later, Bob pulled in to the parking area and noted the car sheltering under the trees. He parked the Seat some distance away before taking the same path to the beach. Tourists were not plentiful and he would certainly attract attention. There was only one person on this section of sand – it had to be his man. He looked carefully and made sure before progressing. Without obviously taking notice of him he walked to the end of the jetty and sat looking out over the water. The sun warmed him. He waited a few minutes before turning and walking back; he deliberately looked away from Roy so that eye contact would not be made. By the way Roy had settled himself he assumed he would be there for quite some while.

His assumption was correct; his quarry remained there until 4pm. The shadows had lengthened gradually and Roy found himself in the shade. The colour of the sea had grown a darker green. It was time to leave. He collected his things and returned to the flat. That night he would drink with his friends; it might be the last opportunity to do so that he would have for some time.

***

Jim Bentley walked briskly down the sand hills facing his room and placed a white square card against one of the taller hills, anchoring it with two sticks; it was about two hundred metres away. He looked back, adjusting his eye line with the window and the target; satisfied he returned to his room. The beach had emptied of sunbathers as the late afternoon sun was now low. It was time to zero the sights on his rifle. Normally he would fire five rounds at the target and then check the group, making adjustments on the sight; this time was no exception. The suppressed shots were silent and there was no flash from the gun. The only signs were the small eruptions of powdery sand that ejected skywards with the force of each shot. He checked the grouping carefully, readjusted the sight and fired one more shot. He checked this against the group. It was set. Removing the telescopic sight he replaced it with the laser sight. The LEI-100 laser sight was one of the most powerful red dot lasers. It could clearly spot a target six hundred metres away, showing clearly the point of impact. The dovetail mounting enabled this to be done swiftly and quietly. The red dot was visible on the target and one round burst fractionally below and to the left of the red dot. A slight adjustment punctured it perfectly. He then unloaded and reloaded each magazine checking the springs; old habits die hard but they brought results. Superstition also played a part although he would deny it; only then was he happy.

***

Even after a heavy night of drinking Roy failed to sleep. The thought of the next day brought a feeling of restlessness he had never experienced; doubt, excitement, fear, were all mixed and churned together. He moved to the balcony and appreciated the peace and the beauty of the stars. What would tomorrow bring, just what would it bring?

He stirred himself from a sleep that he had been denied for so long and felt ill; his head spun and the nausea tormented his stomach. He drank some fresh orange with paracetamol but felt no better. Coffee was needed. Of all the days to feel like this! His mind was blank, he knew the symptoms and alcohol might have some part to play but by no means was it totally responsible for his emotions and mood.

The phone rang but he ignored it and returned to bed. He had to be right, he had to feel better.

"Bob, our man's moving but there's little action. He's failed to answer the phone and now all is quiet. Some night he had." Pippa walked through the bedroom, coffee in one hand and a bread roll in the other. From her ear dangled the wire; she was tuned in to Roy's every move.

***

Toes moved from his resting place and walked into the pine trees. He rubbed his legs to increase the circulation before stretching and yawning. It had been a long night. He moved further from his spot and dug a toilet. He felt better and returned to see what delights there might be in the bag for breakfast. He put a brew on before peeking over the edge. There was no activity, not even from the Turkish troops.

By 12.30 Roy began to feel human but he was more tense than he could ever remember being. He would have given anything to speak to Joan but she would be teaching. He opened his wallet and looked at her picture; it threw his mind into complete turmoil. Any clarity of thought became a complete maelstrom. Images of happy times blended with the horrors of the Gulf, Joan's smile contrasted with the anguish he had wrought. His mood changed. He slumped into a seat questioning himself. He had to carry on. He focused all his thoughts on the photograph, convincing himself that he had done it for the best; even though he might never see her again, he had done it for what he believed in, what he was convinced was justified. The thoughts cleared like fog in the sun and that seemed to give him a boost. He flicked on the stereo and loaded a CD. Bob Seger bellowed, causing Pippa to flinch, as the earpiece filled.

He had left all his kit ready; the packed black clothing, gloves and balaclava might seem over the top but he could not predict whom or what would be waiting for him. In his bag was a change of clothes, a passport and the night sights. He checked his wallet and then dressed.

He left the flat, mentally checking that he had everything that he needed. He loaded the bag into the boot and drove away.

"He's moving!" called Pippa.

They collected their things and found the blue Vitara. Bob climbed into the driver's seat and swung the car in front of the hotel entrance. Pippa was not far behind and hopped in.

"He's on the Nicosia Road, there's no need to go too quickly." Traffic was never bad. They were soon out of the centre and travelling along the plain. It was 14.35. Some five kilometres ahead was Roy, cautious but totally unaware of the vigilance.

Turning off the main road, Roy swung left following the signs for the capital, Lefkosa, a divided city for the past twenty-five years. He pulled up in Ataturk Square and nudged the car into a small space. The centre of the square was dominated by a large Venetian column surrounded by a small garden. He crossed the road, entered the travel agent's and purchased a single ticket on the late ferry to Tasucu under the name of Eric Miles. He left the office and moved towards the market where he bought bottled water, dried fruit and chocolate.

Bob and Pippa had found the car but were unable to find a parking space. Bob had jumped from the car and waited by the bank on the corner, a position that allowed him a view of the square. He could not fail to notice the large bust of Ataturk mounted high on the opposite building, dominating the area. A shoe cleaner set up stall next to him, the highly polished brass of his box catching the sun. Bob turned and raised his shoe onto the box. He waited.

Roy walked casually into the square and opened the car boot. He noticed the tourist with the shoeshine boy, it made him take another look. Tourists seldom used them, there was a fear of being overcharged or mugged whilst standing with their back to the passing people. He took a careful look at the man's face and Bob turned instinctively, knowing full well that Roy was looking directly at him.

Roy eased the car out into the square and returned along the road on which he had entered. He travelled only slowly and pulled in watching the tourist who had, on his departure, paid and run across the square to a waiting jeep. Roy moved off again. His senses prickled and he was concerned. He immediately pulled sharp right and sharp left into a cul-de-sac and stopped the car. Roy climbed out and slipped down one of the narrow passageways. He could now watch the road. In less than a minute the blue jeep turned in.

"Oh shit! Is this a fucking set up? Let's just get the hell out of here and wait!" screamed Pippa. "We shouldn't be this close anyway."

"Pull up and stay calm, he's not onto us. Trust me."

Roy had witnessed the farce from the moment they turned the corner. Although he did not get a clear look at the driver, Bob's face confirmed his suspicions and the obvious strong exchange brought a satisfying smile to his lips. What would they do now? He had time to make them wait but it was really his chance for them to orchestrate the next move.

The passenger door opened and he saw Bob slip out and walk across the road towards his Vitara before disappearing down one of the side roads. Pippa reversed her car towards the traffic and drove away. Roy knew these lanes well and checked on Bob's progress. He was obviously on the search.

Swiftly returning to the car Roy removed his bags before leaving the area in the opposite direction from Bob. He stayed clear of the main street where he believed the blue Vitara would be waiting and then hailed a cab.

"Girne," was all he said initially, before throwing his bags into the back of the yellow Mercedes. He jumped into the front. The taxi pulled away into the traffic and before long was heading away from the centre. Ahead Roy noticed the Turkish flag painted large on the mountainside. He would, in one hour, be over on the other side.

Pippa watched her GPS e-mailer for a communication from Bob. Nothing came and in the end she pulled back into the cul-de-sac and waited.

Roy was approaching Girne. The taxi pulled into a garage and Roy paid and removed his bags. The garage had a number of cars for hire and he only hoped they would have a 4x4 and a dark one at that.

Pippa was growing frustrated with the wait, something was wrong. She typed in the short message and pressed 'send'. Ten minutes later she received the answer, Bob was returning. Walking towards the black Vitara, Bob again looked inside before shaking his head and crashing his fist onto the roof. The space that had contained two bags when he had first looked was now empty. He ran to the jeep.

"He's away. He had bags in the back when I first looked but now it's empty. I take it he was watching us all the time and just waiting for you to leave."

"There's still time to approach the castle road. He's got an appointment, remember?"

Roy had succeeded in hiring a rather old Suzuki, in red. It had to be inconspicuous and this was the best they had. It had not been washed for weeks and the colour had darkened significantly. He signed the forms and left a deposit. He had secured its dubious services for three days. He pulled away and headed back out of Girne onto the forestry roads that he had previously reconnoitred. He found himself whistling for the first time in days. He must be on top of the game.

Chapter Twenty-Six

The single Land Rover had broken away from the convoy as it left the Turkish barrier. The money had been loaded into the Bergen in the Ledre Palace Hotel, once a beautiful Nicosia hotel, now the headquarters of the UN. Its walls and general façade were pock marked by the fighting of '74. Dressed in UN clothing were Colin and Stan. Colin was the passenger. He was wearing very dark goggles that shielded his eyes from daylight. They knew the route. Toes had been aware of their role and had, to date, reported his sightings. In the back sat the standard SAS Bergen rucksack holding the two million pounds. They drove carefully, aware of the time; they did not want to be early. It was 17.10. The sky was turning the colours of evening, the first stars were beginning to appear as they started the climb into the mountains. The overhanging trees brought an early darkness, they would have light for another ten minutes, if they were lucky, and no more.

The mountaintop was eerie as the white Land Rover's lights blazed the narrow road. Toes could see the treetops illuminated as it swung round corners before blackness returned and then another area of trees came into view. Within minutes its lights were clearly visible running past the jousting area then twisting towards the castle car park. From his vantage point it looked like a child's toy. The car park and the castle were totally deserted. Toes knew he would not be the only person watching the Land Rover's progress. Somewhere out there would be Roy Hanna, if only he knew where.

Stan let the engine tick over whilst they organised themselves out. Once ready they switched off the lights. Colin removed the goggles and was rewarded with immediate night vision. His partner would struggle to achieve the same depth of vision in the time they were out. Colin lifted the Bergen onto his back and started the uphill walk to the drop point. Toes, from his vantage point and with the aid of the Eagle long-range night vision device, could see quite clearly in the green, hazy field of view. So accurate was the device that he could tell who was carrying the Bergen. He constantly swept the castle, eager for any sign of Hanna but so far there was none. His partners kept disappearing into the ruins as they threaded their way along the inclined path to the spot marked by the 'X' on the map; it had to be exact.

Roy deliberately stayed low, away from the ridge. He had seen the headlights search the now-dark sky on more than one occasion as the UN vehicle threaded its way along the twisty roads and made its climb to the castle. He pictured the two soldiers moving through the ruins. He was happy to wait until the lights signalled their departure and then he would delay again. He was in charge, no matter who or what was out there, he would control the moves.

**

Bob and Pippa could not compromise the operation that was now taking place around the castle. Although they were not party to the details, they knew they had no business near the castle so close to the drop time. They had returned to the hotel, crest-fallen. Their role now would be to monitor the apartment for his return. Reluctantly, Bob called England and reported the situation. The displeasure was clearly indicated in the conversation. Bob said little after the initial report only listened, raising his eyebrows at Pippa occasionally. They both had a strong drink before organising the listening watch for the night.

**

Colin looked at Stan and nodded. This was the place; even in the dark they recognised it as the drop point from their earlier sortie. The Bergen was placed in the middle of the flat area.

"It's a lot to leave to the dark and the elements." Stan patted it before they both retreated into the ruins and began to follow the descending path.

On reaching the Land Rover they both instinctively looked across to where they knew Toes would be watching before climbing into the white vehicle and moving off down the twisting road. The whole valley seemed to light up and for a moment, the huge increase in light through the night sight dazzled Toes. Roy too noticed the lights filter white into the sky as the noise of the diesel rattled the still evening away in the distance. Roy waited, confident that no one would be in the castle in the dark.

He moved back to the jeep that was nestling in the pinewoods; his eyes were accustomed to the darkness and he moved quietly. From the bag he removed his black clothing and dressed quickly. The balaclava and gloves were the last items he retrieved. Over the top of the balaclava he placed a face mask onto which he clipped the night vision goggles. They were lightweight and comfortable. He flicked them on and the whole area brightened into a green, clear world.

The walk up the northern side of the castle was quite steep but the path that Roy had planned was known to him and he moved with confidence. As it grew steeper he needed to use his hands more, even the injured hand was an advantage to none at all. His breathing deepened and he began to sweat. He had climbed this same route three or four times over the previous few days, often in the full heat of the day, and had not felt like he did now. He checked upwards and the crest was close.

Breaking over the ridge, he was immediately faced by the crumbling castle wall. There was no need to scale it, he simply moved through one of the many holes. He took a breather.

Toes continued to scan. He moved further away from the castle searching outcrops of rocks, trees and bushes for the smallest movement, hoping for a glimpse of his man, but so far nothing. "Come on, you greedy bastard, show yourself!"

he muttered to himself over and over again. A slight movement wavered and stopped in his peripheral vision; it was he. He could not be sure at first but when he swung round and focused all his attention on the figure, he knew it was his man. "If I had my weapon now, you'd be a gonna, pal," Toes thought as he continued to watch the figure creeping along the edge of the wall. It only took him three minutes from first sighting to Hanna getting to the Bergen; he moved well for a man in the dark.

Roy touched the bag cautiously. He covered his mouth with a black rag just in case they'd booby-trapped it. He expected to be sprayed with a gas on moving the bag. They had not. Lifting the money onto his back he hauled the weight upwards following the same path and disappeared over the ridge. Toes removed the sights from his eyes and stared into the darkness. He filed his radio report and within the blinking of an eye the message was sent, "Money has been collected. Your man is on the move." The listening station not twenty miles away collected and de-coded it before sending another encrypted message to GCHQ in England.

Roy struggled more than he thought he would. The bag was difficult to carry over the rough, loose terrain and he rested many times. On reaching the car he dumped the Bergen onto the ground and removed his gloves; the night vision goggles remained on. From the bag in the boot of the car he produced a small, electronic, anti-bug device. He switched it on and immediately it flashed. Roy now knew that hidden in the bag was a transmitter. It had been placed so that his moves could be followed. It either sent a satellite signal or someone was rather too close for comfort, ready to monitor his moves. It would not be in the bag for long. He carefully tried to root it out, only to find it stitched into the fabric. He sliced it out and left it in the back of the car; it would be disposed of later.

He lifted the Bergen and moved into the forest, bound for the ruins of the shepherd's hut. The door hung from its lone hinge but the corrugated, rusty roof brought some protection. It was obvious from the plants growing round the door that it had long been abandoned. The door moved after he lifted and pushed, twisting it inwards. Roy stepped inside lifting the bag after him. The place was dry and that was his main concern. He stashed the bag high onto one of the thick wooden rafters, ensuring that it was covered with old hay and straw that he gathered. There would not be much light in the building at any time of day and he felt that it was in a secure place for the three days that he would need. Before he left he rechecked the position of the bag.

The jeep started first time but he left the lights off, relying on the goggles until he was away from the forestry road, only then would he select the full headlights and stow the goggles on the passenger seat.

Toes continued to monitor the area but he neither saw nor heard Hanna again and he settled in for his last night in his eyrie.

Roy drove down from the mountain, pulling in to the side of the road after a few minutes. He climbed out and placed the transmitter he had taken from the bag in the hedge and quickly returned to the car. Girne looked quite beautiful, its streetlights twinkling, the sea, a dark mass, stood out in the darkness, the sky awash with millions of stars. He drove to the old part of town and stopped. He changed in the car before finding a place to eat. His persona was now that of a tourist, leaving Northern Cyprus for Turkey. Two ferries ran from the new port. The catamaran halved the journey time between Girne and Tasucu but he had time to spare. His ferry would be the larger, slower one. It would take, weather permitting, the full six hours. It departed at midnight. Roy looked at his watch, it was 10.30. He parked his car and checked the booking, showing his ticket. He was in a long line of young soldiers who were travelling home on leave. There was little noise apart from the rattle of backgammon boards and voices.

By 11.10 the queues had begun to form at the gates and were soon boarding. Roy followed a group of soldiers. Their uniforms were untidy and ill-fitting and they cared little, a far cry from his time in the army. Once on board he settled on a reclining couch, lay back and drifted off to sleep.

The sea was calm and the ferry arrived ahead of schedule. Roy could not remember the last time he had slept so soundly. He had not stirred since leaving Girne. He found the gate and walked down the steps onto the harbour side and continued to follow the crocodile of soldiers into the customs building. There was a brief look at his passport and little else.

Tasucu had developed with the tourist trade and a number of cafes and bars filled the area. He pulled up a chair outside the first he came to and ordered a coffee. The sky was a deepening blue and the roads were alive with traffic. He watched the movements of the people coming from the ferry terminal, some heavily laden, others travelling with fewer possessions than himself. He felt free. He would telephone Joan; that would be his first task. His second was to fax the list of bomb sites and times. That could wait a little longer.

***

The news had reached Robin Carey, The Director General of the Security Services, that the money had been taken but the transmitter, it seemed, had been discovered. As the signal was static, it had probably been dumped. However, the two operatives were still monitoring Hanna's flat and an SAS officer was still in the field.

"I want that transmitter finding. It may give us a clue as to where he's been. The bag in fact may have just been stored."

The telephone rang next to Pippa. She answered and immediately swung her legs out of bed. She had not been asleep; it had been her turn to monitor the flat in case Hanna returned. He hadn't. She would do as instructed immediately. She wrote down the co-ordinates given over the phone and hung up. Bob was awake and read the piece of paper before looking up. Pippa switched on the bathroom light and removed her shirt. Bob continued to stare until she moved into the shower.

***

The phone beside Joan's bed rang a number of times blending with the dream she was having. Only its persistent ring woke her.

"Roy? Where are you? How are you? I've been trying to contact you the last couple of days but you haven't been answering your phone. Is everything all right?" Joan's anxiety flooded out and she burst into tears.

"I'm fine, really." There was a long pause. "When are you coming out here?"

Joan calmed herself and told him about the flight details and times. She would be arriving on the Saturday night. "I'm missing you so much, Roy. I just get so worried when I don't hear from you. You promised to call me every day."

He told her he would ring her in the evening when they could talk more. "I'm out of the flat for a few days, doing some travelling but I'll get in touch so stop worrying. I'm fine."

She cradled the phone after Roy had hung up and looked at the clock. Its red numbers glowed. It was 5.15. The wind blew and the blinds rattled, knocking the bowl on the ledge. She burst into tears. Knowing that there was something wrong, that she was losing him.

The tape machine recorded not only the conversation but also her anguish.

***

Roy had hand written a note giving all the relevant information about the next ten bombs, the ones that were due to explode within the month. He faxed it to the Editor of the 'Daily Telegraph' in London who immediately forwarded the details to the police.

At 9.15 a copy of the fax was distributed to the few people sitting around the conference table.

"The message came through yesterday that the money had been removed, almost without doubt by Hanna, and nobody has seen sight nor sound of him since. His girlfriend received a telephone call early this morning from Tasucu, a ferry port on the south eastern coast of Turkey. I've made enquiries and Roy Hanna didn't pass through so all we can assume is that he's using an alias." Robin Carey, Director General of the security services looked across at the Commissioner and then at Alexander Smythe. "You're aware of the consequences of the note? Our man has taken the money and has run without fulfilling his part of the agreement. From the look of this we have details for fewer than half of the bombs supposedly planted."

Smythe spoke without taking his eyes from the facsimile. "We've a third person on the island and I'm sure you are all familiar with his background. He is fully equipped and ready should you feel you need him. The movement into Turkey shouldn't pose problems as we've a number of NATO airfields for a drop of equipment. This would, of course, have to be the final answer to our problems."

"But that could be the start of our problems. If Hanna was telling the truth, and right now, it would take a brave person to argue to the contrary, there are a large number of bombs waiting and we've neither the locations nor the times to be able to make them safe. I think it's time Joan was brought into this equation and furnished with a few facts. She will, according to the telephone conversation, be going over there in a few days which probably means he's going to return or ..." Sheila Dewar broke off. She did not need to complete her thoughts.

After further discussion the meeting ended and it was agreed to speak to Joan Johnson. Their investigations had confirmed that she was likely to be the innocent party, unaware of the crimes Roy had committed.

***

Roy was on a rather uncomfortable bus travelling from Tasucu to Mersin. His view from the window seat was breathtaking as the road hugged the side of the coast. This part of the Turkish mainland had suffered little from the ravages of tourism and vast stretches of unspoiled Mediterranean beaches met the crystal, turquoise sea. The curtains at the windows blew as the bus bumped its way eastwards. In a couple of hours, he would be in Mersin.

Chapter Twenty-Seven

Joan was called from her classroom and walked towards the Head's room. He had told her she had two visitors who needed to speak with her urgently. He would take her class. The door to the office was open and two people were sitting on the chairs that faced the desk. As she entered the room, both stood.

"Please sit down, Miss Johnson." He pointed to the Head's chair. "My name is Stephen Walsh and this is Pat Peters." They both showed her their ID.

"Are you police?"

"In a way, yes we are, but our role is more in line with the security services. We deal with terrorism, Miss Johnson." He looked at her and he could clearly perceive her total and utter surprise.

"Is this a wind up? I have a class to teach." She stood up as if to go, she would no longer be part of this game.

"Sit down, Joan," instructed Pat as she rested her hand on her shoulder. "We want you to talk about Roy Hanna. I can assure you it's not a wind up and we are certainly not joking."

Joan sat down and stared incredulously at the two people opposite her. Her mind raced as the word terrorist filled every cavity.

"We have cleared it with your Head for you to accompany us to the police station. A police officer will take your car home if you leave the keys with the school secretary. May I remind you that you are part of an investigation of great importance and we believe you may hold the key we need. You're welcome to bring a solicitor, if you wish. You're not under arrest or suspicion, but that is your right."

Joan could hardly believe what she was hearing but stood up and was led out. Pat dropped her car keys at the office and explained the situation.

***

The co-ordinates were showing on Pippa's GPS but she could not find anything. She continued to walk along the roadside, kicking at the odd crushed drinks can and lifting litter but she found nothing. Her military GPS was accurate to metres but in the search out there on the hillside she felt the manufacturer's claims were rather optimistic. She moved backwards and forwards sweeping the area visually, she certainly did not want to put her hands into the holes in the ground or under stones if she could help it. On the second sweep of the area she noticed it, the small grey stick that looked more like a stubby pencil than an extremely expensive transmitter. She had found it. She drove into Girne, located the cafe where she had met Roy Hanna and ordered an orange juice. The tree offered her shade. After drinking she phoned Bob and he relayed the news Home. They were now sure that Roy had the Bergen without the transmitter.

***

The room in the police HQ in which Joan was seated was comfortable. She had a coffee brought and the two officers remained with her and chatted. Although she was still naturally tense, she felt herself relax a little.

"What's all this about?"

"Joan, we have reason to believe that Roy Hanna is responsible for the bombs placed on the motorway bridges, in fact we now have little doubt. We have no reason to believe you are implicated other than by the fact that you live with him."

Joan could not believe what she was hearing or maybe she just did not want to let the cold facts percolate the fears that she had held. She had observed the change in Roy at the outset of the bombings, of his callousness and fascination with the media reports.

"We would like you to show us your house and let some of our experts check for any traces of explosives and we'd like you to be present."

Joan had no objection; in fact, she longed to get home, away from this.

The truth facing her clarified many of the doubts that she had felt, doors suddenly opened in her mind and answers tumbled freely. It was possible that what they were saying was true. Her intuition told her it was and her fear turned to anger.

Her car was already parked when the police vehicle pulled up outside their home. She fumbled with the keys and they followed her.

"Please sit through there. Could I get anyone a drink?"

"Forensics and representatives from other departments are on their way. Please relax if you can." Pat went through to the kitchen with her and helped.

Before long three vehicles were parked outside the house and a hoard of people swarmed through the property systematically. It was the cellar that attracted the most attention and it soon became evident that explosives had been stored and assembled there, but the results would have to be confirmed in the lab.

One of the officers in the cellar was Sam Phelps. He had checked to see if there were any remnants of a bomb factory but he found few. He climbed the steps and approached Joan. He shook her by the hand and introduced himself.

"I'm sorry to put you through all of this Miss Johnson. Are you all right?" His manner was of genuine concern and she warmed to him immediately, she felt as though she could trust him. "Do you know if Roy had a machine like this?" He held up the palmtop and she immediately recognised it.

"He has used one of these all the time I've known him. There should be one in the study upstairs."

They both moved to the study and there on the desk was the computer. Sam picked it up and opened the lid. He pressed 'ON' and the screen responded with the words, 'Password Protected.'

"The password's V," said Joan.

Sam pressed the letter and the 'agenda' file flashed on screen. There was little information within any section.

"Is this the only one he has?" Sam placed the computer back onto the desk.

"I really am not sure. There's always one here so I guess he must have one with him."

The investigation lasted most of the day. Forensic had confirmed their earlier suspicion that plastic explosives had been handled in the cellar. The search brought little further information.

Even when Roy's travel logs provided by Drew were analysed, they found little evidence to trace the remaining bombs. His journeys did not include the south and yet bombs had been placed on the M25.

***

The bus pulled up on the dual carriageway that ran the length of the promenade at Mersin. The palm trees certainly gave the resort a Mediterranean feel. The large shops, restaurants and hotels faced the sea. Roy made his way to the docks and located the ferry building. He booked a ticket for the return to Famagusta the following evening and then booked a room in a hotel facing the sea.

The room was bright with double windows and a balcony overlooking the main street and the public gardens. The wind blew the curtains as he moved away to shower and change before heading out to the shops. The market was busy and noisy and the air was filled with an overpowering stench. Roy looked into the back of one of the open backed trucks to be greeted by a hundred staring eyes; it was full of sheep's heads, no bodies, just heads. Flies settled on the nostrils, gaping mouths and lolling tongues. Even he was repulsed and he thought of the men who had stared in the same way after the missile attack. His whole crew, one minute laughing and alert and the next, after the dust had settled, nothing. The memory was as fresh as the blood in the wagon.

The rest of the day passed slowly and lazily as he sat in the garden area in front of the sea enjoying the view. It was a far cry from Bradford. His time there was now a lifetime away. He would eat and go to bed early after telephoning Joan.

***

After returning to the Police Station, Joan was questioned for the rest of the day and her co-operation was surprising considering the shock she had faced six hours previously. They failed, however, to take into consideration the anger that had been released within. She could never have believed that Roy could have stooped so low. She remembered the photo images of the train and the funerals for those killed; children with flowers for lost parents. No cause, no amount of anger, no vendetta was worth that. The two million pounds stunned her, Roy was never truly materialistic and that seemed to be a wrong piece in the complex jigsaw. Everything else could be seen to fit but blackmail was just not credible.

"You said Roy will be telephoning you this evening?" enquired Pat Peters. "We'd like you to carry on as before. You're aware there's the possibility he is holding back on information about other bombs. Earlier he mentioned fifty-seven and we have information on fewer than half."

"I don't think I can even speak to him, let alone appear normal. What you ask is impossible."

"You have to. Your planned visit at the weekend may give us the information we need. It may also help Roy get this resolved before anyone else is killed. As I'm sure you're aware, the Governments of Northern Cyprus and Britain have no extradition treaty and he can stay there with his two million safely in the banks and let the world go to hell. For some people that might mean literally." Pat paused and looked Joan in the eye. "You're our only real chance to obtain the rest of the information. You have to think about this whole situation. We'll be there to support you in any way we can but you have to help."

"A man called at the house, he was in charge of the bombs, Sam I think his name was. Would it be possible to talk to him before I make any decisions?"

Pat nodded at Stephen Walsh and he left the room. Minutes later, he returned. "Sam will meet you at your house as soon as possible. He can't give a time but he will be there."

"I'll do all I can tonight if Roy rings before I speak with Sam."

A car took Joan home and she sank into a chair and wept. She clutched a card on which Pat had written her phone number in her hand. She would help day or night. She stood up and went to the phone looking through the personal directory until she found the telephone number for Bill O'Brien.

"May I speak with Dr O'Brien, please? Tell him it's Roy's girlfriend, Joan, and it's urgent." Music drifted down the line.

"Joan, how are you?" Bill's voice was slightly high-pitched conveying either anxiety or concern, she could not discern which.

"Bill, what do you know about Roy?" She paused before taking a breath to say the word she hated. "Could Roy ever be a terrorist, a cold, calculating killer?"

"Roy is not only very confused but he's also ill, physically as well as mentally. As you're aware he experienced some dreadful things in the Gulf, and may well have been exposed to chemicals that could, given the way they were administered, act in different ways with various people. It seems too much of a coincidence that so many troops suffered strange and unexplained illnesses after the war. Roy suffered terribly, as you know, and was extremely frustrated and angry by the lack of support. To answer your question, Joan, yes, I believe he could but I really don't think it was to vent his own feelings, I feel it would be for reasons other than that. I didn't know Roy all that well after the two sessions, he was only beginning to relax in my company. More importantly, what do you feel?" There was silence on the other end of the line. "Joan are you there?"

"Yes, yes. I just don't know anything any more."

"Would you like me to come round?"

"No thanks, I'll be all right. I knew there was something wrong, but I never guessed it was this." She laughed more to release emotion and then started to weep. "I thought he'd found another woman ..." She recovered her composure, thanked Bill and hung up.

Bill stood looking at the wall where the picture had hung, the one that Roy had so admired, and questioned his own position. Could he have done anything? Should he have spotted the signs on Roy's first visit and done more? He would never know. He put the phone down and cleared away. His night would also be full of consternation.

Joan paced the room, and then settled onto the settee and curled up. She had left the phone in the other room; she would need time to answer its ring.

Chapter Twenty-Eight

The streetlights cast a yellow film over the main street in Mersin. The traffic moved freely along the road that headed from the port. Roy ambled along the side of the shops staring in at the windows. Families walked, stopping occasionally to look at the displays. The place had warmth, a friendliness that appealed to Roy. He opened the door to a coffee shop. Huge glass counters displayed pastries and chocolates, sweets and cakes. He ordered a coffee and a cake from one of the trays before settling into the seat near the window. The tinted glass gave the outside world a strange appearance. He drank his coffee and nibbled at the cake, its sweetness defeating him, before going to the phone in the corner of the shop. He dialled Joan's number.

The ringing phone brought with it an oozing fear that choked, convincing her she was going to vomit; the phone continued to ring. She moved through to it taking deep breaths and considered quickly the lines she was going to deliver.

"Joan, it's Roy. How are you?"

Joan managed to get through the call. She led Roy onto their holiday and convinced herself that she could not wait until the weekend when they would be together. Everything went well until Roy closed with, "I love you, Joan." She just put the phone down and wept uncontrollably. Roy put it down to the fact that she was missing him. He had no idea of the hatred she harboured, no idea that she knew that he was on the run. He left the cafe and walked through the streets for an hour. If her thoughts could kill, he would be in the gutter.

The security services now knew his location and searched credit card company details to try to locate his hotel or onward travel arrangements but to little effect. He had not used his credit cards since England. They would wait in the firm belief that Roy would return to Famagusta.

Joan tucked herself up on the settee again, feeling totally alone and vulnerable. She heard a car stop outside, followed by a knock on the front door, it was Sam Phelps. She moved to open the door.

"Good evening, Miss Johnson. I believe you wish to speak with me. Are you all right?"

"Fine considering the circumstances, thank you for coming. Please." She pointed to the lounge and offered Sam a seat. "Could I get you something to drink? I have some beer in the fridge or red wine if you would prefer."

She poured two glasses of wine and returned to the lounge. Sam was looking at a photograph of Joan and Hanna taken in Cyprus the previous year. He looked away when Joan returned.

"How may I help you?"

"It looks like Roy has done all of these dreadful things. Is there any way Roy never planned to hurt anyone? You see I just find it so out of character for Roy to contemplate hurting the innocent."

"Miss Johnson I can't answer for Hanna, or balance his motives against his obvious anger, but I can say that anyone who plans and plants bombs does so in the knowledge that someone could be killed or injured. I'm aware that the bomber gave warnings to some but not to all and he also planted anti-handling devices to some. I lost a key man to one such device. Joan, this bomber knew he would kill and I personally hold little sympathy for him or for what he thinks he's fighting for." Sam looked Joan in the eye. "If Hanna planted these bombs, and right now everything points that way, he needs help and we need to know the position of all the other bombs."

Joan stared long and hard at the carpet and then at the photograph of Roy on the fireplace.

"Tell your people I'll do all I can to help. Thank you for your time." She looked at Sam. His eyes were compassionate and understanding. She moved her hand into his and thanked him.

"If I can help in any way, don't hesitate to ask. I'll do all I can." He stood up and moved to the door. "One thing before I go, it's been a long day. May I take Hanna's palmtop? Maybe our computer boys could find something hidden in there that we may have missed."

Joan slipped upstairs and brought it to him. He left and she smiled and waved. It was the first time he had seen her smile. He liked it.

***

Roy moved through to the ticket booth, showed his ticket in the name of Eric Miles and embarked. He stood on the deck watching the cars and wagons load. The ferry was larger than the previous one and he had booked himself a cabin. He took some of the chocolate he had bought in Girne from his bag, it would be all that he would eat until he returned to his flat. There were fewer soldiers on this boat and although the holiday season was at an end, he was surprised at the number of Europeans he saw. He moved through to his cabin that proved small but comfortable. The crossing would take all night and they would arrive in Famagusta at around 7am. Once the ship left Mersin he walked the deck, marvelling at the brightness and sheer quantity of stars in the night sky; the starlight almost cast shadows it was so strong. The sea breeze brought a chill that he had not felt since leaving England and he soon returned to the warmth of his cabin. The slow drone of the engines vibrated along every surface but it brought comfort and he slept.

Bob had been allocated the task of monitoring all ferry arrivals, the morning ferry from Mersin was to be no exception. It appeared in the early haze far in the distance. He sat on the old walls overlooking the harbour. He could see the activities from this vantage point.

The ferry from Mersin to Famagusta swings round the pan-handle and the sight of the ancient city in the early, clear light of morning is something to behold. Roy, feeling refreshed after a good night's sleep, watched its slow approach. The pilot boat darted through the waters and guided the ship into the harbour. It took twenty minutes before the ship was secure and the cars began to stream from its open stern. Roy collected his belongings and walked towards the exit. He knew a number of the officials at the port and they waved as he came through. It was this friendliness that attracted Bob and he immediately recognised the man who had spotted him in Lefkosa. He turned, not wanting to repeat the incident.

Roy walked up through the port and stopped at a cafe near the mosque. It was good to be home. Bob had followed as closely as he dared before sitting in a small park opposite. From there he could see both exits of the cafe. Within twenty minutes Roy was on the move. He turned right and walked up to the square. A line of taxis waited, sheltering beneath the large branches of an ancient tree. Roy walked to the third in the line and smiled at the driver shaking his hand firmly. They spoke briefly before they drove out of the square. Bob could only watch. However, he presumed correctly that Roy was going to collect the Vitara.

***

The plain was warm and the cooling breeze from the open windows was refreshing. The car was where he had left it. Roy opened the boot and dumped his bags. From one he took the small anti-bug device and walked around the car. The light flashed as he past the rear bumper. He found it, it was similar to the one planted in the Bergen. Removing it, he walked down towards the local taxis and bent as if to pick something up, sticking the transmitter to the bumper. "That should keep them active." He returned to the car and drove out towards the castle.

***

The Bergen was where he had left it and, as he had hoped, the contents were intact. He walked back through the forest. No one would see him as Toes had been collected twenty-four hours previously. He loaded the bag into the Vitara and drove to Girne to sort out the other vehicle before heading back towards Gazimagusa. It had all gone as planned.

Bob and Pippa had responded to the activation of the transmitter they believed was still attached to Roy's car but they had learned a lesson. They monitored the car's progress and only when they felt it directed them away from Famagusta would they take up the chase. Initially confused by the erratic movements after monitoring the vehicle for some hours did they put two and two together.

"He found both transmitters; you'd be wise to shut down the infinity device in the flat in case he sweeps that too," suggested Bob. "We can get a visual when he comes home."

Pippa dialled the flat's number and the bugs were deactivated, even the one in the kitchen responded and slept. It would be the most strategic move they would make.

The black Vitara pulled up near the flat and Roy climbed out. He was tired and looked forward to a shower. However, he waited and watched, ensuring he had not been followed. He carried his bags into the flat as quietly as possible and checked the room for bugs, there was nothing. He paid particular attention to the telephone but it appeared clean. He stripped and showered. He would make contact with his friends in the Bank of Northern Cyprus later. He had a rather large deposit to attend to.

Chapter Twenty-Nine

Joan did not return to school; she was not expected. She prepared herself mentally for her ordeal. Pat Peters and Stephen Walsh had called early to take her to the station, they had little time to prepare Joan for what was in store. Now that she had agreed to co-operate there was a warmer atmosphere, she felt amongst friends and that helped her. They had heard the conversation between her and Sam the previous night, they had heard the turmoil that the long and lonely night had brought but they were amazed by her resolve to co-operate and if possible, help Roy come to terms with the problem and face his responsibilities.

They needed the computer that Roy carried; that, they felt, was the key. If he were never parted from it all the timings and details would be there. They explained that she would not be alone on the island; already there were two people monitoring Roy, they lied. They were there to support her and collect the computer from her if and when she managed to locate it. They had decided the best possible way would be to do a swap with the one Roy had left in the study, he might not notice until after Joan's departure if he purely used it for the one purpose.

She was given a series of telephone numbers and an identity of May, she laughed at the thought of being some kind of agent. They assured her that it would receive an immediate response whomsoever she called. They also gave her a small mobile telephone that would connect her to the army HQ in the South of the island; this should only be used in an emergency. It would never ring and so, she was assured, it could be easily concealed. They showed her how to use the phone and requested she familiarise herself with it; they even told her the opening sentence she must use.

Her head began to swim more with the covert nature of her visit rather than the information she had to remember. In twenty-four hours she would be travelling there for real and that brought her to earth with a bump. She suddenly began to feel scared and insecure.

"Remember, Joan, it's the same Roy you're going to see, the guy you've lived with for months. Remember too that he still loves you and wouldn't harm you. Remember it, Joan, and let it give you strength. What you are doing you are doing as much for him as anyone."

***

The flight was uneventful. She did not have to change planes, landing in Izmir briefly before continuing to Cyprus. There was a ruling that planes could not travel to the northern side of the island without first landing in Turkey. Formalities concluded, she continued on the final leg. It was dark when the wheels kissed the tarmac and another forty minutes before Joan met Roy. They were right: this was no monster, just a man alone, waiting in the corner of arrivals. His face said it all and his eyes sparkled when he saw her. He moved through the small crowd and held her tenderly. They kissed a long greeting and when she pulled away she could see there was a tear in his eye.

No matter now what he had done, what evil had been perpetrated, she had to help him. Standing there was the man she had loved dearly, a man confused and injured. She felt ashamed that she had damned him.

"You'll never know just how much I've missed you." He kissed her forehead. He put his finger below her chin, lifted her face and kissed her wet eyes. "Come on home, the flat's cold without you."

After a brief chat about the flight they were quiet, Roy concentrating on the unlit road. The landmarks were bringing back memories. There was no real uneasiness and Joan felt more comfortable than she could have hoped.

"I thought you'd have been bronzed from your days on the beach." Joan looked across and slipped her hand on his knee, more out of habit than a sign of affection.

"The autumn sun is not that strong, but I'm darker skinned than I was, believe me."

The flat was as she remembered and before long they were sitting drinking tea in the kitchen.

"Tired?" Roy covered her hand with his.

"It's a long flight, it's been a long half term and I'm bushed."

"To bed with you then young lady." He moved the cups and led her through to the bedroom. He brought in her case and laid it on the bed. "Shout should you need anything." He left the room. Joan sat on the bed and sighed. She had planned different strategies for coping with the awkwardness of this night, the physical contact and eagerness were a small part of the overall charade, if, in the cool late evening, it was a charade; she was so confused.

The shower was warming and the tension drained from her, the scent of soap filled her nostrils and she relaxed. Roy stood in the doorway; the cold glass of the cubical condensed the droplets until they ran in rivulets down the glass. Her hazy body was seductive in its mystery. He removed his clothes.

"Is there room for me in there? It looks so inviting."

Joan turned to see Roy naked in the bathroom. She opened the door and he stepped inside. She wrapped her hands in his hair and kissed him. This was no make-believe and his tenderness betrayed the evil that he had become. For the moment she closed her mind to the past week and indulged in the present in which she felt more in control.

The morning was bright and sunny as Roy brought in the breakfast. "Where to today?"

"Take me to your castle, again. The one with the views of Girne."

"There are other castles just as beautiful that I'd love to show you. I think you need some time on the beach.

Salamis is inviting and the water is still warm. I'll take you to the castle on Thursday."

Joan could understand his concern at travelling back to St Hilarion. She knew that he had used this for his collection point and she was determined that they should go there, that the bombings come out in the open. Until then she would try to locate the computer. "You told me I could choose today and I'd love to visit your castle, but the swimming sounds good. Maybe a day on the beach is what I need right now."

"Your wish is my command."

The deserted beach was ideal. Joan swam in the clear water and looked at the ruins of the sea wall below her. Roy watched her from the sand. She was a strong swimmer and spent almost an hour drifting up and down. The water was calm. He called to her, waved the flask of coffee and she swam towards him.

For the rest of the day they lay on the sand and enjoyed the sun, later they walked through the ruins of Salamis to the car. She kissed his hands. It had been a perfect day.

The following day Roy went out to see friends and Joan searched for the computer but it was not there. She even looked in the Vitara when she drove alone but with no success.

On the Tuesday, Roy woke early and as usual brought breakfast to bed.

"I've a surprise for you today, my girl, so you need to be in the jeep in thirty minutes."

Joan looked at him. "Where are we going?"

They drove away from Famagusta and again into the mountains but then dropped through the pine forests. Throughout the journey they talked but never about the future, only of the present and there were silences, not uncomfortable or upsetting in their length, but silences. They passed through a number of small villages until they approached Esentepe, the road broke into three and Roy followed the coast. In the next small village he pulled up outside a large house that was surrounded by a high wall. The whole estate had been renovated and the gates that Roy opened shone with new paint. He climbed back in the car.

"What's this?"

"Close your eyes until I ask you to open them, it's your surprise."

He stopped outside the front door and helped Joan out. He placed a large, cold, metal key in the door and helped her turn it. He pushed open the door.

"You may open your eyes," he whispered. "Welcome home."

Before her the marble floor in black and white squares opened into a large hall. The stairs led up to doors on the right and the left. Before entering she stepped back looking at the weathered face; a house of beauty and charm.

Roy went round opening the wooden shutters, light flooded into every crevice sullying its cosiness. Although devoid of furnishings, the plasterwork and polished wooden floors brought a feeling of warmth. Roy led her from room to room without saying a word until they reached the master bedroom. French-style windows opened onto a stone balcony above the front door. The view was endless, stretching to the coast and the sea beyond.

"They say on winter days it's possible to see the mountains of Turkey. Do you like it?"

Joan continued to look at the view and then turned to look at the room. Her face shone with pleasure at the thought of living there. Its seclusion and beauty were perfect.

"The house is the most beautiful I've seen on the island, Roy, but why are we here?"

"The house is ours. I've had my eye on it for a while and the price was good. I thought you'd fall in love with it immediately and you have, haven't you?"

Roy turned Joan to face him and it was only then that she realised that she would never live there, never spend nights in front of its large fires or entertain their friends. Soon they would have no friends, soon there would be no house. She felt like running down the stairs and out into the garden and screaming but that would not help. She had to remain in control, she had to remain normal, if only she could remember what that was.

"Show me the kitchen and the gardens, Roy." She again tried to ooze enthusiasm and she felt sure that Roy, totally in love with his house, detected nothing.

They walked round the overgrown gardens, the fruit trees and patios. It would fill their conversation for the rest of the time they were together and it was only Joan who knew that the talk was worthless.

Bob and Pippa had re-connected the transmitters in the flat, assured that they had waited long enough. They were also concerned about Joan; they were aware of her role and the potential danger she might face. They had no way of knowing where they were but were not too concerned, they would soon find all the information they required when they returned to the flat. They were relieved to see that there was still a relationship, that Joan had kept her head and had not immediately confronted him. They listened to their conversation and their lovemaking, amazed at the façade Joan appeared to maintain, but concerned that she might now not co-operate with the police; there was always the chance that love would prove too strong in the end.

Chapter Thirty

Thursday morning was clear and Roy loaded the car for the St Hilarion visit.

"Sure you wouldn't prefer the house?"

Joan just shook her head. "A promise is a promise."

The drive was as she had remembered it, breathtaking and unspoiled. The view of the castle perched so high made her gasp.

"Stop here please."

Roy pulled into the side of the narrow road and Joan stood up leaning on the windscreen as she had done in the summer, marvelling at the magnitude of the ruin.

"Drive on!" she called, still standing up.

Roy drove carefully up the winding road until he pulled up in the empty car park. They walked slowly through the ruins, Roy explaining to her again the history of the castle. She held his hand. The sun was warm and she wrapped her sweater around her waist. They reached the highest part and sat, appreciating the view.

"Why have you destroyed all that we have, Roy?"

Roy's face did not register what she had asked. "Destroyed what?"

"Why have you destroyed us, what we had, our love, our hopes and dreams? Why?" She was amazingly controlled, as if she were chastising a four-year-old for betraying a teacher's trust. She looked him squarely in the face, unflinching and intense. "I know about the bombs and I know about the money but I don't know, and I can't really understand, why you feel that our lives are only worth money, that the lives of innocent people are counted out in pounds. Why, for God's sake, why?"

Roy's body stiffened and shook. The thought of Joan knowing everything was beyond his comprehension. He looked at her and his mouth moved but no words came.

"Do you really know what you've done? Do you have any idea of the pain and suffering you have caused to people, innocent people? It's been a huge game to you, a personal battle for revenge, to get even for what you think the country has done to you. You couldn't get any satisfaction the legitimate way so you decided on this obscene course of action which has now claimed more than your life, more than mine and Christ only knows where it's going to stop. You've got to give it up and give it up now, Roy. Try to reclaim some dignity. You said you loved me, but how can you when you live your real life in the shadows?"

Although the sun still shone brightly, the atmosphere was cold. Joan shivered.

Roy's body was rigid and his eyes were hard. He lifted his head and moved his face close to Joan's and stared into her eyes, a piercing stare, a stare of a stranger and one that brought fear. There was anger and hatred there. He took a long, slow breath and then stood; leaving her he moved down through the ruins to the Vitara. She sat and watched as he started the engine and drove away furiously, the wheels kicking up the dust, the engine screaming his anger.

She could not remember how long she sat staring at the blue of the water far below, the houses, the fields. She could not remember the thoughts that stirred in her mind for that was as thick and dark as treacle. She was numb; she had no senses or thoughts.

"Are you all right? Has he hurt you?"

Joan turned and saw a young woman kneeling behind her. She had neither seen her arrival, nor heard her approach. She turned away without a word.

"Joan, I'm a friend, I know what you're going through, what you're trying to do. My name's Pippa."

Joan turned and looked at her. Pippa smiled. "Please let me help."

Without any show of emotion, unnerving in its delivery, she spoke. "We are beyond help, everything has gone, screwed up like waste paper and thrown away. He doesn't even know why. Can you believe that, 'cos as sure as there's a God somewhere, I can't?"

Joan kept looking out over the forests and fields. Pippa, aware of her anguish, moved a little away and sat watching the road in case Roy decided to return. An hour passed.

"Can you get me home? I don't want to go back to the flat, I don't want to see him again, it's gone, it all died today; up there on the wall the bomb that was planted in me has done its job."

Pippa held out her hand and moved across to her. She wrapped a friendly arm around her shoulder and helped her down the path to her car. The drive back to the hotel was long and silent. Joan just sat staring blankly at the road.

"I'm not alone here, Joan. Bob, a colleague, is in the hotel. We've been keeping an eye and an ear on Roy for some days. What do you know of all of this?"

Joan remained silent for some time and then told Pippa what she knew, she also told her something of his past; she recounted the good and bad.

They parked the car and went into Reception. Pippa directed her to the terrace where she ordered coffee. They sat overlooking the beach that in turn ran to the dead area, The Maras; the emptiness seemed to mirror Joan's feelings.

"What do you want to do next, Joan? You'll need to give it some thought. If you need out, it can be arranged. You'll need neither money nor passport."

Joan looked up. "I want out, the sooner the better."

Pippa showed Joan to their room before organising another room. Bob was curled on the bed listening to the activity in Roy's flat and was startled when Pippa entered with Joan. They were formally introduced.

"Joan's on her way out, there's no computer and we need to tell Home."

"I've a phone in my bag, I was taught how to use it in an emergency. Would the time be right now?" Joan delved into her bag and brought out the phone. "I have a code."

She punched in the numbers that she had memorised and answered as requested. She told the voice the situation and then Pippa joined in. It was agreed that she would be collected in the regular UN convoy through the northern side the following day and a flight would be organised to return her to England.

***

Roy busied himself and waited. He knew she would come back to the flat. He did not know what had got into him and when he had returned to the castle after a beer in Girne, she had gone. He paced the lounge, kicking at the odd piece of furniture and drinking from a tumbler of Scotch. All her things were there, her passport even her money. She had to return. The bottle got the better of him and his pacing became a stagger and he finally collapsed into oblivion.

"What will happen to Roy?" There was genuine concern in Joan's voice. Even though he had betrayed her she wanted to know he would be safe.

"There's nothing we can do other than monitor the situation and hope to goodness he either gives us the information on the remaining bombs or we find the computer. We're now monitoring the flat and hoping for clues. We'll get the information, but as for Roy it's unlikely he will return to England. He cannot be extradited from here and he does appear to hold a second passport in another name, which means he might try to leave the island at some future time. However, you are our main concern for the moment. I'll nip into town and get you some toiletries. Write me a list of things you need. Help yourself to my limited wardrobe."

"Thanks."

The organised convoy stopped on time at 10.15 the next morning by the Salamis ruins. The Fiat was waiting. Joan stepped out, walked to the leading vehicle and climbed in. She was handed a UN uniform, jacket and cap. By nightfall Joan would be on a military flight from Akrotiri to Brize Norton and by morning she would be home.

The bright light hurt Roy's eyes but it compared little to his thumping head. "Joan!" His shouts went unheard. He staggered to his feet and checked the bedrooms; his worst fears were realised. There was now a confusion that tore at his conscience. It was he who had left her alone, he had not tried to find her and she had not returned. The anxiety of not knowing where she was was unbearable. He washed and drank black coffee before returning to the castle. Ironically, he passed the UN convoy travelling out towards the border and failed to see her, but why should he look? If he had it would have been the last time he saw her. In his heart there was hope, a slim chance that she might have gone into Girne and travelled back to the castle to teach him a lesson, but it was only slight.

The castle was empty and he stood on the highest part shouting her name. The word echoed loudly. He approached the very spot where they had sat the previous day, when they had walked together and chatted. He even answered the question she had asked but it sounded hollow and without sincerity. All that he had done had been worthless, he was alone and he had brought this on himself. There was no time for self-pity, he would check Girne.

The bars and restaurants proved time consuming and useless and he checked the hotels but without luck. He returned to the flat. The half bottle was still on the table and he poured a generous measure.

The next two days were a haze, an indistinct period of smudged thoughts; suicide had loomed without menace at times but he had battled through, a trait that might be responsible for his present predicament. He had telephoned Joan's home and mobile number repeatedly in England throughout this time, but he had no reason to believe she was there. The answerphone with her voice gave some comfort and the fact that she did not answer personally still gave him hope that she was on the island, the fact that her passport and belongings were still in the apartment did not seem to convince him.

The confusion was clearly audible as Pippa and Bob monitored the apartment, the crashing and banging, the periods of silence and the telephone calls. It was these that upset Pippa; she had never heard such desperation as Roy talked to nobody down the phone and to himself afterwards; the intrusion of his privacy was painful.

"What do you want to do, Pip?"

"I want to get this thing over as soon as possible. At times this job really is the lowest." Pippa moved out onto the balcony and took some deep breaths before turning to Bob. "How long would it take you to search the apartment thoroughly?"

"Two hours at least, why, what do you have in mind?" Bob moved out to the balcony and sat on one of the wicker chairs. There was no sound from the apartment; Roy was sleeping off the alcohol yet again.

"I've bumped into Roy on two occasions, the first by accident but I contrived the second. He believes I am here with my husband. He can't be locked up for long and I'm sure I can meet him again. He's at a low and if you put two and two together I might be able to give you some safe time to search his apartment."

"You mean you're going to screw the poor bastard on top of all this and then bugger off, that will really bring more joy into his life! Sounds good to me and I'd be happier searching the apartment at night." Bob imagined the lucky guy between the sheets with Pippa and for that short time he would have loved to swop places. "I think he'll bite, if you don't mind my saying so." He looked her up and down and smiled.

"Give me another idea."

"What about just calling in the guns and then you'll have all the time you need to look through the apartment?"

Pippa's look said it all. "Don't tell me, you don't think the computer's there." Pippa was nodding.

"There's always that chance and we just can't risk that."

They were interrupted by sounds of movement from the speaker. They both paused and listened. Roy had dialled and the phone was ringing, the dialling tone told them it was to England. It rang for some time and was answered by Joan.

"Hello."

There was a silence and then a click. Roy had obviously put the phone down. He now knew that she was home. He moved into the bedroom and dragged out the drawer until he found her passport. He held it in his hand, staring at the photograph.

Bob and Pippa were now on the bed as close to the speaker as they could get, frightened of missing anything.

"Bitch!" Roy threw the small booklet at the wall. "Just what were you doing here?"

He moved out of the bedroom and into the kitchen and from the back of one of the cupboards he removed some plywood. His hand delved inside; it was a tight squeeze and he extracted the palmtop.

"Where do you think he is now?" Pippa asked Bob.

"He's in the kitchen and quite close to the bug."

Roy returned it to its hiding place, happy it was still secure and moved back to the bedroom. He pulled out everything that belonged to Joan and went through it. He threw most into a pile in the centre of the bed, tipping small bags out haphazardly. There was nothing. He picked up the box of tampons flipping the lid; he had found what he was looking for.

Joan had sensed that it was Roy after she heard the receiver fall. She had waited, nervously listening to the silence before putting down the phone. She considered ringing him but quickly dismissed the thought. As far as she was concerned he was on his own.

The black palmtop nestled in the half-full box. He withdrew it, scattering the remnants of the box over the floor.

Joan hated computers and seldom used his. He now knew why she had come. He flicked open the cover and pressed 'ON'. Immediately he knew it was his own from home. That too went the way of the passport and crashed against the wall. The batteries flew in one direction and the sturdy little box dropped to the floor. Roy moved over and trod on it, trampling it on the floor. "Screw you Joan Johnson!"

Pippa looked at Bob and raised her eyebrows. "That's one mean man."

Roy bagged all of Joan's belongings, packing them into the back of the Vitara before driving towards the town. He would dispose of them all as quickly as possible.

Chapter Thirty-One

Two days later Bob followed the black Vitara out through the town and towards Salamis. He again watched Roy unpack and move to the beach before contacting Pippa. She prepared and set out for Salamis, passing Bob on the way. Pulling up in the car park behind the small wooden bar that was now closed, she strolled towards the ruins of the old Roman town. She could not see Roy until she climbed the ruins and looked towards the jetty. He was sitting on the sand staring out over the water, beside him a bag and a book.

Pippa watched him for some time before moving through the ruins to the sea edge. She walked up the beach towards her prey, her bag and sweater over her shoulder. As she had hoped, Roy spotted her first and watched her move towards him, her footprints in the soft sand were washed by the sea.

"On your own again?"

Pippa paused, more for effect; she was neither surprised nor startled by him.

"Hello, we seem to meet quite often. Yes, unfortunately, is the answer to your question."

Roy stood and moved towards her, offering his hand. "Roy Hanna, we met on the castle."

"Pippa Mason."

"Is your husband finding Turkish Cyprus to his liking?"

"He did but I'm afraid he's been called back to the office. Some crisis or other, it often happens, and in his world, work comes first."

Roy could only think that some men were stupid; his own actions he never questioned.

"So, what brings you to the beach?"

"I've been looking at the ruins behind for some time but I really wanted to splash my toes in the sea."

Roy sat and she did the same before removing her shoes and lifting her skirt.

"Is the water warm?" Not waiting for an answer, she walked into the sea. She turned and smiled. "Lovely!" Her words laughed as she waded in a little further. The small waves ran up her legs.

"When do you fly home?"

"I have another week planned but I don't know if I'll be here that long. I feel a little vulnerable on my own, so restricted at night."

"There's no need to, the island is safe and women are able to walk the streets at night here. It's one of the pleasures you find. They still believe in family values, respect for elders and women so you should have nothing to fear."

Pippa came out of the water, holding her skirt higher than necessary to keep it away from the water. She noticed that Roy enjoyed the view. She sat next to him.

Roy took a flask of coffee from his bag and poured a cup offering it to Pippa. She took it and smiled before drinking. She handed back the cup and stood up collecting her things.

"Going so soon?" Roy's voice clearly reflected his disappointment.

"I'm going to walk to that hotel along the beach and then back. Thank you for the coffee, it was lovely to meet you again."

"May I walk with you?"

"Feel free."

They walked up the beach stopping occasionally to chat, throw pebbles into the sea and laugh. It was the laughing, the lightness of mood that attracted him more and more and by the time they had returned to the car park, Pippa was in control.

"I'm eating out tonight, would you like to join me? It will be a typical Turkish meal," Roy suggested.

Pippa thought for a moment as if not sure. "That would be lovely, Roy. Thank you."

"If I remember correctly, you're at Palm Beach? I'll pick you up at eight."

She climbed into her car and waved before driving off down the straight road. She watched him in the mirror standing where she had left him, like a kitten left alone, vulnerable.

Bob was waiting in the room, eager to hear if she had made contact and whether she would entice Roy that night. She needed three days at the most but she assured him that tonight would not be the night and he could relax. She wanted to have his Vitara parked outside the apartment when Bob searched so that any lights or sounds could be attributed to Roy and she knew just how to achieve that target.

***

Roy was waiting in the lobby of the hotel exactly at eight and Pippa was not late. Her little black dress was perfect and it was clear from Roy's expression that he approved.

"Is this OK Roy? I didn't know what to wear."

"If I may say so, you look stunning." She handed in her key and they left. The meal was quiet and most enjoyable. She was surprised to find Roy's company far more congenial than she had dared hope, the chore she had imagined had evaporated as the evening progressed and it was late when they left. Roy opened her door first and she relaxed in the car.

"Have you any plans for tomorrow?" Roy looked at her inquisitively.

Pippa wrinkled her brow as if in thought and then shook her head. "No, I've nothing planned."

"Would you like me to show you a little of the area? Maybe we could have an evening meal in Girne."

"Sounds lovely but on one condition, you let me drive."

"I'd consider that a pleasure. Say noon. You could pick me up from the Victory Monument, the black statue on the roundabout."

Roy dropped her off and she bid him goodnight before moving away. He watched her enter the lobby before he left.

"We're on for tomorrow night." Pippa smiled at Bob. "I'm collecting him at noon and we'll be out all day, meal in Girne and then back here for as long as I can keep him occupied!" She stripped off her black dress and threw it over Bob's head; she was wearing nothing underneath.

"I wish you wouldn't do that," Bob complained. She only giggled and ran a shower.

"We'll need the room we booked for Joan and you'll have to clear all your things out. You might leave a tie on the dressing table so I can say it's one my husband left. You'll be free to search the apartment when you can. Give me a ring when you're back in the hotel, if I'm busy I'll ignore it but I'll know when to stop!" she shouted above the running water.

Bob looked at the two beds and heard himself whisper, "Lucky bastard, he doesn't deserve this."

The sound of the water stopped and within minutes Pippa emerged from the steam-filled room wrapped in a large towel. Bob was already in his bed, the bedside light illuminating just a small area of the room. Pippa was silhouetted against the light of the bathroom.

"The black widow emerges from her lair," Bob said, his face hidden in a novel.

"More like the Portia spider whose elaborate masquerading lures many spiders within striking distance. Are you safe there?"

Bob looked up from his book and then down again. "Unfortunately, yes. Good night, sleep well."

***

As arranged Roy was waiting by the monument and waved as she approached the roundabout. He opened the door and climbed in.

"Good morning. Thank you for a lovely evening last night, Roy. I enjoyed it immensely."

"My pleasure. We need to head towards Salamis and I'll give you the directions from there."

They drove out along the coast road before turning inland, the same route he had taken with Joan. The road took them into the mountains and to Kantara, another of the island's Crusader castles. From there they travelled to Esentepe before ending up at the house he had recently shown Joan.

"I want to show you my new home, it still needs work but it's close to completion."

They walked first through the gardens and then the house. Pippa made all the right noises, complimenting Roy on his choice of colour. He led her into the empty master bedroom and again opened the balcony windows. He knew she would delight in the view; she did not disappoint him.

"It's really out of this world, Roy. You're a very lucky man. Do you plan to grow old here, marry, have a family?" She knew she had trodden on sensitive ground, pushed to the quick, but that was her aim. He looked across at her, there was sadness in his eyes and she thought of the kitten-like figure in the road at Salamis.

"Who knows, but it's doubtful." Instinctively she leaned across and chastely kissed his cheek. "Your new house is lovely and will soon be a home. You have all the makings of a family man."

"Do you have children?"

"Neither have nor want. I'm not the maternal type Roy, too selfish really. Robert, my husband keeps trying to suggest it would make our relationship but with the demands of work I rarely see him now, he's hardly a husband so I can't really visualise him being all paternal. No, I'm happy as I am."

Roy lifted his hand and turned her face before planting a fuller kiss, this one on the lips. Instinctively she felt as though she must pull away and look hurt before continuing. She did and it had the result she had hoped for. She then returned his kiss. They stood on the balcony, his tongue touching her lips gently, exploring as if testing the ground. To his amazement she responded, penetrating deeply into his mouth. She felt him grow against the light cotton of her shorts. She pulled away.

"I'm sorry, Roy," she hung her head." Much as I'd love to, we shouldn't, I'm sorry. It was my fault."

Roy was flattered if not confused but the pleasure had left him unhurt. He took her hand and led her back through the house and to the garden. "Let's move into Girne. Are you ready to eat?"

Pippa nodded and smiled. "Thanks for understanding." The coquetry unseen, the thought of the Portia Spider came into her head. She knew she was doing her job well.

She linked Roy's arm as they walked to the car. The drive into Girne was straightforward, Pippa followed the signs. She pulled up on the front, the Dome Hotel to their left.

"I know just the place," muttered Roy as he climbed from the car.

They walked along the sea wall to the old harbour, it was growing dark and a chill had blown in from the sea. They rounded the corner and Roy directed her to a large busy restaurant and chose a small table for two in the corner. Roy ordered drinks and was surprised when Pippa insisted on driving home after he had offered; she wanted the alcohol in Roy not herself. The meal was good and so was the dancer who wiggled and strutted to cheers and applause. Surprisingly, Pippa enjoyed it and found it quite a turn on. She had never witnessed a real belly dance before.

It was 9.30 when they left and started the drive back. As they approached Famagusta Roy suggested she drop him at the monument.

"Will you come back to the hotel for coffee and drinks? The bar is lovely and it's too early for home."

She did not need to ask twice. She collected the key and left Roy in the bar whilst she went to her room for a sweater. On the bed was a book. She had not remembered leaving one there. She collected her sweater and picked up the book, "The Merchant of Venice". On the flyleaf Bob had written: *To the Black Widow, much love and appreciation*. She laughed out loud.

Chapter Thirty-Two

Bob had entered Roy's apartment without difficulty and the shuttered windows afforded him the privacy he needed. His search started in the kitchen, he felt sure that the computer was somewhere there. He carefully checked all cupboards and drawers but without success; it was going to be more difficult than he had anticipated, particularly as his imagination kept returning to the moves being played out in the hotel.

***

"It's been a lovely day, thanks. You'll never know just how much I've appreciated your company. You must be tired? I'll be leaving."

"I'm sorry about earlier today Roy. I guess I was caught a little off guard."

"Don't worry about that. As I say it's been lovely."

"Will you see me to my room. We have some unfinished business?" Pippa took him by the hand and Roy made no protest. They took the lift and as the doors closed she stretched and kissed his lips tenderly. "If I could wind back the clock I would," she breathed.

Roy took the key from her and opened the door. They moved inside and locked it. Pippa switched on the bedside light and looked across at Roy and smiled. Slowly she unbuttoned her cotton blouse and slipped it from her shoulders.

***

Bob tapped the backs of all the cupboards until he found the one. He carefully moved the backing and slid his hand behind it. His fingers wiggled in the darkness for a touch and there it was. The fit was tight, giving little opportunity to get a firm grip, but he eventually moved it closer until it emerged into the light. The computer was his. He now had to ensure everything went back just as he had found it; that was the easy bit. One final check and he switched off the lights and left the building.

***

Pippa moved gently above Roy her breathing fast as a rivulet of saliva trickled from the corner of her mouth and fell on Roy's chest. The phone rang.

"Roy, Roy!" gasped Pippa as she moved with greater force almost in time with the ringing phone. Her body convulsed and stiffened in orgasm as the phone fell silent. They both lay there. Roy's eyes were closed. Pippa was awake, staring at the ceiling. She felt dirty, Bob's words rang through her mind, 'You're going to screw the poor bastard and then bugger off.' She turned to look at Roy, his body relaxed. She leaned over and kissed his forehead. "I'm sorry, Roy. I'm sorry."

***

The sun splashed yellow throughout the room and the fine white curtains blew like wisps. It was the sound of the door closing that made Pippa wake. Roy had gone. Next to her was a note. "Thank you for a lovely day. If you're free tonight I'd like to see you. Have a good rest. Give me a ring 54391. Roy."

She slipped her legs out of bed and the musky smell of sex surrounded her. She had to shower, to cleanse herself of the act. The phone rang again, this time she answered it.

"Hello."

"Bingo, Pippa, Bingo! We've got it!"

"Good," was all that Pippa said and replaced the receiver. She tore up the note.

Within half an hour they had arranged the pick-up point and time and by lunch they would be on the Greek side of the island. Mr and Mrs Mason would not be seen in the hotel again, they would check out, drive towards Salamis and make contact with the convoy. Both hire cars would simply be left outside the hotel and payment made to Reception. A taxi would drop them at the desired location. The computer would be safely stored and its secrets soon known to all.

***

Jim Bentley had made the most of his time in Cyprus but was now beginning to feel restless. He had not received any communication. His consolation was the weather, which was kinder than that of home, and he was paid very well. However, he would not have much longer to wait.

The palmtop retrieved from the kitchen was handed to the main computer experts based at RAF Akrotiri and with their skill it took little over twenty-four hours to hack into the system, break the passwords and extract the information. The detail found was staggering as it gave a clear indication of the devices, their nature and those with anti-handling mechanisms. The information was sent along a secure line to GCHQ and from there to ACPO where it was immediately acted upon. Bomb disposal sections of both military and police responded and the careful process of making the devices safe began.

Sam Phelps and his team were allocated three intended targets and were issued with the relevant details. At pre-determined times, the motorways would be closed late at night to cause the minimum disruption. He personally was relieved that the GULF's bombs were about to be terminated. The successful retrieval of the information, he believed, had been through Joan's co-operation. He thought of the last time he had seen her, the distress she had gone through and the smile as he left. It made him stop what he was doing. He would call round to see her, to thank her personally.

Chapter Thirty-Three

Roy woke late and felt excited. He lay, still dressed, looking at the ceiling and whistled to himself. He tossed in his mind the culmination of what had been a perfect day, eager to re-live every sound and every feeling He went for the telephone directory, found the number of the hotel and dialled. It was answered in Turkish.

"Please connect me with Mrs Mason, room 225."

"I'm sorry, sir. Mr and Mrs Mason checked out today, this morning in fact."

"Mr and Mrs Mason, did you say?"

Roy's body stiffened as he crashed the phone down and he ran into the kitchen. He tore off the back of the cupboard scattering glasses that fell and shattered to every corner of the room. He groped eagerly into the cavity behind the cupboard, the force tearing the skin on his hand.

"Empty! You fucking whore!" He crashed his head against the door in pure frustration and anger as he withdrew his hand, oblivious to the pain and the blood that trickled through his fingers before splashing a pattern on the floor. He could feel the bile rise in his throat and he vomited onto the tiles. It mixed with the droplets of blood as he too slumped to the floor. He had been used; he had not seen through the masquerade, he had been drawn hook, line and sinker. She had flattered him and he should have known, should have suspected something. He could clearly see the coincidences now, but it was too late.

***

Jim Bentley answered the phone in his room. He had just finished his swim and run. He listened and chatted freely as if to a business colleague.

"You will be glad to hear, Jim, we have finalised the business and we only need your signature when you can. I thought you'd be pleased to hear."

"That's joy to the ears, my friend. I should be home soon and we can sort everything out. I'll ring in a day or two." Jim put the phone down and moved to the window, looking at the area where he had placed the target. "We only need your signature," he repeated. He looked up at the case on the wardrobe.

***

The knock at the door made Joan jump, she had finished reading the paper and was about to clear away the breakfast things. The sight of Sam Phelps shocked her. She smiled suddenly.

"How lovely to see you, please ..." She opened the door and Sam entered. He sat in the same chair and she asked the same question.

"No, I've just had a coffee. It's been a long night but I wanted to let you know that we're in the process of sorting out all of the bombs. The information we received has done the trick. I just wanted to say thanks for your help."

Joan looked across at Sam. The puzzled expression triggered Sam's response.

"You've no idea what I'm talking about have you?"

"Yes, I imagine the computer has been found."

Sam nodded. "And right at this minute the bombs are being stripped and disposed of. I just thought ..." Sam stopped himself as he noticed the look on Joan's face. It was he who put his hand on hers. "It's over and that's the main thing. There should be no more casualties until the next nutter who comes along."

Joan looked up and smiled. "Thank you for letting me know."

Sam stood and moved to the door. Joan opened it and he stepped onto the street.

"I think you've been a very brave woman, Joan, and we have a lot to thank you for." He looked at her and the smile that he had seen on the first occasion returned. He stopped and walked back to the door. "If it's possible, I'd love to see you again, maybe a meal?" Sam took a card from his jacket and handed it to her. "When the time is right and you feel like company it would be my pleasure." He walked back to the car, waved and drove away. Joan looked at the card and moved it to her chest. She knew it would be sooner rather than later.

***

Roy did not know how long he had been sitting in his own vomit but the blood had congealed on his hand and the lights were on in the street; the room was in darkness apart from the dim glow of orange from outside. He stood and cleared up the mess before showering. He dressed casually and checked the flat before locking the doors. The Vitara was parked outside and he walked past it. Tonight, he would get horribly drunk, he would see his real friends.

In his anger he failed to notice the figure who walked behind, stopping to give a clear distance. Even as he trudged through the narrow, ancient streets his pursuer hugged the shadows. Roy crossed the narrow bridge that forded the now dry floor of the moat eight metres below and vanished into the darkness of the ancient gate. The archway, although small, allowed the passage of cars and vans into the old city walls. Jim watched the silhouetted figure move again into the light and he continued to follow after taking a good look over the bridge wall. The music and light from the bar spilled onto the pavement, giving a warm welcome as Roy approached. Soon he was in.

He drank *Efes* from the bottle followed by cheap whiskey. He laughed with his friends and as he was paying, they drank with him until late; his circle of friends grew as the evening went on. Jim sat at a small, round, metal table, sipping at his beer; he ate pistachio nuts and watched Roy slowly drink away his troubles until he could hardly stand. He paid by dumping money onto the counter, shouted his goodnights and laughed before staggering out. His meandering path took him close to Jim's table which he missed before entering the toilet. Jim followed. Roy stood at the urinal, his head against the dirty wall. His shoes shone as urine splashed the dusty surfaces. Roy turned slowly to look who had followed him in and a yellow stream of piss followed before he corrected it. He uttered some indistinct sound and then placed his head against the wall. Jim said nothing; he entered the cubicle and bolted the door.

Roy staggered from the toilet and out onto the street. Black, wet patches marked his trousers. He tried to focus and balance but did neither well. Jim followed, passed and walked ahead taking the route he had walked earlier in the evening, only this time he stopped in the darkness of the gatehouse arch and waited. His wait was long but he was patient.

The pathetic figure of Roy staggered up the quiet, narrow street. He stopped and vomited occasionally before continuing. His real friends were still back in the bar, he was still alone. He was too drunk to care. Traffic was light; one or two cars passed but paid little attention to the drunk. He tried to whistle to himself but found it too difficult to find a tune and concentrate on his path at the same time. Jim watched; he was nearly there. He moved further into the darkness and settled his backside onto the low parapet wall of the bridge and waited. Roy continued to make progress until he too arrived at the wall which he used to guide himself, keeping safe from the road.

He approached Jim and stopped. He moved his head backwards and forwards as if trying to focus on the object that appeared to block his way. He swayed gently. Jim stood away from the wall and Roy began to move.

"Excuse me, but am I correct in thinking that you are an expert on the destruction of bridges?" Jim's sarcastic tone was wasted on Roy's swamped mind but he did pick out the word bridges and stopped to look at Jim. Roy's face was creased in confusion as his thoughts tried to swim in his soaked mind. He desperately tried to pull himself together, to understand what had been said for he knew it was important. There was a threat, he was not too drunk to ignore that instinct and he felt a sudden chill of fear.

"I believe I'm talking to GULF." He let the words linger. "You bastard!"

Roy felt Jim's strong arms hit his chest and his head spin as he began to bend backwards out of balance. The bridge wall at his buttocks formed a perfect fulcrum as Jim moved sideways, still applying pressure, and kicked Roy's legs out from the wall with all the strength of his right foot. His arms pushed again and Roy lashed out in a desperate attempt to grasp anything solid but there was only the warm evening air. A shallow scream started to erupt in his throat but this was soon stopped as the acid taste of vomit was forced into his mouth. The streetlights flipped uncontrollably downwards as he fell backwards his arms flailing and feet kicking.

"Goodnight, GULF, goodnight," were the last words he heard but it was doubtful whether his brain unscrambled their meaning. He plunged into the darkness until his head hit the sandy ground, forcing it forward with terrific force. Jim would have heard the neck snap had he been closer but the impact of the body hitting the ground drowned the subtle sound of the break. He saw neither the body twitch nor the trickle of vomit soil the ground around the body. He assumed death had arrived instantly.

Roy's spinal cord had snapped between C1 and C2. He could not feel his body; his arms and legs would not respond and he found his breathing laboured but his eyes still focused on the arch and the outline of the figure leaning over. His mind was suddenly clear as he gasped for air against a paralysed diaphragm. Sweat was the only thing that would run freely and his face grew wet. He tried to scream but he had no control of his voice and he began to choke on the vomit that now flushed into his mouth. The arch of the bridge and the artificial yellow of the street-lit sky grew more dim as the panic swelled in his head. If he could have screamed out loud, the word 'Joan' would have been audible throughout the quiet town; he put a final effort into it but a gurgling rattle was all that emerged. Roy's now sightless eyes stared at the span of the bridge; he twitched once more.

Jim walked through the town and back out towards his hotel. He would have liked to have used his rifle but this was cleaner and certainly would be easier to deal with, after all, accidents happen all the time!

***

Roy's body was found in the early morning and it was clear that he had fallen over the bridge. The vomit stained clothing and urine-soaked shoes gave all the clues as to the reason. It would be only later when the pathology report detailed the bruising to the chest cavity and severe grazing to the Achilles' tendons, that they would suspect any kind of foul play.

Jim waited, as his two colleagues had previously, on the main road. Two white UN vehicles approached and pulled up. He handed the case to the passenger, who slid it into a small compartment behind the seats and then climbed into the back. There were a number of boxes and he settled down. He had particularly enjoyed his final run and swim that morning but was ready for home.

Chapter Thirty-Four

Joan stared at the ceiling and felt fully contented. The light wind clashed the blinds against the Venetian bowl on the window ledge; its crystal ring chimed intermittently, unobtrusively. The body next to her oozed warmth and slept. She was fully awake and slipped out of bed, grabbing her dressing gown before walking downstairs. It was 7.14 and the wintry morning was dark and misty. A drizzle fell and coated the cobwebs that draped the few shrubs in the garden with opaque droplets. She marvelled at their structure before moving into the kitchen.

The kettle soon boiled and she sat in a chair, feet curled up tightly, sipping at the steaming hot tea and viewing the damp world. Since her return from Cyprus she had come to terms with all that had happened. She had, after the initial trauma, remained philosophical and the police had supported with counselling. However, the news of Roy's death had been devastating, particularly as it was so out of keeping with his general lifestyle. In her heart of hearts she had suspected some foul play but of that she would never be fully sure. The official report suggested Roy had been mugged and that either by design or accident he had fallen over the bridge. The Cyprus police would make enquiries but she knew that they would lead to nothing. Her return to work had given her the necessary distraction that she needed to overcome her loss and her friends had rallied round. The legal aspects were handled by Louise and it appeared Roy had left everything to Joan, both houses and the contents of two insurance policies.

The sound of the letter box and the crash of the paper on the hall floor broke her thoughts. She particularly enjoyed the time with the paper at the weekend, it was a relaxing moment to savour. It was the headline that shocked. A group of Gulf War veterans, known as 'The Stormers', a small group in contrast to the 1,000 who had registered with the Ministry of Defence as suffering from the illnesses associated with their brief service in the Gulf, had taken out writs against the Ministry of Defence claiming compensation. However, this was only the advance party and should they be successful, then the floodgates to compensation for all would, they hoped, naturally follow. Earlier in the year, lawyers had completed their research and presented their evidence and now, according to the headline, had been successful in their fight. It appeared that the MOD admitted to errors in both the allocation of major drugs and a cavalier attitude to the supervision of insecticides.

It was the spokesman for 'The Stormers' comment that made her heart stop, made her re-read the passage:

We have been fighting for years but proceedings are expensive. We have been supported by many generous financial gifts; we've even recently received a donation of £2,000,000 pounds from a foreign supporter with the instruction that it should be used to help the families of those who have already lost loved ones. It is such a generous gift and we would like to thank all those who continue to support our struggle for recognition and compensation.

Immediately Joan knew where the money had come from and she remembered that Roy had always tried to put his friends and colleagues first, but this? Could he really have planned all of this? Could this have been his goal all along?

She looked at the drizzle and grey cold outside, the dark clouds low in the lightening sky and remembered what Roy had told her about the desert weather on the night before he was injured. She remembered the warmth of his smile and it seemed to lift her; she read the words again and smiled. Maybe he had won after all.

I hope you enjoyed my first novel, **'Bridging the Gulf'**.

To commemorate the centenary of the conclusion of WW1 I wrote a short story entitled **'The Penultimate Man'**. I thought it might be fitting to add it here to help us remember the sacrifices paid by our armed forces.

This story is taken from my collection of short stories 'Shadows from the Past'.

The Penultimate Man

B ells rang in his ears and people shouted words that he didn't understand as they thrust flowers into his hands. Girls tried to kiss him but he only had one person on his mind, Emilie was the one he must see. His 303 was haphazardly thrown across his shoulder and only occasionally did he experience discomfort from his old wound. His greatcoat flapped at his legs like an eager dog. He had not felt so excited since his arrival in 1914. The road to the bridge seemed to stretch away for ever as he pounded the cobbled road of Ville-sur-Haine; on each side people had gathered, their homes in disarray from days of shelling but still jubilant on hearing the welcome news. More people, more bells and more cheers. It was soon to be over. His body seemed distant, numb, and his heart beat in tune with the bells. Tears of joy ran down his cheeks and suddenly his effort was rewarded, he was at the bridge that stretched across the Canal du Centre. He knew she would be near the chateau gates, away from the dressing station, enjoying the celebrations. Through blurred, watery eyes he spotted her. He called her name, waving one hand full of tightly held flowers. As he called again she turned, a smile forming on her lips as her hand shot into the air.

***

The needle produced a burning sensation as it traced the tail of the small bird that seemed to follow the line of his thumb to his wrist. The blue ink, mixed with the deep red of beading blood, appeared to make the tracing more purple than he had imagined, distorting his idea of the image he had been promised. It was only when the rough cloth held in the tattooist's hand wiped away the residue that Henry saw the outline of the small bird, the painful love token he had promised her he would take back to the Western Front.

He had been there before, of course, on a harrowing number of occasions. Each time seemed worse than the last. It was the knowledge of what was to come that proved more of a nemesis. Gratefully, his memory seemed to conveniently numb the horrors and he was only left with an innate sense of self-preservation. He had an almost blasé approach to the next day. "What will be, will be," he often heard the cynical voice whisper.

There was only one visit to the Western Front that he recalled with great clarity: he remembered his first, excited encounter in 1914 and he smiled to himself at his naivety. Mons didn't sound as attractive as he had imagined the distant continent to be, but at the dawn of war and in the light of the rising sun, he remembered how beautiful the area really was when the morning mist gently blotted the landscape into a blur, smudging the sharp outlines like an artist working with pastel. It had, he thought, a certain magic, a mesmerizing mystery all of its own. The air smelled differently back then, fresh and clean, unpolluted by the stench of the bodies of troops and horses. The trees, he recalled, ran militarily straight along the horizon before gently falling into the valley where late corn dipped its laden head as if in homage to the dawn and birdsong mixed mellow and comforting. He gently shook his head as he remembered feeling angry that this beauty brought about a dilution of his enthusiasm for the anticipated fight. Was this it? Was this the killing ground, the place where the Bosche had killed and pillaged? The fight, the war, *'that would be over by Christmas'* they had told all recruits, bringing about an eagerness to join the fight, seemed so remote. Only the news of the occasional confrontation suggested it had started.

Swiftly, the riders of the Apocalypse had come; within their wake, danger, pain, suffering and death concealed behind many early morning golden veils and in their turn, the deadly clouds of poison gas. He knew that now only too well as it took only a short time for the cork from the innocent looking Belgian bottle to be removed and for the Genie to turn this idyll into a monumental hell.

His reflections changed as he looked at the red, swollen hand that appeared to be supporting the blue ink swallow, his bird of love, and his thoughts quickly turned to Emilie. In the bleakness he had found her. Unable to communicate, their eyes had spoken, fleetingly at first, like timid birds, but as trust and confidence developed, so too had their eye contact.

Henry soon realized that the success of life was chance. Even as a naïve recruit full of enthusiasm and eagerness for the fight, he had begun to realize that the bullets and the bombs were not specific but casual, indiscriminate, random reapers of death. It mattered little to a bullet; your status in life meant nothing, your previous profession, nothing, religion or persuasion nothing, your bravery or your timidity had little to do with the daily roll call of death. Survival was determined by one element, the element of chance. It was some greater being's toss of a coin or roll of the dice. However, he believed strongly in luck. He was superstitious and always performed the same personal ritual each morning and nobody could tell him anything differently. So far, his life and his limbs were intact, unlike many of the others who had been but inches away from him when they lost eyes, arms, faces and more often than not, life itself. This was his fortune and how long it should last was only in the hands of his God. He now had a new amulet and he touched the tender skin. It was chance too that had brought him to Emilie.

The first day of July 1917, after a week of heavy rain, seemed to last for ever. Although severe bombardments had taken place, the heavy shelling had failed to cut and blast away the barbed wire as intended and much of the German trench system was still in place. As a consequence, on that day the British army suffered more casualties than any other day in its history. The machine guns reaped a deadly harvest. The toll of the bell was not enough. When you survived that day there was another and then another. In the trenches, the rain was either wet or deadly; each in its turn took its toll. It was what the generals, safe, warm and far away expected. *"The path of duty is the way to glory"*, were the words that tolled in tune with the Grim Reaper's bell.

It was three days after the worst day of his existence that Henry's life changed. It was his turn for respite, which meant carrying the dead and wounded away from the front. His billet for the next forty-eight hours would be a barn. It was a place to rest, to eat and to write letters home, a haven where some degree of normality might be snatched. It was hard to put into words what these days away from the fighting meant to the battle fatigued, the scared and the wounded. Each saw them as a different blessing or a curse, a place to find oneself again, for nerves and immediate fear to evaporate. To some it was the start of their journey home. For many, life had changed. Excitement, spirit and fight were replaced by fear, exhaustion, uncertainty and the worst disability.

For Henry, it would prove to be serendipity; after all, it was in the relative beauty of his temporary home that he first saw her. She was chasing an errant chicken that had fled the coop housed within the barn. He watched her from his own roost, high in the hayloft like some voyeur, some higher being. She cornered the cockerel but it fluttered, squawked and flew amongst the rafters before landing next to Henry who quickly seized his moment and the bird. It was then that their eyes first met.

Henry climbed down the ladder, the bird expertly hanging by two locked feet held by strong hands, its wings fluttering in protest at its lost freedom. He proffered the protesting bird with extended arm. Neither spoke as the gift was exchanged but he was sure he saw her smile. Was it his clumsiness or his agility to catch and retrieve the bird? He knew not, nor did he care … she had smiled and that had injected him with a warmth of humanity that he had lost, alongside his youth, out in the muddy trenches. Emilie put the bird inside the wire and turned to leave. Just before she went through the small aperture cut within the large barn doors, she turned to look at Henry. It was there again but this time he could see it clearly. His heart jumped and that warm glow filled his body one more time. He knew he must see her again before he returned to the hell that was the trenches.

Elfi Behrans had met Albert Price in the Black Forest near Freiburg in the summer of 1894. The farmer's daughter became enthralled with the handsome young English traveller who stayed on the farm that summer helping with the harvest. When he left, she left too. She travelled secretly with him back to England, to Southport, to begin their life together. Henry was born in 1896, to this German mother and English father, brother to Inga. It was with his sister that they learned from their mother the skill of making the 'corn mother' or 'dolly' and now Henry started to weave a special gift for this girl before he had to return to the front. He shaped it like a small bird, twisting the stems and plaiting the shape. For the first time for as long as he could remember he felt that his life might have a future, a purpose.

He wrote his name on a small piece of paper before tying it to the corn bird and attaching it to the coop before he left; it was his token, his gift for those brief moments of normality. He could smell the field kitchen and he suddenly felt hungry.

***

The irregular, white-hot piece of shrapnel emerged from the mud after separating from the exploding shell-case before continuing its journey through the cordite-fumed air. It burned its way into Henry's shoulder, tearing cloth and flesh with ease before boring through muscle to find greater resistance on striking bone, changing its projection significantly. Within seconds it exited part way down his arm, rending a larger exit wound, and from there it simply ploughed impotently into the churned soil.

As he lay on his back in the mud, knocked there by the force of the explosion and cascade of clods of earth, he noticed that his webbing and uniform were torn and a small, dark area of blood spread. He moved his hand and felt the torn material. He tried to move his shoulder but that proved more difficult. He decided to roll into the crater made by the explosion, out of sight of the enemy guns, and investigate the numbness of his arm. Water already sat in the very bottom and the remnants of an arm lay partly buried, the gold ring contrasting with the brown soil. His heart fluttered and he immediately looked at both his hands; luck again had played its part. The grey sky above was where he sent his whispered, small prayer of thanks.

***

The dressing station was clean and the smell pure. Henry's senses had decreased in sensitivity since his arrival at the beginning of the war. He could now tolerate the stench of rotten and burning flesh, the almond odour of gas, the stink that bubbled from the duckboards of the trenches but this fragrance, this subtle incense of cleanliness, proved difficult to comprehend. It was as if he had enclosed himself in a defensive wall and something gentle sought entry. The white bandaging and the clean clothes also proved an anathema to him but it was here in these strangely hostile surroundings that he saw her again. Briefly. She passed the passageway that led to the dining room of a large chateau, now the temporary first-aid post, and another sense concealed deep in his soul brought him to an abrupt halt. He was immediately alive again.

When he turned, holding his injured arm, his heart fluttered again. Above his bed, as if a protecting presence, he saw the corn bird.

The following morning, she was at his bedside, organizing and arranging, straightening sheets and checking his temperature. Their eyes danced and smiled. He turned and looked at the bird as she rested her hand on his.

"Merci," she said as her eyes smiled. "My name is Emilie."

Her broken English made him smile back. She turned, removing a small enamelled dish from his bedside table. It was then that he noticed the small posy of flowers.

After a week he was well enough to sit in the garden. He was able to move his arm; the wound was healing well. They met every day and although language was an initial barrier, bit-by-bit their understanding of each other and their love grew. She put the corn bird into his breast pocket and kissed him.

"Sois sauf."

One particular warm day she met him by the bench in the garden, accompanied by another young man. Henry's heart fluttered, partly out of jealousy and partly because it always did when he saw her. She perched on the garden bench. Henry could see the facial injuries of the young man who offered his hand.

"Andrew Lloyd. I've heard about you from this lovely young lady. I'm sorry to intrude but she asked me to be here to act as her mouth and ears. I speak the language and she thought it would be good for you both to chat."

Henry could see the excitement in her eyes as he learned more about her. It was hard telling a stranger just how he felt about Emilie and she him but it worked and Andrew soon became known as Cupid by many of the other casualties. He laughed at the requests for him to find them a lovely, Belgian lass.

Over the coming months, whenever possible they met, sometimes only briefly as he travelled back from the front. Slowly, as the face of war changed, the meetings grew less frequent but their love grew stronger.

The war seemed to be never-ending but the rumour mill suggested a light at the end of the tunnel and that it was all soon to end. The years of death and destruction, the agony and pain were to cease. It was said that the German powers were in consultation and if all went well a ceasefire could be imminent. Henry felt suddenly invisible, he had been through the worst and survived, but more than that, he had found the one woman he truly loved. An energy came to him as if he had been revitalized and he thought about the one thing in the world he had to survive for: Emilie. He let his mind wander as he remembered that special moment when he and Emilie had explored each other's bodies for the first time, innocent youths naïvely caressing and forging their own intimacy. And even in the sodden trench whilst on watch he felt his body stirring.

"Bloody hell, Henry, asleep on duty? You were miles away then. I've come to relieve your watch."

Henry, started at the intrusion, looked at his relief and smiled. "Made me jump, Tom. All's quiet. Let's hope it stays that way. Do you believe the rumours that it could soon be over ... maybe even by Christmas?"

"Heard it before, mate. Show me the holes is what I say, show me the bloody holes. Tom by name, Thomas by nature. I don't know if I can do much more. Get some rest."

He inhaled on his cigarette.

Henry was just collecting his things. He saw Tom pop his head over the parapet. "Yep all seems ..." He didn't finish. The crack of the rifle had found its mark and Tom slumped back into the trench like a hessian sack of potatoes, a jagged hole where his left eye should be. Henry let out an involuntary scream as he stared at the dark, oozing chasm where blood mixed with the slippery mud. He then noticed the glowing cigarette hanging from his lip, smoke rising like the man's soul heading heavenward.

"You bloody, bloody fool!"

He picked up the periscope and looked out across no-man's land but he saw nothing. It was a lucky shot from the alert enemy, attracted by the glowing tip of a careless cigarette. One forgetful moment, that was all it took, that was all it ever took. He tapped his breast pocket and whispered another prayer of thanks.

During the next few days the barrage and fighting were hectic, as if the Allies and Germans had to exhaust all their weapons. Casualties mounted and no thought of a ceasefire was discussed again. The second battle of Mons grew more fierce. The push was to the North East.

On the 9th November, the Kaiser abdicated, slipping across the border to the Netherlands. It was only then did the newly formed German Republic seek to extend a hand in the hope of finding peace. At 05.10 on the morning of the 11th November 1918 the armistice was signed and it was agreed that a total ceasefire should commence at 11am (French time).

At 09.30 Henry found himself under heavy bombardment. Machine gun fire completed the cacophony and he settled into his trench. It was the runner, braving the firing, who brought the news:

'Ceasefire to commence at 11am.
No further movement from present position.'

Most men sat back and relaxed as much as possible but it was clear that others had grievances to air and the intensity of shelling increased. Henry looked at his dirty hand, traced the swallow and thought of Emilie. She was back at the aid station, twenty minutes away, and in that moment he made up his mind. He would go to her. Bells began to sound out from the direction of Mons, men patted each other on the back whilst many still kept their heads low. Others simply fell to pieces and wept. Picking up his weapon he followed the trench to the rear and spoke with his Senior Officer, who held the paper declaring the ceasefire.

"One hour and you're back here."

Strangely the officer suddenly and desperately grabbed Henry and they hugged, an outburst of sheer relief and emotion. Henry could feel the tension fall from the officer's shoulders.

"One hour, Sir. There, a kiss and back, I promise, thank you."

He smiled and left. The village of Ville-sur-Heine was his initial destination, from there the bridge and then the dressing station and then … Bells rang in his ears and people called out with words that he didn't understand as they thrust flowers into his hands. Girls tried to kiss him but he only had one person on his mind, Emilie was the one he must see. His 303 was haphazardly thrown across his shoulder and only occasionally did he experience discomfort from his old wound. His greatcoat flapped at his legs like an eager dog. He had not felt so excited since his arrival in 1914. The road to the bridge seemed to stretch away for ever as he pounded the cobbled road of Ville-sur-Haine; on each side people had gathered, their homes in disarray from days of shelling. More people, more bells and more cheers. It was soon to be over. His body seemed distant, almost numb but his heart beat in tune with the bells. Tears of joy ran down his cheeks and suddenly he was at the bridge that stretched across the Canal du Centre. He knew she would be at the edge of the road by the bridge, away from the dressing station, enjoying the celebrations. Through blurred, watery eyes he spotted her. He called her name, waving one hand. He noticed the swallow tattoo, proud and blue in the light, his love token made just for her. The same hand gripped tightly the floral gifts that would soon be hers. He called her name again, his lungs bursting. She turned, a smile forming on her lips as her hand shot into the air as she recognized the sprinting soldier, his arms aloft, his face a picture of happiness.

The German sniper lay behind the bloated, stiff carcass of the horse, he was impervious to its stench. His colleague lay dead beside him, killed an hour earlier but even in the November cold the flies had found the congealed blood. Anger brewed inside him. He had received no message of surrender and only death and revenge filled his mind. The bells, however, confused him for he heard the continued sound of shelling battling the bells. He had heard rumours of a ceasefire but the sight of Lothar's body quashed them instantly. However, in his heart of hearts he knew that this day would be the end of the atrocious war. Flies buzzed, a small black cloud, around the gaping wound in the side of the horse.

It was then that he saw the Tommy running from the village towards the bridge. People were out shouting and the noise drifted across the water like a hymn. He took aim. He watched the man raise an arm and saw a female respond in his peripheral vision but his finger was squeezing the trigger.

Henry picked up speed on seeing her and she started to move towards him. Had he not increased his pace the bullet would have passed harmlessly, a foot in front of him. As it was, it entered his left breast pocket, travelled through the corn dolly and collected a piece of straw turning it into cupid's arrow. The bullet ricocheted from a rib and travelled through his back to lodge in the wooden stock of his rifle but the piece of corn found its true target and punctured his heart. His vision blurred, temporarily filled with the face of Emilie. He carried on for two strides before crashing to the bridge, flowers spreading like the confetti he would never see, his life-blood anointing the cobbles. He twitched as the sound of the bells diminished in his ears and only Emilie's scream from the far side of the bridge resonated through his final thoughts. Emilie sank to her knees. The time was 10.58, on the eleventh day of the eleventh month of 1918.

The sniper looked at his dead friend and spoke softly, "Auge um Auge, Lothar."

He would not be the last to die. One more Allied soldier was to die at 10.59, a Frenchman a few miles away. Sadly, many more were to make the final sacrifice through over- zealous, vindictive commanders pushing for selfish glory after the hour of eleven.

***

A short distance from the now non-existent bridge over the canal is the small cemetery of Neuville. Buried there are five soldiers from the first ever assault in August 1914 and four from the last morning of the war, 1918. It is a poignant reminder of the foolishness of war. Staggeringly, the war to end all wars started and ended almost at the same spot, North East of Mons.

***

Officially over 10,000 men were killed, wounded or went missing on November 11th 1918.

Acknowledgements

'Bridging the Gulf' was my first attempt at writing and I thoroughly enjoyed researching and travelling to bring reality to this piece of fiction. I have always felt concerned at the lack of Government support for our veterans, particularly those who exhibit few or no physical scars for their years of active service but who daily face difficult ongoing battles.

November 11th is an important date in my calendar but I do try to support those in need 365 days a year. If you have enjoyed these two stories, I would be grateful if and when you can, to give a moment's thought to the many charities supporting our soldiers.

I would just like to thank my wife, Debbie, for her wonderful support.

Thanks to Helen Gray for her guidance. To Andy and Isabelle Clark and Dan O'Brien for technical support.

I must thank my many friends living in Northern Cyprus who showed me the true meaning of hospitality and friendship.

Dee Groocock – Your support has been amazing. Thank you.

May I also thank you, the readers. I do hope 'Bridging the Gulf' has given you food for thought.

If you would like further details of my writing then you can always find me on:

Twitter: Malcolm Hollingdrake@MHollingdrake

Website:
www.malcolmhollingdrakeauthor.co.uk
www.malcolmhollingdrakeauthor.com

Bridging the Gulf

Printed in Great Britain
by Amazon